Playtime's Consequences

"I'm sure we can manage. But Eric…there's something you might not be considering here."

"Such as?" Eric asked.

"Well," Sam began, "I think you're aware of this, but you may not realize how deep it goes. The sad truth is…there's a lot of suppressed science out there. Many workable technologies are not allowed to go forward, because they threaten some established power center. Stuff that has to stay on the fringes, for its own safety. *Real* solutions to our energy needs, snuffed out by Big Oil. Inventions that would cause governments to lose their grip on power. And more immediately…the autonomous cybernetic intelligence you want, that could lead to widespread panic about a robotic rebellion. And all of it kept in check by lack of funding. If you're willing to support this…you could unleash forces of unstoppable chaos."

"We already *have* chaos," Eric reminded. "We have riots in the street, widespread breakdown of civil order, and common sense being cast aside for foolish notions. Besides, the chaos we'd bring wouldn't be *all* bad. Remember, freedom is chaos put to good purposes."

Sam let out a long, drawn-out chuckle. "I'm sorry I doubted you, nephew. You're right…you haven't mellowed out at all."

"I'll forgive you for using the m-word in my presence," Eric joked.

Playtime's Consequences

Steven Boswell

Version 1.1
© 2021 by Steven Boswell.
All rights reserved.

This is a work of fiction. Names, characters, businesses, places, events and incidents are either the products of the author's imagination or used in a fictitious manner. Any resemblance to actual persons, living or dead (or artificial), or actual events is purely coincidental.

Prologue

Jimmy ran out of the liquor store, holding two twelve-packs of beer in his hands. He could hear the shopkeeper behind him, cursing up a blue storm. Jimmy dove through the open passenger door of his car, slid across the seat, and placed the beer behind him, all in one swift move. He gunned the engine and pulled away; the passenger door obediently slammed closed. He laughed openly; damn, he was smooth.

As he got to within two blocks of his apartment, he suddenly found himself surrounded by police cruisers. The cops jumped from their cars and advanced on him with batons. Jimmy smirked; he knew the drill. He held his hands up in the air, fully visible to anyone outside the car. They opened his door and let him exit slowly and deliberately. He stood passively, flaunting an air of arrogance, as the police searched him from top to bottom, finally satisfied he was unarmed. Then, in a flash, they handcuffed him.

"Hey! What's going on?" Jimmy protested. "You can't detain me for petty theft! You have to cite and release!"

The police started laughing among themselves. Jimmy's brow furrowed. "What's so funny?"

One officer held up a picture to Jimmy. "Is this you, from two days ago?" It showed Jimmy driving back into town. "Sure, what of it?" Then he blanched. "How long has that camera been there?"

The officer pointed to something in the picture. "Don't you see the sign?" Jimmy squinted. Below the "Welcome To Skeeter" sign was a new one; he hadn't noticed it before. In the picture, the writing was too small to read. Jimmy scowled. "What *of* it?"

"Those are the new terms and conditions for living here. Stealing that beer was a violation. You've voluntarily given up your permission to live here, and will be expelled immediately."

Jimmy was aghast. "You can't do that! I have rights!" Again, the police rolled with laughter. Jimmy smoldered angrily. "What *now*?"

"You must be thinking of the *town* of Skeeter. This is the *corporation* of Skeeter. The local gated-community association bought the town after it defaulted on its debt. The sign you passed explained it all. Guess you should have read it, huh?"

Jimmy steamed. "You can't do this! I'll get a lawyer, and beat this rap!" Again, uproarious laughter.

"Just by being here, you waived your right to a jury trial, and agreed to submit to binding arbitration. Of course, *we* hire the arbitrators, and they only meet *here,* and you're not *allowed* in here, so…"

Jimmy sputtered. "This…this is *un-American!*"

"The government won't do *anything* about this. Skeeter incorporated as a city management firm *and* a social-media company. These sorts of terms and conditions are *extremely* common with tech companies. Nothing out of the ordinary at *all.*"

The officers continued to chuckle. "What about all my stuff?" Jimmy pined weakly.

"Can you honestly say you *own* any of it? Or was it stolen, like your beer?" Jimmy looked down sullenly. "It'll be returned to its rightful owners. Anything you actually *owned* will go towards restitution."

Jimmy pouted, but could think of nothing. "So, what now?"

The officer grabbed him gently and led him to a squad car. "Now, we escort you out of corporation limits."

As the squad car pulled away, Jimmy could see the remaining officers making obscene gestures toward him. He slumped in his seat and stared forward vacantly.

He spoke after some time. "How did this all happen?"

The officer looked at Jimmy through the rear-view mirror. "Beg pardon?"

"The takeover. Whatever this crap is."

The officer snorted. "People like *you,* that's how."

Jimmy sulked. "But nothing like *this* has happened before. What changed?"

The officer threw back his head as he laughed. "My buddy was in the bar the day it started. He said it was some hotshot law student on break, one of the rich kids in town. The regulars were drowning their sorrows about how bad things have gotten around here. Then he mentions the 'terms and conditions' used by tech companies to treat their users any damn way they pleased. One thing leads to another, the beer keeps flowing, and before they knew it, they had a plan! The next day, the town declares bankruptcy, his daddy and his friends buy the place…and the rest is history."

Jimmy scowled. "Damn rich people," he muttered.

The officer smirked. "Normally, I'd agree. But it sure makes *my* job easier." They neared the town limits; the car began to slow. "That kid's daddy isn't stopping there, either. He says this thing is ready to explode nationwide."

The squad car came to a stop; the officer uncuffed Jimmy and gave him a light shove. "Don't come back."

He knelt to look at the sign. The writing was too small to read without a magnifying glass. He wondered if that was legal. Sourly, he realized it was probably authorized by the terms and conditions.

Glumly, Jimmy began walking to the next town. He wondered if there was one.

1

Jamie opened the door to the apartment complex's multi-purpose room. Rows of timeworn fold-up tables spanned from one side to the other, surrounded by a variety of mismatched, antiquated chairs. Many were the collapsible, metal type; any cushions had gone flat long ago. Some looked like grade-school surplus, too small for adults, their plastic bucket seats a glaring orange. A raised platform in back served as a stage; the faded white paint failed to conceal the poor condition of the ancient wood. A dingy tarp covered a vertically mounted roulette wheel; three times a week, a collection of nearby senior citizens would use it to play bingo, sponsored by the local Parks And Recreation department. But today, this would be the site for Jamie's project.

A few like-minded folks were already here. She smiled as she saw Ronald, donating his own cleaning supplies to wipe down the tables. Kathy struggled to hang some colorful garlands on the back wall, her dilapidated ladder too short to make the task safe. The fire-exit doors were propped open, hoping to catch a breeze that might flush out the putrid smell left behind by the once-overflowing trash cans; Garrett continued to empty them.

Carrying a rolled-up poster, Jamie ascended the stage and began to unfurl the paper. Floundering with its tendency to curl back into its original shape, she eventually managed to tape down the corners. Finally, its message became clear: "Sunny Day Suites" in large letters, "Tenants Association" in smaller letters below that. With minor reproach, she noticed the roulette wheel blocked the view of her poster from a large portion of the room. She sighed and looked around.

"Garrett? When you get a chance, could you give me a hand?"

Garrett tried to shake the odor from his hands, to no effect. "Sure. I needed a break from that stench anyway."

"I can't believe they let the garbage pile up for so long in here," Jamie bemoaned. "Just another example of why the tenants need to make a stand."

"I guess the bingo players don't notice," Garrett shrugged as he hopped up onto the stage. "Maybe their noses fail around the time their eyesight does."

Jamie hesitantly gripped the roulette wheel. "I can keep it from falling over, if you can scoot it. Want to try that?"

Garrett found that it wouldn't slide over the deck. "Little bits of the wood keep catching the bottom." He turned to look into the room. "Ronald? Little help?"

Ronald was already bounding onto the platform. "Yeah, yeah. I saw this coming." Without further trouble, Ronald and Garrett managed to lift the roulette wheel an inch from the floor, and waddling under the strain of its mass, labored to move it to the side. Jamie tried to help keep the load steady, but mostly got in the way. She smiled sadly as she thanked her helpers.

Kathy descended the ladder, preparing to move it to another spot along the wall. "Hopefully this goes as well as we expect it to."

"I think this has been a long time coming," Jamie agreed. "The landlord just doesn't seem to care about us. We need to make our voices heard! And the only way we can do that is to band together!"

"They really need to cut us some slack," Ronald groaned. "I asked if my son could stay with me for a while, after he got released. They expected him to fill out a formal application! Is that *really* necessary? Sure, he's gotten into trouble in the *past*, but that's all behind him now. Like I can't keep an eye on him?"

"And all because Mrs. Johnson's youngest got out of control," Kathy commiserated. "Somehow, that makes us *all* bad parents."

"You should have seen the property manager when I asked to reserve this room," Jamie grimaced. "She demanded to know the reason. I can't forget the look on her face when I mentioned wanting to form a tenant's association! She made me agree to all these terms and conditions, just to get an hour's time. It was like I was asking for the keys to the kingdom!"

"I'm sure she thinks this *is* her kingdom," Garrett pointed out. "No matter how run-down it is. She just wants to hold on to every scrap of authority, and wave it in our faces. What a bully."

"It's *definitely* long past time for some real change around here," Kathy opined.

"Well, today's the day we turn it all around!" Jamie gushed. "I can feel it!" Her shoulders drooped. "Just as soon as someone actually shows up."

They heard the door open; they turned to see one of the property manager's assistants poke his head in. Jamie sighed. "Hello, Mr. MacNeill. Come to check on us? I hope this is all to your satisfaction."

The lackey glanced around briefly. "Oh…yeah, sure. Listen, I wanted to let you know that this meeting has been moved. Sorry for the short notice."

"*What*?!" Jamie hollered. "But we've been prepping *this* room! We don't have time to start over!"

Mr. MacNeill's eyes swept over the room. "Not a bad job! Maybe we'll hire you to do this *all* the time." He chuckled to himself.

"Don't patronize me!" Jamie insisted. "This is *exactly* the sort of behavior that makes us want to form a tenants' association!"

He turned to her absentmindedly. "Right…that's why it's being moved. There's a lot of interest in your meeting! It's been moved to the concert hall. People are showing up in droves! That's all. There's just not enough space here."

Jamie's face beamed. "That's great news! It may take us a few minutes to move our stuff."

Mr. MacNeill gazed at the back wall. "Nah, leave up the garlands. They look nice in here."

"But they were for *our* event!" Jamie protested.

"It's just, I think that's been taken care of, too," Mr. MacNeill explained. "There's probably not room for any more decorations." He made his way back to the door. "Come by anytime. Oh, be sure to close the fire exits before you leave." He walked out.

"Did you hear that?" Jamie thrilled. "We've hit the big time! Things are going to be *very* different around here!"

With a spring in their steps, Jamie and her cohorts marched to the other side of the apartment complex, through the common area between the buildings, across the divide between the older structures and the newer ones, towards the concert hall. That was the name given to the longer room, in one of the more recently constructed buildings, with the permanent rows of seats. It was used frequently to show movies; more recently, it had hosted a variety show put on by the local elementary school. It could easily seat four times the people of the multi-purpose room. Jamie's heart soared with delight as she heard a roar erupt in the distance from the assembled crowd. They hurried their pace.

Jamie flung the door open to reveal a packed house, then stopped and frowned. She didn't recognize most of the people here; they must have been the recently-arrived tenants, mostly young professionals that worked nearby, like the one presently speaking on stage. In the back of the room, she saw her friends and long-time neighbors, standing against the wall, looking unsettled. She rushed to join them as the speaker continued.

"How much longer are we supposed to put up with the bad apples? With criminals and flakes? They break into our cars, they spray graffiti, they harass us as we come and go! We're just trying to live here in peace and comfort! Somehow, *they* have all the rights, and *we* have none!" The crowd roared again. Jamie felt a shiver run down her spine.

The speaker pounded the lectern. "We don't have to live like this! We outnumber them! The first step is to pass new rules that all tenants must abide by! It's obvious who's trying to behave, and who isn't. And if they can't live like civilized human beings, they get the boot!" He leaned in, gazing levelly at the audience. "People that cannot regulate themselves deserve to get regulated by *others*!" Another loud roar of approval.

Jamie and her friends finally made it to the back of the room. She found Eleanor there, wide-eyed and fearful. "Who *are* all these people?" Jamie implored. "When did we get crowded out?"

"It happened slowly, over the last few months," Eleanor mused. "The place changed after all those new businesses opened up nearby. I've heard of gentrification before, but I never thought it would happen here."

Jamie gestured angrily with her hands. "Are you *serious*? So we're going to find ourselves priced out of the apartments where we've lived for years, to be replaced by...*them*?" She motioned across the room, referring to the well-dressed throng.

The speaker was joined by the head property manager, a beatific smile on her face. Jamie's mouth gaped as the speaker beheld the audience. "In consultation with Mrs. Rhatigen, I've drawn up a code of behavior that all tenants will have to abide by, once we vote to approve it. You all had a chance to read it if you're on the tenants association e-mail list." Eleanor pushed a paper copy into Jamie's hands. "These were piled on the table as we entered."

"*What* e-mail list?" Jamie asked. "That's nothing *we* did!" Eleanor just shrugged.

Jamie skimmed over the proposed rules. All misdemeanors, and most property crimes, subjected the tenant to immediate eviction. Certain nuisances, like hoarding, unruly pets, or littering, were punishable by steep fines. And an across-the-board rent increase, to take effect immediately, would pay for increased security patrols, electronic surveillance, and "necessary" renovations. Further pages went into more detail, with ample usage of words like "reasonable", "professional", and "civilized". The fear that had started in Jamie's spine spread to the rest of her body.

Mrs. Rhatigen now stood at the lectern. "It's time to vote! Make your choice *now*!" Jamie saw several people noodle with their cell phones. Eleanor pointed out the printed QR code on the last page of the packet of papers. Glumly, Jamie realized her phone was too old to allow her to vote. Even Eleanor's senior-oriented flip phone could scan the matrix barcode.

A few minutes later, Mrs. Rhatigen gestured to the totals on the projection screen behind her. "The results are in! 605 in favor, 74 opposed! The motion is *carried*!" A cheer rose from the crowd as Mrs. Rhatigen beamed. "Today begins a new era for Sunny Day Suites! And if you're one of the few that don't like it…your time is short!"

Jamie skulked along the side of the room, heading to the exit. The gloom in her eyes went unnoticed by the people in her way. She could still hear the cheering from a fair distance down the corridor.

◊ — ◊ — ◊

Tyler drove up to the gate of his neighborhood. He saw the leering grins of the three security guards on duty. Oh great, he thought to himself as he slowed down. *This* again.

He rolled down his window as he came to a stop. "Hi, fellas. How's your day going?"

"License and registration?" The red-haired guard's eyes burned with ferocity.

Tyler already had that ready. "*Really*, guys? We go through this every time. You *know* I live here." He handed over the paperwork.

The hairy guard shuffled nearby; he scrutinized Tyler closely. "You match the description of someone who just knocked over a liquor store, out in the nearby town." The burly guard already had his trunk open, and was rifling through it.

Tyler sighed. "You *know* I'm not like that. Besides, you can see what's in here."

The red-haired guard punched up something on his PDA. "This isn't your car."

Tyler let out a small chuckle. "No, it's my stepdad's car. We don't have the same last name. You know that *too*."

The burly guard slammed the trunk shut. At that instant, the hairy guard whipped out his baton and held it menacingly, twitching. "Don't sass us! We could strip this car down to the frame if we wanted!"

Tyler smiled wryly. "My stepdad would be *pissed* if you did that. Do you *really* want to answer to him?"

The security guards froze. None of them spoke for several seconds. Tyler gazed at them, unimpressed. "Can I go now?"

As the red-haired guard handed Tyler his paperwork, a growl stirred from the burly guard. "We've got our eyes on you. Don't get out of line, you little punk!"

"Guys, look, if you're *really* this bored, I can bring you by something. Some of my mom's cookies? Games and puzzles? Comic books? *Whatever* you like!"

"*Move along, sir!*" The hairy guard waved Tyler through, as another car pulled up behind him. He drove off without saying another word.

This was getting out of hand. He'd have to talk to his stepfather about this.

As Tyler approached the gate the next morning, the security guards were nowhere to be found. He was surprised to find gleaming metal robots jump out of the guard shack. They stopped him.

"License and registration?" The metallic voice vibrated with authority.

Tyler smiled as he handed them over. Finally, some impartial justice! He could get used to this.

An alarm sounded from within the robot guard; the other two followed quickly with their own. "You are wanted for felony vandalism! Hands in the air, *now*!"

Tyler's heart skipped a beat as he thrust his arms upwards. What was going on?

All three robot guards belched a staccato imitation of a laugh. "Just kidding. We hope our fun-loving antics have endeared you to us. On your way, citizen!" The robot guard handed Tyler his paperwork and motioned him forward.

Tyler couldn't leave fast enough. He missed the old guards already.

◊ — ◊ — ◊

Carl Beaumont entered the large conference room; a majestic oval table dominated the center. He found the other executives already sitting there.

"Good morning, chairman!" one called out.

Carl smiled. "Good morning, Drew." He swept his arm across the room. "I'm glad to see you all arrived early!"

"It may have had something to do with your meeting notice," Drew replied acidly. "The one alluding to a crisis? And how the meeting would start *exactly* on time?"

Carl chuckled. "I admit, I was pretty stressed when I wrote that. Hopefully you all had a good night's sleep in spite of it." He looked around the room and smiled sympathetically. "I need you all at your best." He grabbed the remote-control clicker from the table and pressed a button. The television on the wall stopped displaying the property-management firm's logo, and in its place was a handful of sedate bar charts.

Carl sighed. "As you all know, the company is at a crossroads. We've had decent success adapting to the new trend of private government ownership. We own our fair share of gated communities and small towns. But expansion has stalled; there are other national property-management companies doing the same thing. Finding a town to take over is becoming more difficult, since a lot of prime targets are snatched up by others before we can close the deal."

Carl clicked the button, and the slide was replaced with a riot of colored graphs. "We could continue to bid on small towns, but prices are rising on the most desirable ones, and the overall effort is too small to make much of a difference in our bottom line. To make matters worse, profit from them has ceased to grow. Very little followed the initial windfall that came from reforming governance."

Carl clicked again; the next slide showed a pareto chart of possibilities. "We need larger profit centers, if this venture is ever going to be worth the effort. The types of large-scale industry that can be enticed to set up shop in a small town are pretty limited. The plethora of small businesses to be found there are *nice*, and one of them might become a big business *some* day, but it hasn't happened yet. We're already investing in some of these smaller concerns, but it's not clear if we should ramp that up. We're unsure of the odds of seeing a return on such a diversified portfolio; this isn't really our area of expertise. To be blunt, the next step is not clear."

Carl clicked a button on the remote control, and the screen resumed showing the company's logo. He turned to face the table. "I don't need to tell you how the rest of our business is doing. Home prices are high, and tenants are milking the seemingly endless eviction moratoria for all they can, to stay in houses they can't afford. This stops us from selling the houses and reaping a pretty good profit."

Carl grimaced. "I'm afraid the only sure way to make money in the current environment is to assume things will continue to slide downhill, and to somehow find a way to profit on that decline."

Carl rested his hands on the table, supporting himself. "To put it mildly…we've plateaued. Without some big ideas, this venture may have hit a dead end." He looked across the room, which greeted him only with nervous silence. "So…does anyone here *have* any big ideas?"

The room became deathly still. "Oh, come on, people," Carl anguished. "I've worked with some of you for *years*! We've always made it through the tough times. Granted, we never had to deal with such insane levels of unbridled chaos. But we've gotten to where we are because we always managed to pull a rabbit out of the hat. Is that over? Has the well truly run dry?"

Carl stood still for a moment. On the other side of the table, he could see someone with a shock of red hair look to his left, then to his right, then stare directly at Carl. As a smile washed over his face, he raised his hand.

Carl nodded and gestured towards the gentleman. "Why don't we hear from one of our junior executives? What's your name, son?"

"Eric Thompson, sir," came the confident reply.

"Pleased to meet you, son," Carl proclaimed. "Of course, that's just a nice way of saying I don't know you from Adam." A smattering of polite chuckles flitted through the room. "Why don't you tell us a little about yourself?"

"I'd be happy to," Eric declared as he stood up. "As you pointed out, I'm a junior executive…but not for *this* firm. I work for a hedge fund, one of your largest partners. I was embedded here, not only to keep an eye on their investment, but to learn this business."

"Well, I wish you could have joined us back in our better days," Carl lamented. "This can't be a very prestigious assignment for you."

"Oh, I assure you, sir, quite the contrary!" came the enthusiastic reply. The board members shook with a start.

"Really?" Carl snorted. "You *enjoy* being part of our slow-motion crash?"

"I don't see it that way at all, sir," Eric assured. "I'm utterly *fascinated* by what I've learned in my time here. I've seen this firm expand from owning homes, to owning gated communities, to owning entire towns. I never would have believed I'd see *anything* like this, and yet here I am, in the thick of it! I find it *far* more interesting and motivating than just counting beans…I'm awed by the *possibilities* here! And what you see as a crisis, I see as a great opportunity." He paused for a moment to behold Carl, who seemed dumbfounded. Eric continued. "Would you allow me to explain?"

"Of course, son," Carl asserted.

"Yeah," one board member chortled, as he turned to a colleague. "I can't *wait* to hear this one." A few scattered snickers erupted.

"To me, our next step forward is clear," Eric declared. "I propose taking over an entire city…the one we're in."

The board erupted in guffawing laughter. The chairman covered his mouth, but finally couldn't stop himself from letting out a disrespectful giggle. Eric stood stoically, unmoved, and continued to scan the room slowly with his eyes. Finally, the clamor died down.

"I'm sorry, son," Carl explained. "I should have been clearer…I wanted a *realistic* idea."

"The way to make money in real estate is to buy a depressed asset, one whose value isn't appreciated by others, and refurbish it," Eric interjected. "Wouldn't you agree?"

"Well…of course it is," Carl stammered. "That's true for *most* investments. But how is that relevant here?"

"I'm *glad* you asked!" Eric crowed loudly, causing a few to wince. "May I show my presentation?" He motioned towards the television screen mounted on the wall.

Carl shook his head and chuckled softly. "Sure, son. Knock yourself out. Here you go." He put the clicker down and, with a flick of his arm, slid it along the table. The clicker sailed over the smooth surface, spinning gently. Abruptly, it hit some barely visible imperfection on the surface, causing it to pirouette into the air, loudly tumbling end over end, before coming to a graceless stop, somewhere near the middle, in front of a young lady.

Eric gestured to her. "Ma'am? Little help?"

She beheld Eric for a moment. Then, with a smirk, the young lady grabbed the clicker and flung it down the table with great force. It slid noisily, and as the board members watched it, the clicker collided with a wire strung across its path, sending it into the air, bouncing and cartwheeling clumsily. As it threatened to sail over the edge of the table, Eric nimbly snatched it out of the air, the slapping sound it made with his palm echoing faintly through the room. "Thank you, ma'am," Eric chirped as he saluted politely. "Excellent assist!" She returned a warm, beaming smile.

Eric pressed a button on the clicker; in the company logo's place was a montage of riots, spirited street protests, and clouds of smoke billowing from fires. The members of the board reared at the abrupt transition. "I don't need to remind you of the current state of affairs," he quipped. "But I did anyway."

He clicked a button, and the next slide showed before/after pictures of apartment complexes and small-town business districts, depicting how each had been cleaned up and refurbished. "Of course, there's some good news. People at the grass-roots level are self-organizing *against* the macro-trend of decay; the ownership of gated communities and small towns is just the beginning. The recent stories of apartment complexes coming up with social-media inspired 'terms and conditions' for their residents are a new phase of the same movement." He panned his eyes over the room. "Unfortunately, this isn't the story of *our* city."

The next slide showed an aerial photo of the metropolis at dusk, looking dingy and dilapidated. Overlaying the image was a depressing collage of sobering statistics. "Foot traffic is down a stunning *eighty percent* in the city center. Consumers and tourists simply don't feel safe in an area beset by riots and criminal violence. Our police departments have been defunded; gun violence has skyrocketed. Our firm has had to hire private security to make up the difference, and although we're safe for the time being, that cost comes *straight* out of our bottom line."

Eric surveyed the room; everyone remained dead silent. He continued. "Businesses less blessed than ours are losing fortunes to looters, and are pulling out. Citizens are fleeing the soaring crime and high taxes. Ever since the city council decriminalized property crimes involving less than a thousand dollars, shoplifting has risen to epidemic levels. Insurance for retail businesses has become unaffordable, and many won't pay for damages unless their client relocates to a less crime-ridden area. The collapsing business and tax base have left the city unable to pay its bills."

Eric clicked a button; the slide showed the state capital complex. "The state government isn't much better off. They can't afford to bail out the city, because their finances are *also* hanging by a thread. Without a dramatic reversal of fortune, we can expect to lose everything we've worked so hard to build."

The room was silent for a moment, then Carl spoke up. "We don't debate *any* of this. But what do you propose to actually *do* about it?"

"We need leverage over the city," Eric explained. "The real-estate-rental business is relatively low-margin, especially factoring in rent moratoria, depreciation from unruly tenants, and the ongoing civil unrest. On the other hand, home prices are near all-time highs, and inventory is very low; this is the time for us to sell our holdings. We need to change the law so that we can evict non-paying tenants, but trying to get a bill through the city council, with all the corruption and vested interests, simply isn't feasible. But I ask, why bother owning the houses when you can own the infrastructure itself? I propose we replace the city code with the same sort of social-media-inspired terms and conditions that so many of our gated communities, and small towns, have utilized to such great effect."

"And what leverage do you suggest we use?" Carl challenged.

"The oldest leverage there is," Eric trilled. "Creditors!" He clicked the button; the next slide revealed a pareto chart. "It turns out that five firms own eighty-five percent of the city's outstanding debts. All of them are quite aware the city can never afford to pay it off. That gives the debtholders *great* leeway in demanding major concessions. And the biggest one they can demand…is assuming total ownership and control of the city. We follow *that* by replacing city law with our well-vetted set of terms and conditions. That gives us the foundation we need to turn around the decline."

"You know," Drew began, "one reason we were able to purchase gated communities and small towns, is because the money came from our *own* funds; we didn't have to get anyone else's buy-in. What makes you think these debtholders will go along with your plan?"

"Because I've already discussed it with them," Eric revealed. "And they've agreed to go along with it."

"They have?" Drew asked incredulously.

"Well, tentatively," Eric admitted. "Providing I can make good on the *other* parts of my plan."

"And what might *those* be?" Carl demurred.

"I'm *glad* you asked!" Eric answered brightly. Carl put his hand to his face and winced as Eric continued with his spirited presentation.

"I will need this firm's permission to deal with our delinquent tenants," Eric explained. "I'm confident I can get them evicted, allowing us to sell the houses. I've already made all the connections I need to make it work, from beginning to end. I just need money to put it into play."

One board member raised a single eyebrow. "How much will *that* be?"

"It can vary," Eric offered. "But the more you commit to, up front, the more broadly I can operate. And I'm happy to tell you that the hedge fund I work for has already committed to matching the funds that *you* pledge. Keep in mind, the amounts I'm talking about are large, but relatively minor for a company like yours. Plus, I already have informal commitments from all the people, and companies, that I need; as soon as I can get it funded, we can move forward almost immediately."

"Just how informal *are* these commitments?" Carl countered.

Eric's face became serious. "Sir, I wouldn't waste the board's time with a plan unless I had done all of the legwork to put it together; everything about the plan is in place, *except* for the funding." Carl didn't speak; Eric continued. "I project that the money made from selling houses currently rented to delinquent tenants will pay back the seed money in relatively short order, at which point the company can decide to take their profits, or plow them back in to make an even bigger profit."

"And once you've sold the houses?" one board member piped up. "What then? The city is still in terrible shape."

"And it must be refurbished," Eric agreed. "I've identified a corporate takeover target that would be of great use to us." He clicked a button on the remote, bringing up a video of gyrating robots. "No one will ever forget *this* synchronized dance routine! The rest of their product line is just as eerily sophisticated. But they've been bought and sold a few times since then. Sadly, their prospects have been kneecapped by widespread opposition from the workers that their robots would replace. Their parent company is regretting the investment, and has begun making noises about unloading it, but with uncertain future prospects, the odds are low that anyone wants it." Eric smiled as he beheld the room. "I propose we buy them. Given the bleak consensus on their future, it'd be an incredible bargain. I have a *different* opinion of their worth. I believe they're *just* what we need to reclaim our infrastructure!"

"I'm afraid I must disagree, Mr. Thompson," a board member chimed. Eric turned to look at the elegantly dressed middle-aged lady. "My husband works for an investment firm that lost the bid to take over that company. He's seen their internal documents. While their robots make for a good viral video, it takes a lot of programming and preparation to even make a canned demo work. Their sophistication is simply not up to the level of autonomous intelligence you need."

"Intelligence," Eric quietly said to himself, his eyes staring off into space.

"And without that, you'll need a skilled labor force capable of wielding them. Their manufacturer doesn't have enough people to do that, not even if every last one of them decided to uproot their lives and move here, and work solely on *your* tasks. And without autonomy, this part of your plan won't work."

The chairman smiled. "Thank you, Mrs. Verhage. I'm grateful you were able to inject some sanity into this far-out plan." He turned to Eric. "I'm sorry, son, but your ideas are simply too fantastic. We can't go forward with this."

Eric continued staring into space. Carl frowned. "Mr. Thompson? Can you hear me?"

Eric suddenly turned his head, staring intently at the chairman. "My apologies, sir. I was thrown a curve ball; I had to come up quickly with a backup plan. I believe I've done so." He gestured to Mrs. Verhage. "Your objections are noted, and gratefully received."

"That's hardly good enough," Carl grumbled. "Frankly, your plan sounds like a house of cards. Magic robots aside, you must concede that one reason acquiring gated communities, and small towns, has worked so well is because the people that live there are largely law-abiding and self-sufficient. Large cities attract people that need public services in order to survive, and as we've learned recently, far too many are irresponsible and criminally oriented. You can't scale up from small towns to a big city; the situations aren't comparable."

"With all due respect, sir, I disagree," Eric countered. "I truly believe that most people are decent. Scaling up to a big city involves hiring the decent people, so that they can unleash their potential, and, inspired by what social media and other technology firms get away with all the time, impose terms and conditions that effectively banish the wrongdoers. One big advantage we have here is the widespread public surveillance network, already installed by the city. We're not lacking for information on the bad guys, the city simply has no ability to *do* anything about it. Once the law is changed, the ne'er-do-wells can be imprisoned or deported."

Carl paused for a moment, and then sighed. "OK, I can see how that would work. But I still believe your project is too risky to do under our banner. We have a nationwide reputation that could be tarnished irreparably."

"Completely understandable, sir," Eric concurred. "I suggest forming a separate corporation for it, of which this company, and its financial backers, would be the early funders and primary shareholders." Eric smiled as his eyes glowed with revelation. "And I'll give it the name I've always wanted to use."

"Which is?" Mrs. Verhage asked, raising one eyebrow.

Eric raised his head and looked into the distance. "Unlimited Partners."

Carl snorted. "Sounds pretty generic."

"I disagree," piped up a voice. The room turned to look at the young lady, seated near the center of the table, the one that assisted Eric with retrieving the remote clicker. "I think it has the perfect combination of sensible and messianic." At this, the room burst into laughter.

"Son," Carl challenged as the noise died down, "give me one good reason I should approve of your insane plan."

"Because it'll work," Eric replied confidently. "Because it captures the spirit of the times. *And*...because it's the only idea anyone's offered you."

Carl looked around the room. "*Please*, someone present a competing idea." Several tense moments passed. "Anyone?" The board members just looked uncomfortably at each other.

Carl's shoulders slumped. "Fine, kid. So how much are you

asking for?"

Eric smiled. "A lot, but not compared to what you can afford." He clicked a button on the remote, leading to a spreadsheet that broke down the up-front costs. At the bottom loomed a rather large figure. The board members collectively gasped.

Eric pounced. "That noise you all made, *right* then, tells me why this company is in so much trouble." He turned to Carl. "You *said* you wanted big ideas."

"Not quite *that* big," Carl countered. "I might approve about half that."

"I'm sorry to hear that you continue to think small," Eric grimaced.

"*Fine*," Carl glowered. "Half your figure, *but* your project gets approved."

"*Deal!*" Eric shouted, grinning ear to ear.

The chairman looked around uncertainly. "Did I just get scammed?" He turned to Eric. "How can you agree to that, when you acknowledge it's not enough?"

"I'll accept the additional challenge, if it means I get to put my lifelong vision into action."

"You were *expecting* the collapse of civil order?" one board member mocked.

Eric turned towards him. "Our country has been in a slow-motion crash for decades. Are you saying you hadn't noticed? When was the last time we even won a war? Or *didn't* abandon our allies at the end?" The board member glumly looked down.

"You really don't know your place, do you," Carl growled. "Just a loose cannon. You don't sound like *any* businessman I've ever run into."

"You're right, I don't," Eric countered. "And that makes me sad, because *I* think I make a lot of sense."

"I'm still making up my mind about that," Carl declared. "So, while this might be your project, and your idea, you won't be in charge. You *will* be the senior vice president, responsible for the overall direction and the day-to-day activities, but you'll have your own bosses, and board of directors, to answer to. A board staffed with more sober minds, that *I* approve of. Catch my drift?"

Eric swallowed. "I can work with that."

The room was still for a moment. Then Mrs. Verhage spoke up. "Congratulations, you have your funding. Now, how exactly do you intend to make your plan *work*?"

"I'll put together a team to do it," Eric explained. "After all, if I can't put together an effective team, I have no business sitting at this table."

The chairman shuddered. "Well, we now have our one big idea...God help us all. Unless someone wants to propose another one, this meeting is over." The silence in the room revealed the faint murmur of the city outside. The chairman threw his hands in the air and wordlessly turned to leave. Most of the rest of the board followed, throwing reproachful looks at Eric on the way out.

Eric sighed happily, pulled his phone out of his pocket, and began to dial. He became aware that someone had walked up to him. Looking up, he saw the young lady that had previously been sitting at the center of the table.

"Hi, I'm Danielle," she opened.

"Pleased to meet you!" he beamed. "Thanks for the assist back there. I literally couldn't have done it without you."

Danielle smiled. "That was the most stunningly visionary idea I've ever heard in my life. It has a rare combination of solid foundations, force multiplication, and optimism."

"I'm glad you even understood it!" Eric laughed. "I'm not sure anyone else in the room grasped it beyond the up-front cost."

"I heard somewhere you were putting together a team," she ribbed. "I'd love to be part of this project."

Before Eric could reply, a shout stopped him cold. "Danielle! Stop dawdling and get back to work!" Eric caught a glimpse of the interrupter's name badge; he was Ted Danbury, vice-president of something illegible.

Danielle turned towards Ted, incensed, and looked him right in the eye. "I need a few more minutes."

Ted's eyes shot open in surprise, but an expression of anger quickly washed over his face. "Two more minutes! Then you'd *better* be back at your desk!" He turned around and stormed away.

Eric watched him leave, then turned to Danielle. "It takes all kinds, doesn't it," he deadpanned.

"No it doesn't," she shot back. "He's just a bully." She looked up with a deflated expression in her eyes. "I'm not just a secretary, you know. I *have* my business degree, and got *very* high marks in college. But all Ted cares about is that it wasn't one of the 'top 20' schools. I can only find work as a glorified file clerk; no one will take me seriously!" She stared at him fiercely. "I'm *dying* for a chance to show what I'm capable of!"

Eric faced his palms forward in a pleading motion. "If you're applying for a job on my team, you just got it." A beaming smile flooded across her face. Eric continued. "Now, I'm *not* going to bully you…but I *will* ask you to put up with a completely different kind of pain."

"I accept the challenge," she replied stoically. "When do I start?"

Eric typed something on his phone, then touched his phone to hers; Danielle's phone chimed. "Go pack up your desk. Here's the location of your new office. I'll see you soon. But now…I have to make a call." He stared into the distance wistfully. "One I've wanted to make for *years*."

Ted appeared at the door to the conference room. "Danielle! What are you still doing here? I said *move it!*"

Danielle strode confidently towards the door, pushing past Ted, who just gaped at her. She gestured to her rear. "You're no longer my boss; I work for *him* now." Eric slipped past Ted, smirking as he went by.

"How dare you!" Ted exploded. "I'll fire you for this!"

Eric continued to walk away, turning to look at Ted. "She's not yours to fire any longer."

Ted gaped speechlessly for a moment. "Uh…you can't just leave! You have to give notice!"

Danielle stopped walking and turned to face Ted, arms akimbo. "But my employment is at-will…as you're so fond of reminding me whenever I 'get out of line'."

Ted marched right up to her, but stopped short; the fierce look on his face melted into uncertainty. "You…you need to hand off your job to someone else."

"You only gave me menial secretarial work," she retorted. "That hardly needs to be handed off."

Ted's face fell; his eyes filled with sorrow. "OK, I admit it…I can't do this without you."

Danielle looked incredulous. "What?! If that were true, why did you treat me so poorly?"

Ted didn't respond; tears slowly welled in his eyes. "I'm sorry…I'm so sorry. I promise never to do it again."

"You're darn right you won't," Eric interjected as he stepped between them, throwing a steely look at Ted, holding it for a few seconds. Danielle strode away without saying another word.

"So, I see you finally decided to do the right thing," Eric told Ted, "after exhausting every other possibility."

Ted burned with rage. "I'll get you for this. I'll get you if it's the last thing I do."

Eric shook his head sadly. "So you *really* have nothing better to do with your time." Ted didn't respond; Eric continued. "Maybe I can find something worthwhile for you to do. Your combative nature could be really helpful, in the right setting."

He then turned to walk away, leaving Ted standing there, speechless.

2

Eric sat in his office; his door was slightly ajar. He sighed as he looked out the window, at the overhead view of decay and desperation. Even at this height, he could see trash strewn around the streets, some of it blowing in the wind, forming lazy tornadoes that dissipated quickly. "My God," he muttered to himself. "What have I gotten myself into?"

He gazed into his phone, and a smile crept over his face. "Time to find out!" He brought up his contacts, filtered it by family, and punched an entry near the bottom. It rang several times before being answered.

Eric was met with a pregnant silence, then a voice spoke. "Eric? Is that really you?"

"Uncle Sam!" Eric gushed. "It's been a long time! How have you been? How's Aunt Angie doing?"

"What do you want?" Sam's voice seemed nonplussed.

"Do you have some time? There's something I really want to discuss with you."

"There *is*? We have something to *say* to each other?" Sam countered. "It's literally been years. You went your way, I went mine. You got yourself a fancy business degree, put on a suit, and now you're the Wolf Of 7th Street, or wherever the heck your office is."

"That's all true," Eric agreed. "But I'm still the same person inside! I remember how well we used to get along, especially during my teenage years."

"How can I forget?" Sam replied, sounding pained. "Like some of the stuff you and your friends would get into. I can't believe you got away with it."

"And *I* can't believe you suggested it!" Eric laughed.

"I did, didn't I," Sam groaned.

"Hey, let's not mince words here," Eric ribbed. "You *paid* us for some of it!"

Eric could hear Sam wince. "Yeah, I admit, I had a lot of responsibility. But what did *you* do with it? Seriously, I never saw you as the businessman type. You had all the makings of a wild-eyed rebel, but traded it for a company car and an expense account." Sam's voice dripped with sarcasm. "How's the view from your office?"

"Hey, don't sell me short, Sam!" Eric protested. "You've always been something of a mad scientist; how is that fundamentally different from being a mad financier? Same mentality, different field!"

There was a pause. "I might concede that."

"I might walk like a duck, talk like a duck...even *quack* like a duck...but that doesn't mean I'm a duck." Eric eyes twinkled. "I *could* be a loon."

Sam laughed. "OK, this is starting to sound like the nutball nephew I used to know."

"I really am, I promise!" Eric pleaded. "And I can't wait to tell you why I called you. You won't believe it."

"You're right, I don't believe it," Sam quipped. "So what is it?"

"So, I mean this as diplomatically as possible," Eric assured, "but...how is your career going?"

Sam let out a long sigh. "About as well as can be expected. I still think it was the right decision to sell my business and get a corporate job. But that was years ago, and the tedium and powerlessness have really gotten on my nerves. Even more so, lately."

"Not much room for growth, is there," Eric sympathized.

"There's not a lot of imagination among our so-called leadership," Sam related. "They won't fund any project that isn't absolutely a sure thing, which kind of defeats the purpose of doing research and development. Support for even the most *promising* project dries up whenever they need to 'make their numbers'. And if by some miracle we can preserve funding long enough to actually *complete* something, our competition has run circles around us, and already has the market locked up. And don't even get me started on the piffling raises, or how smooth-talking grifters get all the promotions."

"Hey, you knew what you were signing up for," Eric reminded. "Glacial progress at best, in exchange for your paychecks not bouncing."

"I try to tell myself everything is OK," Sam confessed, "but my career really wears on me sometimes. I wish there was an alternative."

"What if I told you there *was*?" Eric trilled.

Eric could hear Sam snort in surprise. "What? At your hedge

fund? Doing what? Shaving microseconds off transaction times? Trying to speed up cryptocurrency-mining apps? My job might be a grind, but working in finance would be much worse."

"It's not for the hedge fund," Eric explained. "It's not even for the property-management firm where I'm embedded. It's for a spinoff that *they're* funding. They're leaping straight past small-town ownership…and are poised to take over a large city."

"Is *that* what you do for a living?" Sam groaned. "Pretty much a big disappointment, as far as I can tell. The idea has *so* much potential, but no one is doing it right."

"My feelings exactly," Eric agreed. "That's why I want to bring you on board. So we can do it right."

"Me?!" Sam protested. "I'm not a businessman, and I'm *definitely* not a politician. What the hell do you expect *me* to do?"

"I have some thoughts," Eric hinted. "How's your research into cybernetics going?"

Sam let out a hollow laugh. "As well as can be expected, given no funding and no time. The basics are all there, but not much more."

"The last I heard, you and Angela had perfected neural implants in cats. That let them communicate with each other, and with you! They can follow orders, they can effectively hunt in packs…you were even able to bypass spinal damage."

"I've gone further than that," Sam revealed. "For a time, we dabbled in completely repurposing cranial tissue. Angie and I actually managed to get a cat brain to unpattern itself; we then reprogrammed it to be something else."

"That's incredible!" Eric guffawed. "I had no idea you'd progressed so far."

"Not far enough," Sam lamented. "We got them to do some amazing things, but they could never quite forget they were once cats. They'd follow their new programming for a while, then they'd go rogue. Finally, we stopped trying."

"That's too bad," Eric consoled. "That sounds like a really promising research direction. Too much for the straitjacketed types running the firm, I guess. But that's exactly the sort of cutting-edge research I can use in my venture. I need autonomous intelligence for a lot of the advances I want to make. Would you and Aunt Angie be interested in starting that up again?"

Sam let out a long sigh. "Angela doesn't want anything to do with it anymore."

Eric gasped softly. "Why?"

"She had a change of heart after seeing her creations go rogue. She said she couldn't justify putting a living creature through that kind of torment. It's been a long time since she's done *anything* in the field of biology." Sam paused. "She's a lot more bitter than you remember her."

Eric took a deep breath. "I'm really sorry to hear that. Someone with her gift for bioengineering deserves far better." Eric looked down sadly. "I guess you can't help me *after* all."

"Actually," Sam corrected, "she agreed a long time ago that I can use her notes. She just doesn't want to be personally involved with any of it."

"Well, that's *something*, I guess." Eric sounded relieved. "But to make this work, we'd need to find someone that can replace her."

"I might know a few people," Sam offered. "I met several bright young graduate students as part of my company's collaboration with academia. They like to form short-term partnerships with universities, to share knowledge as well as expenses. But colleges are just as conservative; anything truly innovative is inevitably treated as a threat, not only to the status quo, but to the egos of more senior researchers." Sam chuckled to himself. "But that doesn't mean some of the kids don't have potential!"

"Are you still in touch with any of them?" Eric asked.

"A few," Sam revealed. "I recognized them as kindred mad-science spirits. We stayed in touch after one of these partnerships. I became something of an unofficial mentor to them. Sadly, most of that devolves into convincing them to lower their standards, and to become more cynical."

"Well, maybe we can offer them something better," Eric hoped. "What sort of project did you do with them?"

"Oh, it was the usual sort of overly-conservative go-nowhere retread," Sam deadpanned. "It was what they were doing, on their *own* time, which was fascinating. They managed to grow neural tissue in a lab, and induced it to form basic patterns in response to stimuli. They were able to get some of their synthetic brains to play games, sort patterns, even learn rudimentary language. But the college cut off their funding too."

"For something *that* promising?" Eric mourned. "What a stunning lack of vision."

"It was worse than that," Sam explained. "There was a

significant amount of unstated jealousy from the more senior scientists. And for a few of them, an unsettling amount of sexism from the old guard."

"I'll *never* understand not making full use of available resources," Eric pined. "That's just bad business."

"But how does any of this fit into what *you're* doing?" Sam asked. "What are you up to?"

"I need autonomous intelligence," Eric revealed. "Robots capable of thinking for themselves. Service animals that can communicate with us, and with each other. It takes a lot of effort to refurbish a city, and we don't have the manpower for the expected volume of work."

Sam sounded thoughtful. "I think these kids could pull that off, especially if I gave them access to Angela's notes."

Eric reared. "You mean you haven't done that already?"

"There was no point, not yet," Sam explained. "They already have their hands full being university staff scientists. But if they could get *jobs* doing this sort of thing...well, that's a different story."

"Are you willing to recruit them?" Eric asked. "I mean, assuming *you're* willing to join this effort."

Sam sighed. "I hate to be a wet blanket, but...how well-funded are you? I'd love to cut loose with some *real* research, but at the end of the day, I still need a paycheck. And so will they. The university might not pay much, but at least it's regular."

"Assume funding isn't an issue," Eric implied. "I didn't get the budget I wanted, but I'm confident I can grow it far beyond the initial seed money. Your team's portion will only be a fraction of it, of course, but rest assured, I have the ability to ramp up your funding anytime."

"If you don't mind me asking," Sam probed, "how much are we talking? What's your budget?"

Eric told him.

"My God," Sam gasped. "I thought you were only a *junior* executive!"

"Keep in mind, I asked for more," Eric reminded. "But we all have to start somewhere."

Sam was silent for a moment. "Yeah. OK." He laughed. "*Hell* yeah! I'm *sick* of rotting on the vine! I'm sure I can find *several* like-minded people to come along!"

"That's great! I'm counting on you!" Eric gushed. "I'll send you all the details in a few hours. You may all have to relocate to this city, at least temporarily."

"I'm sure we can manage. But Eric...there's something you might not be considering here."

"Such as?" Eric asked.

"Well," Sam began, "I think you're aware of this, but you may not realize how deep it goes. The sad truth is...there's a lot of suppressed science out there. Many workable technologies are not allowed to go forward, because they threaten some established power center. Stuff that has to stay on the fringes, for its own safety. *Real* solutions to our energy needs, snuffed out by Big Oil. Inventions that would cause governments to lose their grip on power. And more immediately...the autonomous cybernetic intelligence you want, that could lead to widespread panic about a robotic rebellion. And all of it kept in check by lack of funding. If you're willing to support this... you could unleash forces of unstoppable chaos."

"We already *have* chaos," Eric reminded. "We have riots in the street, widespread breakdown of civil order, and common sense being cast aside for foolish notions. Besides, the chaos we'd bring wouldn't be *all* bad. Remember, freedom is chaos put to good purposes."

Sam let out a long, drawn-out chuckle. "I'm sorry I doubted you, nephew. You're right...you haven't mellowed out at all."

"I'll forgive you for using the m-word in my presence," Eric joked.

"Then it's settled!" Sam chimed. "I'll start recruiting immediately. Any idea what our first project is? We'll of course need some time to set up the lab, but it'd be nice to know what our short-term focus should be."

"There's an immediate need for two types of cyborgs. One is the construction and demolition bots I mentioned earlier; we have a lot of renovation to do. But the other is security bots. We're already using artificially intelligent guards in some of our gated communities, but their record is...uneven. Biologically-derived intelligence could go a long way to solving that problem."

"Going straight to the killer-droid scenario, are we?" Sam jested.

"Hey, I gotta be me!" Eric trilled.

Sam let out a belly laugh. "Wow. You sure know how to break up my day, kid. Looking forward to the details! I have a bunch of calls I need to make now."

"I'll let you have at it," Eric granted. "I have plenty more to do at this end."

They said their goodbyes and hung up.

Eric looked up to see Danielle hovering in his doorway. "Hope you don't mind me listening in," she apologized. "But I couldn't help myself. I only heard your side, but it sounded fascinating."

"Not a problem!" Eric assured. "Hopefully you got the gist. My uncle is an underemployed tech genius, and he's got plenty of like-minded contacts. They're going to staff up our first research-and-development team. I'm confident he can deliver the autonomous intelligence we need to make this plan *really* soar!"

"What was that I heard about risking technological dystopia?" she asked as she entered his office and sat down.

"Just a worst-case scenario," Eric dismissed. "We should be so *lucky* to achieve something sophisticated enough to risk that outcome!"

Danielle chuckled to herself. "This is *exactly* what I want to be doing. But I have to wonder…why did you choose me? You don't even know me."

"You made a good first impression," Eric disclosed. "I've had quite a bit of success over time reading people. To me, it comes down to a decision, whether the other person is who they claim to be, or if they're hiding their true intentions. And I admit…every time I meet a new person, there's a chance I'll misjudge them and it'll end catastrophically." He settled back in his chair, making himself comfortable. "But I've been doing pretty well for myself. I have a good track record of finding diamonds in the rough."

"Any qualities in particular you look for?" Danielle asked.

"Indeed," Eric explained. "The ability to think for one's self. The willingness to go against consensus." He leaned forward and looked her in the eyes. "I don't want you to only give me good news. I can't solve the problems if I don't know about them. And I *don't* want you to tell me what you *think* I want to hear. That's literally useless. I need you to tell me how it is, with no omissions or soft-soaping. That sort of cowardice is what led to the collapse we find ourselves drowning in. We can't solve the problem by doing what's already being done. We have to be different."

"I can do that," she assured. "I've been waiting for the chance to do that for years. I'm tired of being punished for doing the right thing."

"I won't do that," Eric promised. "But it'll just be our team against a world that still operates with retrograde values. *They'll* still punish you."

"How will we ever overcome such overwhelming odds?" she pined, fear trembling in her voice.

"Because I believe most people are decent," Eric declared. "Many don't get a chance to show their decency; they try to blend in for their own self-protection. I want to create an environment where they're free to be the good people they really are. If we reach a critical mass, nothing can stop us."

"That sounds wonderful," Danielle gushed. "How can I help?"

"Right now, we need to find allies," Eric explained. "People from all walks of life; we have a lot to accomplish, and need a diverse skill set to do it. Hopefully I've just recruited our first science and engineering leaders. I've been cultivating financial backing for some time; today's board meeting was just one small piece of what I'm up to. But one area I've barely started on is political support. Granted, a lot of the plan involves sweeping aside the old order, but then it has to be replaced with something. Ambiguous terms and conditions can quickly go south without sober intellects to judge situations. And I'm afraid I've barely broached that subject."

"Actually, I think I know a few people," Danielle offered. "Quite a few, really. And *they* know people, too. I should be able to stand up a like-minded set of middle managers relatively quickly."

"I look forward to seeing what you come up with!" Eric cheered.

Danielle rose to leave. "At the same time…I'm really enjoying my new office. Finally, a window that lets me see outside."

"I'm sorry the view is so depressing," Eric lamented.

"That's OK," she assured. "It'll keep me motivated." She gazed at the sorry scene below, and smiled. "I can keep tabs on my progress."

◊ — ◊ — ◊

Darren looked out the window of his third-story office; he used to enjoy this panoramic view of the nearby park. But it was no longer filled with family picnics or strolling lovers; now, a jumbled scattering of tents formed a gigantic homeless camp. The smoke that used to rise from barbecues now poured out of flaming garbage cans. Lying openly on the wide paths between tents were filthy, rail-thin people, shivering in the throes of opioid-induced ecstasy. The others simply stepped over them, hardly taking another look.

He heard footsteps pass by his door; whirling around, he caught a glimpse of his office manager. "Carol!" he called out, the fear in his voice palpable. "Are they here yet?"

Carol poked her head through the doorway. "Not yet, Mayor Glenleavy," she soothed. "They've got another fifteen minutes." She looked at him with a concerned expression. "Are you all right?"

He resumed pacing the floor in his office. "I've been dreading this moment for months, but now I wish it would just happen, so I can get this over with."

"Sir, if you don't mind me saying," Carol consoled, "I've worked for this city for over thirty years, and God willing, until the day I retire. I've seen mayors come and go; I've also seen problems come and go. This *too* will pass!"

Darren slumped in his chair. "I want to believe that, I truly do. But this time, I really think it's different." He fixed Carol with an intense gaze. "Can you remember a time when things were *this* bad?"

Carol stood there, pondering for a moment. Darren motioned with his arm. "Please, come inside and have a seat. Pour yourself a drink, if you'd like."

"*Much* obliged, sir!" Carol walked to the liquor cabinet, fetched a bottle of single-malt whiskey, and poured herself a double. Darren didn't say or do anything to stop her. She took her drink and settled into a nearby armchair, smiling at him sweetly.

"I remember things got this bad in the late sixties. Lots of rioting, widespread disrespect for authority…but that finally quieted down."

"Do you remember how?" he asked. "I tried to model my response on what cities did back then, but obviously I've missed something huge."

Carol sipped her whiskey before continuing. "For one, the economy was better in those days. We used to manufacture things here."

"Well, *that's* ancient history," Darren griped. "Heavy industry moved out decades ago; the city's never been the same." He laughed. "Funny, isn't it? We really thought free trade would lead to other nations adopting our way of life. Instead, all it did was fund *their* way of life, and entrench it deeper. We gave away our future and made our adversaries stronger." Darren winced before continuing. "Without employment, workers moved away, leaving behind people dependent on the government, and the criminals that prey on them."

He turned his chair to look out the window. "I tried to appeal to young hipsters — tech workers that could do their job remotely. And for a while, that worked; they liked the scrappy chic of our inner city, as well as the cheap rent. They brought in much needed money. But as the place got cleaned up, rents rose, causing many of them to decamp for *cheaper* locations with a hipster kitsch. The rioting drove out the rest."

He turned back to look at Carol. "So the economy is moribund. Anything else I missed about those times?"

"Part of it was people got what they wanted," Carol recalled. "The military draft ended; elected officials were no longer just white males. But that was then. What do they want *this* time?"

"That's the problem," Darren anguished. "This time, the protesters want to defund the police. And I *did* that. But now, violence has skyrocketed in a way we've never seen before. Things are so bad, even if I *could* get funding to restore law-enforcement jobs, there are very few takers. And the protests have continued, uninterrupted."

"What *else* do they say they want?"

Darren winced. "That's just it. The rest of their demands are *insane*! They want free housing, free food, free money, free everything! They think it's my job to let them live at home with mommy and daddy forever! They're not protesters, they're overgrown babies!"

"That may be," Carol observed, "but it doesn't help that you won't press charges against them. Why *is* that?"

Darren hung his head. "I was too young to be part of the social-justice movement of the late sixties, but I wish I could have been. And when these protests started, I was overjoyed; I thought I could finally lead a massive march against the corrupt establishment, and force historic changes. But these people aren't the revolutionaries of long ago; back then, violence was a way to get attention, and the cause was always more important. These days, the *violence* seems to be more important, and the cause shifts to maintain an excuse for civic destruction. They seem to literally be opposed to *common sense*! And now all we have is chaos, and yet they *still* cry out for more!" Darren sobbed. "I thought I could get out in front of this, but that only let them stab me in the back."

"There's one other major difference between then and now," Carol said, pointing at him. "They deployed the National Guard. Several thousand in each city."

"That would mean I've admitted failure," Darren grieved. "I've spoken out in favor of their cause so many times; by doing so, I lost the support of half the population. If I turn around and clamp down on the riots, I'll lose the other half."

The sound of people outside his office startled them both. Carol quickly downed the rest of her drink. "I admit, sir, you've given me quite a puzzler. But this, too, shall pass."

"Will I still be mayor when it does?" Darren griped.

She only gave him a cryptic smile as she left his office. Darren sighed and pressed his hand to his forehead.

"Good morning, gentlemen," he heard Carol say. "The mayor is waiting for you in his office."

"Isn't it a little early for hard liquor?" he heard one of them say.

"Not if you had *my* job!" Carol quipped. That brought a round of appreciative laughter. Darren took a deep breath and rose from his chair.

Through the door walked a young man with bright red hair, followed by five distinguished-looking older gentlemen. The young man extended his hand. "Good morning, Mr. Mayor, I'm Eric Thompson."

Darren shook the offered hand absentmindedly. "Won't you please sit down."

After all had taken their seats, Eric spoke up. "As you may know, my colleagues here represent investment firms that own nearly eighty-five percent of the city's outstanding debts."

"I recognize them," Darren mumbled. "But who are you?"

"I work for a firm called Unlimited Partners. And, to put it mildly, I'm here to solve everyone's problems."

Darren snorted a short laugh. "Lofty words from a company I've never heard of."

Eric smiled. "Don't worry, you will soon. *Everyone* will." He looked around the room; his colleagues nodded politely. Eric continued. "Mr. Mayor, I've come here today to present you with a deal that absolves the city of *all* of its debts and obligations, and lets you off the hook for any future consequences."

Darren was taken aback. "What? I was expecting to turn over ownership of prime plots of city-owned land, or our landmark architecture."

Eric shook his head. "No, not at all." He raised one eyebrow. "Not in pieces, at least."

Darren looked uneasy. "What are you saying?"

Eric proffered a piece of paper. "This is the deal memo. The full contract will be presented to the city's legal department right after this meeting. Put simply…in exchange for assuming responsibility for *all* outstanding city debt, and any and all of its other obligations…management of the city's affairs will be turned over to Unlimited Partners."

Darren jolted upright. "You can't do that!"

"Actually, I can," Eric claimed. "We've done this with several small towns across the country. This is the largest city for which it's been attempted, but it's not really that different."

"But…what would the state think?" Darren flustered.

"I've already spoken with them," Eric explained. "They have their own problems, and ultimately, they want whatever will make the city's debtholders happy…as in, these gentlemen right here." Eric leaned in. "The bottom line is, the city is bankrupt, the state won't bail you out, civil order has collapsed, your debtholders *own* you, and this is the only way they'll ever see a dime from their investments."

Darren scanned the deal memo frantically. "But what about my reputation?"

"What *about* it?" Eric countered. "As it stands, you're known as the mayor that let it all go to heck. Do you really think it's going to get any better?"

Darren stared nervously at Eric, and swallowed hard. "How can this be legal?"

"Bankruptcy makes a *lot* of things legal," Eric reminded. "A few years back, the federal government saved a national automaker by arbitrarily splitting off its liabilities and forming a new company to own them. Say what you will about the ethics and legality of such a move, but *it happened*." Eric settled back in his chair. "We're not proposing anything that drastic. We intend to keep the *entire* city, and restore *all* of it to be the sort of place good people would want to live."

Darren continued to scan the deal memo. "As you may have read by now," Eric interjected, "the deal is contingent on the city's legal department signing off on it. We're confident they will; it's very similar to the terms and conditions we presented smaller towns when we took over their operations. Your signature just means they can go ahead with their analysis. You're otherwise not agreeing to much...at least, not by yourself."

Darren finished reading; his shoulders slumped. "I can't believe this is happening."

Eric leaned forward and looked Darren in the eye. "I'm offering you a solution to *all* your political problems. You'll be able to walk out that door with a *huge* burden lifted from your back. How can you say no to that?"

Darren stared fiercely at the memo. The debtholders leaned in, expectantly. With a quick flourish, Darren grabbed a pen and scribbled his signature on the dotted line, and finished by slamming the pen down on the desk.

In response to that sound, the debtholders jumped out of their seat, cheering and congratulating each other. Eric, standing, snatched the memo away from the mayor. "Best decision you ever made in your life, Mr. Glenleavy. I'll have Mrs. O'Donoghue make a copy for you." He tapped a few times on his phone, then smiled. "The contract is now in the city's hands."

Without warning, several people in blue jumpsuits entered the office. As Eric and his colleagues walked out, they swarmed all over, taking notes at a furious pace. Through the door, Darren could see similar people in the larger office area, doing the same thing.

"Hey!" Darren yelled. "Who the hell *are* these people?"

"They're taking inventory," Eric explained. "We need to know what we have. As for you, Mr. Glenleavy, you'll probably want to pack your belongings and go home. Just don't take anything that isn't yours...because we'll know." With that, Eric left.

Darren gaped at the throng of blue-jumpsuited workers. He finally noticed each suit had a company logo, a stylized U and P overlapping slightly. He continued to stare in confusion as they went about their business.

Carol entered with his copy of the deal memo, her face awash with a smirk. On her blouse was pinned a shiny badge, consisting of the same logo.

"Welcome to Millenniaburg, Darren," she trilled.

◊ — ◊ — ◊

Dan huddled in his cubicle, staring intently at his computer screen. His eyes moved in quick jumps, the apparent focus belying his true actions. He smiled to himself. One moment he appeared to concentrate on a spreadsheet; for a longer period afterwards, he browsed the Internet, intending to satisfy any of his many shameful addictions. As soon as anyone walked by, he could almost instantly switch back to something work-related. He had spent quite a bit of time and effort mastering this deception, and it was paying off handsomely. He now got paid for doing very little. Everyone is stupid except me, he thought.

His phone rang. Instinctively, he switched back to the spreadsheet, feeling slightly dumb for doing that because of a phone call. He saw his wife's name on the screen; he slid the button to answer. "Hey, babe," he answered brightly. "How's tricks?"

"*Dan?*" The panic in his wife's voice was unexpected. "You need to get down here *right now!*"

She had his full attention. "*Jessie?* What's happening? Where are you?"

"I'm at home!" she sobbed. "They're in our house, packing up everything! I can't stop them! There's too many!"

"Where are the kids? Are they safe?"

"They're spending the night at friends' homes," she cried. "I didn't want them to see this."

He stood up suddenly. "Call the police!" he remonstrated.

"I'm *trying!*" she protested. "I've been on hold for over ten minutes. Just get down here *now!*"

"I'm on my way!" Dan hung up and shut off his computer. It was close enough to the end of the day; what was another fifteen minutes, after all. He grabbed his briefcase and fled down the corridor.

When he arrived, he could hardly believe his eyes. Two large flatbed trucks, each with their own shipping container, slowly filled with his family's possessions. Boxes of various sizes sat on the patchy front lawn; large men in navy-blue jumpsuits carried more out of the house. Tread-driven robots lifted the boxes into the back of each truck; another robot, its upper half looking like a multi-tined forklift, stacked the boxes expertly on top of the wrapped-up furniture, making use of every available space. A handful of large men with dark-gray jumpsuits and serious expressions supervised the activity; curious neighbors and passersby gawked at the spectacle. The street swarmed with people and cars; Dan had no choice but to park several houses away.

As he rushed angrily down the sidewalk, he saw a group of teenagers watching him. It was a few of the neighborhood's surly punks; they smirked as he neared. "Ooooh, mister, you're gonna *get* it now!" one mocked. Dan muttered an expletive under his breath as he strode by. He heard them laugh insolently as one mimicked him; "civilized people obey *rules*!" Dan burned with rage, but the teens were the least of his problems right now.

"What the hell *is* all this?" he demanded as he stomped into one of the few unobstructed spaces left in his front yard. Further away, past a short wall of boxes, he could see his wife with her phone to her ear, speaking intermittently with one of the gray-suited men. Two other ones looked at each other, sighed, and ambled up to meet him.

"I take it you live here?" one asked Dan, his politeness barely concealing his aggressive tone. Jessie approached them, her hollow eyes flush with worry.

"That's *right*! And *you* need to tell me who you are and what the *hell* is going on!" Dan's face flushed with rage; sweat beaded on his forehead.

"I'm Officer Chilcutt, and this is Mr. Randolph. And as it should be clear, you're being evicted."

"But you can't *do* that!" Dan asserted. "I have rights!" Jessie came to a stop at his side.

Chilcutt tapped his clipboard. "According to our information, you haven't tried to assert *any* of those rights; you simply stopped paying your rent. We have no record of any complaint you filed with the local housing authority, and no evidence of any communication with the landlord to try to resolve this."

"Well, they're getting one *now*! And *you* are going to put all my stuff back, right where you found it!" He dialed his phone furiously.

"Dan? Is what they're saying true? Why didn't you tell me?" Jessie pleaded. Dan shot her a fiery look. "Not *now*!" She flinched and went back to being on hold, staring at the ground.

"I'm pretty sure they're closed for the rest of the day," chuckled Mr. Randolph. "But be sure to leave a message."

Dan smoldered as the recorded message played loudly enough for others to hear; he angrily stabbed at the hangup button. "Fine!

You'll all be hearing from my *lawyer*!"

"Do you *have* one?" Randolph brusquely inquired.

Dan gaped wordlessly for a moment. "No, but I can *find* one!" He searched public listings for eviction lawyers.

"They're likely to be done for the day, too," Randolph predicted. "And the ones that are still taking calls, won't be the best and the brightest. They'll just be desperate for business."

"Oh? And how would *you* know that, Mr. so-called Randolph? You some sort of expert?"

"You could say that," Randolph chimed. "I was a police officer too, until the city decided to defund us. Now I work freelance security, and recently started a salaried position at Full Service Evictions."

Dan stopped scrolling through his phone for a moment to eye Randolph. Fury still burned in his eyes. "Really? There's a *company* called that?"

"There is," Randolph answered. "It's a really professional operation…nothing like the old days. We take care of the whole process, from beginning to end."

Dan chose a listing for an eviction lawyer and tapped to make a phone call. "Yeah, well, I'll be taking care of *them* in a few minutes!"

"You had a chance to fight the eviction *order*, but the eviction *itself* is simply a fact at this point. The house *has* been vacated." Randolph seemed weary. "Look, sir, I can tell you how the entire thing is going to pan out, no matter what you do. I've been involved with evictions many times before. Now, what say we discuss this calmly and rationally, before you give yourself a heart attack? I don't relish having to resuscitate you…which, it turns out, I'm *also* fully qualified to do."

The lawyer's voicemail recording could be heard faintly. At the beep, Dan spoke. "Yeah, hello…my family and I are being evicted, and I want you to help me fight this." He finished by giving his name and phone number, then hung up. He glared at the two officers. "*Fine*," he barked sarcastically. "It seems I have time. Why don't you two tell me *all about* it? I swear, if anything I own goes missing or gets damaged, so help me, I'll—"

"There's little chance of that, actually," assured Chilcutt, as Randolph smiled pleasantly. "This team is highly trained in rapidly packing objects of value for transport."

Dan crossed his arms and huffed. "Why, because they're *expert* movers?"

"No," Chilcutt remarked, a twinkle in his eye. "Because they're professional burglars."

"*What*?!" Dan roared. He felt a pain in his chest; he quickly tried to calm himself. A mental image of Randolph giving him mouth-to-mouth was enough to chill Dan's hot fury.

"Hello?" Jessie suddenly interrupted. "Yes…my family is being evicted from our home. They *claim* to be police officers, but…um… Chilcutt? Yes, he's right here…oh, OK…" She proffered her phone. "It's for you."

"Chilcutt here," he began. "Oh, hi, lieutenant! No, everything's fine, it's going smoothly. But yeah, the tenants showed up. Uh huh… yeah…OK, you can tell them." He handed Jessie her phone. "Your turn."

She listened glumly to the voice on the other end. "I see…oh, I see…well, thank you." She hung up, then glanced around helplessly. "They said, even if something *was* going wrong here, they don't have the resources to deal with it." Listlessly, she stared at her shoes. "Something about funding cuts."

"So as I was saying, your belongings are in good hands," Randolph promised. "Each of the movers is under electronic surveillance; anything stolen or damaged would be noted immediately by their A.I.-driven observers, and displayed *here*." He held up a tablet computer; a swarm of green dots indicated that they were all doing their jobs properly. Randolph motioned towards some nearby blue-suited movers. "Have you looked closely at their headgear?"

Dan squinted his eyes; in the long shadows of the rapidly approaching twilight, he could barely make out the details. What had appeared to just be a hat was now more obviously a ring of cameras, microphones, and other sensors. He contemplated them for a few moments. "So…how is *that* legal?"

"It's *not*, for warehouse workers," Randolph answered. "That's how we were able to buy this equipment so cheaply. But it's perfectly legal to use on convicted criminals during work-release. Something of a digital chain gang. But most of them are happy to be out of their cells, getting fresh air, and earning some money. They appreciate the chance to build up a nest egg for when they're released."

Dan looked over the array of boxes now stacked all over his

former front lawn. "OK…but…something *always* gets broken in a move. How can you be so sure nothing will?"

Randolph smiled. "Why don't you come with me, and see for yourself?" He began walking towards the front door, and beckoned Dan to follow him. Dan trailed behind; Jessie meekly brought up the rear.

Inside the house was a whirlwind of activity. Floodlights washed away any traces of shadows. The furniture was already gone; now they were packing the smaller items. Dan watched as two people picked up knick-knacks, sealed each in a plastic bag, lay them into a box, and sprayed foam over them. The foam bubbled and then went still; by the time the next knick-knack was placed, the foam had firmed into something pliable and sticky.

Dan sniffed the air. "I've seen spray-on packing foam before, but it always had a horrible smell."

"This is water-based," Randolph explained. "It's not much more expensive, and it lets us use a lot of it in a closed area. It's mostly corn starch and wheat gluten, so it's not toxic either."

In the kitchen, the dishes, pots, cutlery, and food were being packed similarly, but doing the job was a spidery-looking robot. Its multiple arms worked together like a well-oiled team of several people as it bagged, padded, and packed items into several boxes at once. "That's another bit of warehouse tech. The e-commerce giants paid for all the research, then we buy it when it becomes cheap. Can you believe that's one of their *obsolete* models?" Dan simply gaped at it as Randolph continued his explanation. "It works well in open areas where there are lots of items to pack. It's not so good at going up stairs."

Dan's shoulders slumped. "Well, apart from being evicted, it seems I have little to complain about." He looked down at his clothes. "Hey, what are we supposed to wear tomorrow?"

"We've taken care of that, too." Randolph swept his arm to point at a series of loosely packed boxes near the front door. "In there you'll find a minimal set of toiletries, plus outfits for three days. Granted, they might not be your favorite clothes. And we can only hope they all fit; we had no way of knowing."

Dan and Jessie peered into the boxes; the contents appeared to be what was promised. He shrugged. "So what happens to our stuff now?"

"Well, assuming you want us to store them, not just leave them here on the street..." Dan blanched. "Of course. So, the shipping containers will be kept indoors, in a locked and guarded facility. A full inventory of your belongings will be delivered to you as soon as we're done making it. You'll be able to find anything you own once you find the box with the matching number. And should you choose to sign the contract that provides for repayment of past due rent, storage fees, moving fees, and so on, it'll all be returned to you, and you can go on with your lives."

"How much do you expect me to pay, and how quickly? You *know* I'm in debt."

"True," Randolph soothed, "but you have an advantage you're not considering — lots of collateral." He pointed to an area on his tablet. "Turns out you own several high-value items. Undoubtedly this list will grow once we inventory the contents of your safe. Don't worry, we won't damage it...we have expert safe-crackers on hand."

"Also on work release, I presume." Dan chuckled for the first time this evening.

Randolph returned his smile. "You can get your bare necessities back with very little down, and the rest will be returned once you pay off your debts and we don't need it for collateral anymore. Or faster, depending on your level of cooperation. But confiscating your cars won't be necessary. I'm sure you're glad to hear *that*."

Dan's brow furrowed. "This seems too good to be true. You make it sound like this'll all be resolved painlessly. I'm not buying it. Evictions are a traumatic experience, no matter how you try to sugarcoat it."

"Full Service Evictions intends to be a game-changer in this field," Randolph stated. "We want to earn and maintain a stellar reputation; we plan on doing a lot of these, and in short order. There are a lot of people in houses they can't afford, and a lot of landlords not getting paid, to the point where it's causing widespread social problems. It needs to be solved before the economy as a whole is damaged even more."

Dan shook his head. "An eviction service with a *vision*? Now I've heard everything. This is *really* what your founder has been dreaming of all these years?"

Randolph laughed. "No, not this specifically. *This* company was founded to solve one of many related problems. The parent firm is the one with the vision." His eyes glowed with revelation. "I never would have believed that, at my age, anything could surprise me, or any cause could capture my imagination. But frankly, their presentation knocked my socks off. And it didn't hurt that I really needed the job. Now I'm one of their gung-ho supporters."

"*Who?*" Dan felt slightly unnerved.

"Unlimited Partners." The name rolled off Randolph's tongue like a benediction. "They haven't been around very long, but they've already made several significant moves. You can read about them online."

"I'll do so…in my copious spare time." Dan let out a hollow laugh. "In the meantime…where does my family sleep tonight?"

"We have a deal with several local motels," Randolph explained. "Your family can get rooms for the night at a discount. You'll even get a buffet breakfast in the morning. But after that, you'll have to pay full rates. Hopefully, by then, you'll make a deal with us, and you'll move into your new apartment later tomorrow."

"Tomorrow? Why not tonight?"

Randolph grinned coyly. "Because *they're* in the middle of getting evicted too."

Dan pinched his brow. "You certainly thought of everything, didn't you."

"That's our *job!*" Randolph beamed. "Besides, the place needs to be cleaned first. Maybe some light repairs."

Dan noticed that the lights in his old house had been turned off, and the blue-suits were now removing the floodlights and coiling up the extension cords. Entering the house was a small army of different robots, many with brush and vacuum attachments. The cleanup crew, Dan surmised. "You already have a tenant here?"

"No, an owner," Randolph noted. "The house was bought unseen, contingent on you leaving. The real estate market is *really* tight these days."

Dan threw up his hands helplessly. "So an injunction against this eviction wouldn't have helped — the house isn't theirs to rent any longer."

Randolph's eyes gleamed. "Like I said, I knew how the entire thing was going to unfold."

"Excuse me, sir," one of the blue-suited movers addressed Dan. "Where would you like these?" A few of them were carrying the boxes left by the front door, containing their clothes, toiletries, and other bare necessities.

"Oh…my car's down the block." Dan turned to Jessie. "Well,

honey? Ready to go?"

"I've been ready for a long time," she sighed. "We could never afford this house anyway."

Arm in arm, Dan and Jessie walked down the block, trailed by the movers with their boxes. Dan smiled sanguinely. "You know, I'm looking forward to that buffet breakfast."

The teenage dead-enders were still there, smirking up a storm. One put on an air of politeness. "So how are *you* this fine evening, sir?" The others could barely contain their mocking giggles.

"Laugh it up, flakes," Dan deadpanned as he walked by. "You'll be *lucky* to end up so well. Don't forget; civilized people obey rules." He didn't bother to turn to see their reaction. The sudden dead silence told him all he needed to know.

3

Raymond idly flipped through channels on the TV. There wasn't much on at this hour; the movie channels had the usual assortment of bland, cookie-cutter blockbusters, but the rest were showing reruns of old sitcoms, or talk shows of little interest. A few had already switched to infomercials; that usually didn't happen for another hour, but was increasingly common these days. He winced as one channel played an especially loud advertisement; flipping past it quickly, he stole a look at the hallway, hoping that the noise hadn't awakened his lady.

He settled on an old crime drama from the 1970s. The on-screen guide told him it was a made-for-TV movie. He smiled, popped open a generic-brand 40 ounce malt liquor, and settled in for the kitschy low-grade noir. It seemed like a perfect way to kill the next two hours. Not quite enough to make it to daylight, but close.

From within the walls came scurrying noises; one went straight up and then across the ceiling, between floors. He shivered as he thought of the rats that infested this building. There seemed to be less of them lately, but it was difficult to focus on that when one of them was literally overhead. He tried to hold back his disgust.

Raymond heard shuffling noises coming from the hallway; he didn't turn to see who it was. The on-screen action showed the toughs chasing a lone police officer, panting and wide-eyed with terror. He watched with glazed eyes, not wanting to miss a moment.

"Are you *ever* coming to bed, Raymond?" The shrill harping could only come from one person.

"Get off my case, Clara," he retorted. "It's not like I have to get up early tomorrow."

"Yeah…tomorrow, or any *other* day," she huffed. "Did you even *work* tonight?"

"I got done *early!*" he snapped. "It was just a quick courier job. No hassles. Everything went smooth as a peach."

Clara moved in front of the TV, just as the bruisers caught up with the hapless cop. "More hustles with your hoodlum friends? Are you *ever* going to get a real job, like you promised?"

Raymond bobbed and weaved, trying to regain line-of-sight with the victorious goons. "Damn it, you're blocking my view! Get the hell out of the way!"

Defiantly, she switched off the TV and stood there, her gaze like icy daggers. Glowering, he clicked the remote to turn it back on. Nothing happened; she was blocking the sensor. Clara smirked as she returned his angry stare.

"You bitch!" he shouted. "You made me miss my favorite part!"

Clara clucked her tongue. "Well, isn't *that* too bad. You already missed the good parts of your son's childhood. I don't hear you whining about *that*!"

Raymond threw his hands up in the air. "You *wanted* me to come back, after all these years, to try to help you raise him! And here I am! I bring in money when I can, and I keep quiet about living here so you can continue to collect your child assistance! What does it take to make you happy?"

Clara stabbed her finger in his direction. "How about serving as a better *role model*? I almost had him going to school regularly until *you* showed up. Now he's out on the streets, acting like *you*! The extra money you bring in isn't worth the bad influence!"

Raymond pointed past her, to the TV. "It got you this fancy cable-TV package, didn't it? You know you watch it as much as I do."

"Stop changing the subject!" Clara raged. "Do you even *know* where your son is right now? How can you raise him if he isn't even *here*? He's out on the streets *right now*, following in your disgraceful footsteps!"

"So what do you want me to do?" Raymond snorted. "Leave?"

"Oh, isn't that just *typical*!" Clara exploded. "You're gone for years and years, then one day you show up out of nowhere, promising you've changed and that you'll make up for time lost, but once you run into the slightest bit of static, you want to leave again! You're a worthless excuse for a man."

Raymond didn't reply. He just stared at the ground.

"Why did you *really* come back?" she accused. "Did you just need a place to crash?" Raymond looked up at her suddenly, a sheepish look in his eyes.

Clara gaped. "Really? That's *it*? You're only here for what *you* can get out of it? All your promises were just *empty*?"

Raymond looked towards the hallway. "Look at me when I'm talking to you!" Clara steamed.

"Good job," Raymond chided. "You've woken her up."

From behind the door jamb, a pair of wide eyes peered fearfully into the living room. As Clara turned to look, they disappeared back into the hallway.

"Muriel?" Clara cooed. "Just go back to bed, sweetie."

Muriel appeared again. "I can't sleep."

Raymond gestured angrily. "See what you did? *I* was being quiet until *you* showed up."

"Don't *even* start with me!" Clara turned toward Muriel. "Why can't you sleep, baby?"

Muriel paused, her eyes fluttering shyly. "I smell smoke."

Raymond and Clara looked around nervously, sniffing the air. "Hey, I think I smell it too," Raymond noted.

The building's fire alarm abruptly started to blare. Clara strode towards her bedroom. "Muriel, honey? Get your jacket and shoes and follow me outside!" She turned to look at Raymond, but he had already bounded out the window onto the fire escape. She sighed heavily and disappeared inside her room.

Outside, the tenants gaped as smoke drifted out of the open windows and through the seams of the building's failed weatherproofing. Clara and Muriel walked around from the side of the building, sniffling and coughing lightly. They came to a stop a safe distance away, on the sidewalk opposite their tenement, surrounded by neighbors and curious onlookers. Clara swept her eyes over the crowd for Raymond; he was nowhere to be found. Clara scowled angrily.

"That smoke smelled funny, momma," Muriel piped up.

"What are you talking about?" Clara replied dismissively. "It's smoke. It all smells the same."

"No, momma," Muriel challenged, clinging to her mother's gown. "It smelled...waxy."

A nearby kid turned to Muriel. "Yeah, I noticed that too," he concurred. "Like the kind they have at magic shows. What does it mean?"

A distant din of sirens slowly approached. The crowd watched a convoy of trucks arrive; they looked like police vans, though they didn't bear any government insignia. As they stopped, several people in dark-colored guard uniforms emerged; there were both men and women, though all of them were stoutly built. One of them was taller and thinner; he wore a suit, and observed the action from a distance.

Instead of checking on the tenants, the guards surrounded the building, forming a perimeter. Clara could barely make out a dim emblem on the nearest van, seemingly dark-gray on a black background, consisting of stylized renditions of the letters "U" and "P". She heard one of them remark on their cell phone that all entrances and exits had been successfully barricaded.

A group of security officers, wearing gas masks, ran inside the building. Another addressed the crowd. "Remain calm, everyone," he assured. "The smoke will be fixed in just a few moments."

More sirens converged on the area; before long, a squad of police vans had arrived. Other than their prominent government logos, they looked identical to the vans that arrived before. They parked across the street on both ends, forming a barrier. The officers quickly disembarked and stood in a barricade in front of their vehicles, joined by several of the security personnel. An uneasy murmur emerged from the crowd of tenants, and many of the passersby quickly tried to leave the scene.

Clara noticed that the smoke had thinned out considerably. She also saw that more windows had been opened. Some were at the ends of hallways, but many more were from the inside of people's apartments, windows that didn't lead to fire escapes. Apparently, they had entered the apartments! She raised her hand to object, but quickly withdrew it, and just watched sadly.

The kid that had been standing near Muriel marched confidently up to the waiting police officers. "What's going on?" he demanded. "When is the fire department going to show up?"

"They're not," the officer shot back, haughtily. "The smoke was just to get all of you out of the building." The crowd's grumbling became more incensed. "But it's two-thirty in the morning!" the kid pouted. "That's all right," the officer scolded. "Most of you were still awake." The kid's eyes dropped; he stared morosely at the ground. "What's going on?"

The officer flashed a surly smile. "You're about to find out."

A security guard with a bullhorn spoke. "OK, listen up, people," he barked. "Those of you who are behind on your rent…consider yourself evicted. Those of you who are meeting your obligations… you can go back inside. And anyone with an active warrant for his or her arrest…" Clara noted with alarm that the police officers had drawn their weapons; a few had tear-gas cannons mounted to the top of their shotguns. The overdriven voice on the bullhorn continued. "…will be going away with these fine officers." The speaker stopped a moment to sneer. "And you may as well go quietly…there's no sense in adding 'resisting arrest' to your charges."

A panicked din arose from the crowd. "Now, if you don't know which you are," the voice blared, "form a line in front of the building's entrance."

Clara swallowed hard, grabbed Muriel's hand, and slowly walked forward. A throng of her neighbors meandered in the same direction, joining one of multiple lines. Clara noticed uneasily that a number of the residents, and a few of the passersby, had simply lied down on the ground and put their hands behind their heads. It unsettled her to realize how familiar they were with the procedure for being arrested.

For the first time, she noticed a new group of people had arrived, wearing navy-blue jumpsuits and carrying a variety of packing supplies. They were followed by large spider-legged robots, with platforms where their heads should be, loaded up with collapsed paper boxes. All of them disappeared into the front door. She wondered if anyone else had noticed them; no one seemed to react to their presence, as if giant spider-robots were somehow an everyday occurrence.

The line moved slowly. Most people were simply sent aside, to wait inside the unmarked vans. A few were taken away by the police. Not once did she see anyone allowed back inside. She heard part of the discussion involving the resident in front of her. "But what about all my stuff?" the obese man protested. "It'll be packed up and stored, and treated as collateral, until you make good on your debts," came the gruff reply. "But I can't afford that!" the fat man pouted. "Then it'll probably end up in a thrift store," the guard snarled. "Now go sit in the van, if you want a place to sleep for the night." The portly fellow, looking chastened, slowly lumbered toward the waiting van.

Clara and Muriel were now at the front of the line. "Hold still," she was ordered, as a security guard held up a tablet to her. A few seconds later, her name and photo splashed across the screen. "Is this you?" demanded the guard. "Yes," she replied meekly.

The guard studied the screen for a few moments, her long blonde hair packed tightly into her cap. "You recently caught up with your past-due rent, but we have evidence you've got an unapproved roommate." The guard showed her the screen; there was a photo of Raymond, with a similar first name, but a different last name than she knew him to have. "Yes," she mumbled. The guard pressed a few buttons on the screen, then turned it towards her again. A video showed Raymond inhaling some sort of white powder up his nose. "We recorded this video a few hours ago. We have several more just like it, stretching back about a week."

Clara's face fell. "How did you get those videos? Where were the cameras?"

"They're mobile," the guard explained. "The droids in your walls have extensive sensor packages. You probably heard them scurrying at all hours of the day."

Clara looked alarmed. "I thought those were rats!"

The guard appeared unmoved. "They were, at first. The droids have been killing the vermin, patching up a lot of holes, making other interior repairs, and recording evidence on the tenants."

The guard looked more closely at her screen. "Your son Julio lives with you, right? Where is *he*?" Clara looked down disconsolately. "I don't know. Out with his friends, somewhere." The guard shrugged. "It's just as well. We've amassed a pretty big dossier on him, too. Lots of petty theft." She played a series of videos for Clara, showing Julio hiding his ill-gotten gains in his bedroom. "If he were here right now, he wouldn't be going with you — he'd be leaving with the police."

Clara suddenly became aware of strident caterwauling, coming from behind the police vans. "Don't you *dare* stand in my way!" came the cry. "I'm your boss! I pay your salaries! Now *move it*!" Emerging from behind the perimeter was a smartly-dressed woman with a ruffled collar and a fierce gaze. She marched straight up to the guard interrogating Clara, trailed by two police officers serving as her security detail. "And just what the *hell* is going on here?" She thrust her open wallet into the guard's face.

"You don't need to show me your I.D.," the guard chided. "I recognize you from the news. You've certainly made a name for yourself lately, councilwoman Karen. Now, how can I help you?"

"You can start by letting these people back into their homes!" she demanded.

"I'm afraid that's impossible, councilwoman," the guard demurred. "They're all being evicted for cause."

"But they have *rights*!" she protested. "There are *court* hearings for this kind of thing! And while the details are being sorted out, they can continue to live here!" As she spoke, a few of the police officers ambled towards her. The others remained behind to secure the perimeter and to keep an eye on the arrestees in the vans.

"They've already vacated the premises, and their belongings are being packed," the guard countered. "At this point, the eviction is simply a fact."

"The *hell* it is!" councilwoman Karen blubbered. "How dare you talk to me like that! I can have you arrested *right now*!" He turned back to the police and stared hotly at them. "Did you hear me? Arrest them *this instant*!"

The nearest police officer smiled. "Hi, Sandra; how have you been?" The guard returned his smile. "Hi, Charles! Not too bad, considering. I was worried after our department got defunded and I lost my job, but I got picked up by this new outfit pretty quickly. They were only too happy to hire highly-trained law-enforcement personnel! I think most of us ended up here."

Charles looked around. "Yeah, I recognize a lot of faces. Glad to see you all bounced back!"

"What are you *doing*?" the councilwoman demanded. "I said arrest them this *instant*!"

Charles shook his head. "I'm not about to do that to an old co-worker. She may not be with the force anymore, but that wasn't by choice, and it's obvious she's still one of the few holding civil society together." He motioned to the rest of the security guards. "And that goes for them too!"

"Don't you *dare* defy me!" the councilwoman screeched. "I'll have your badges for this!"

Charles coolly ignored her. "By the way, Sandra…are there any more openings at your firm?"

"Plenty!" Sandra gushed. "They need a lot more trained law-enforcement officers for what *they* have planned. They'll probably pick you up in no time flat!" She looked at the police officers crowding around. "And I'm sure that goes for the *rest* of you, too!"

"That sounds great," interjected one of the officers in the councilwoman's security detail. "We're getting mighty tired of taking her abuse," he added, pointing at Karen.

"So what do you say, councilwoman Karen?" challenged Officer Charles, as Karen gaped. "Do you want to defund the *rest* of us, right *now*? A writ of authority from the government is less important to me than doing the right thing, which these people clearly are."

"I...er..." Karen stammered. Charles continued. "And don't bother threatening us with the courts. You *know* how backed up they are. They wouldn't even get to this for a few months." He leaned in more closely. "Keep in mind...the city council can't even stop the wave of crime on the streets. What do you think your chances are of stopping a supposedly rogue police agency run by a private company? Ultimately, that's just another crime wave that you can do nothing about."

Councilwoman Karen moped forlornly. "We'll all have our day in court...as soon as possible." She straightened herself, and tried to put on a brave face. "I think we're done here." She turned to march away. Her security detail followed, smirking at her behind her back.

Security guard Sandra, staring levelly at Karen's retreating form, muttered under her breath. "You have *no* idea how right you are."

She resumed addressing Clara. "So...we found Raymond's drug stash while we were packing up. I'm sure it comes as no surprise to learn that you qualify to be evicted."

Muriel cried and clutched her mom tightly; tears formed in Clara's eyes. "What must I do to get my stuff back?"

"A few things," the guard commanded. "You need to find a new place to live, we need to make sure you don't have any other outstanding debts, and given what we found, you need to pass a drug test." She eyed Clara warily. "Do you think you will?"

"Yes!" Clara asserted. "I don't do drugs. I didn't even know *he* was doing them."

The guard smiled; her eyes beamed with sympathy. "Then this will probably all be over soon! We'll put you and your daughter up for the night; don't worry, it won't be expensive. We know you can't afford much. Tomorrow, we'll get this straightened out, and you can get on with your lives."

"We can't get our old apartment back?"

Sandra gazed at Clara levelly. "You couldn't afford your old apartment, not without Raymond's money. And we have no record of him being employed. So he was probably getting paid under the table. We'll be dealing with him separately. For now...if you two get in the van, we'll take you to a place you can sleep for tonight." Clara nodded, and she and Muriel slowly made their way to the waiting wagons.

As the guards continued to sort the tenants, officer Charles walked up to the man in the suit. "I take it you're in charge of this operation?"

"Indeed," replied the man. "My name is Jason. How can I help you, officer?"

"So, funny story," began Charles. "We don't actually have space in our jails for all these people. Is there anything you can do to help?"

"Indeed!" beamed Jason. "Let me make the arrangements."

Clara nervously watched a security guard approach the van. He smiled as he caught her eye. "OK, people," he began. "Tonight, you'll be taken to a spare dormitory at the local college. The families with children will get first pick of the private rooms; the rest of you may end up in bunks. If you cooperate with us, you may be allowed to live there for the time being. You'll have to share facilities with others, and keep them clean, and in any case, it's better than being homeless."

"Will we be safe?" Clara clutched Muriel tightly.

"Not to worry, ma'am," the guard assured. "Anyone truly dangerous has already been filtered out. And the whole place is under A.I.-driven surveillance, 24 hours a day. If anything bad happens, it'll get stopped pretty quickly."

"Is that legal?" The obese man Clara had seen earlier looked incredulous.

"You'll have to consent to it, as part of the terms and conditions for staying there."

"What if I don't *want* to? You can't *make* us do that!" The obese man was defiant.

"You're free to take your chances on the street," the guard offered, pointing away. "Though I must say, that alley doesn't look very inviting. What kind of hotel room can you afford right now?"

The portly guy looked crestfallen. "Fine…I accept."

"Why does the college have a spare dormitory?" a young man asked.

The guard demurred. "It's not really my place to speak for them, but it's my understanding that parents don't want to pay for education when their kids never seem to be in class, opting to join protests and the like. So they're having trouble retaining students." He smirked before continuing. "Also, college is so expensive these days, students have begun taking their first few years of undergraduate classes at community colleges or trade schools. Only then do they find a college that'll let them transfer their credits. The place you're going tonight is one of the colleges that *doesn't* allow that. So they're hurting pretty badly." The guard shrugged. "I mean, it works out well for *you*, and for the firm, so I'm not going to complain."

"What firm?" a middle-aged lady asked. "Who do you work for?"

"It's called Full Service Evictions, but they're a wholly-owned subsidiary of Unlimited Partners. They have a vision for fixing the problems that the government can't, and turning a tidy profit while doing so. And unlike the government, *they're* hiring police officers right now."

"Who *else* are they hiring?" the young man interrupted. "I'm more than willing to work, but times are really tough."

"We can sort through all of that tomorrow," the guard offered. "You all need to pay off your debts, and if the firm can make use of your skills, that helps both of us!"

"That sounds great," sighed the young man sanguinely. "I can't believe this eviction might turn out to be a blessing in disguise."

"That's what Unlimited Partners is all about!" the guard trilled. "Win-win scenarios, and making full use of available resources. I think you'll find them a vast improvement over the failing government."

"That shouldn't be too difficult," Clara added. "It's a pretty low bar to start with."

The guard, and everyone sitting in the van, shared a laugh.

"OK, officer Charles, I've got a solution worked out," Jason explained. "There's an older dorm at the same college where the tenants are being housed; it's scheduled for demolition, but that's been delayed, since the college can't afford it. It should be good enough for prisoners. They're certainly nicer accommodations than they'd have in jail!"

"But will it be secure?" Officer Charles seemed skeptical. "We don't want them escaping."

"Not to worry!" Jason assured. "Several security drones are being moved there, as we speak. They're capable of tasing a moving target from fifty yards away. Plus, we're including two drones armed with sniper rifles. And all of them are tied together with surveillance A.I., monitored by human oversight. No one is getting out of there unless we say so."

"Where did you get such amazing equipment?" Charles marveled.

"In bankruptcy, believe it or not," Jason related. "The companies that made these devices intended to sell them to the government, but after a fierce series of protests, the contracts were canceled. They then found they were legally blocked from selling their products to anyone else. But *acquiring* those companies was still legal, which we did for pennies on the dollar, and now we use the equipment for our own purposes."

"Very clever," Charles replied with a smile.

"It's how the system actually works," Jason explained. "If a lawyer can't make a living, finding clients that want to pay for their services, then they go out of business and become a politician. These bad lawyers then write laws that are analyzed by *good* lawyers, who find plenty of loopholes in them, allowing them to continue to do whatever they want, unimpeded by the authorities."

Charles scratched his chin. "I've never heard it put like that before. That actually explains a lot!"

Jason punched a few more buttons on his phone. "We'll send the directions to your vans' onboard computers. Our equipment knows how to talk to them; after all, we own the same kind of vans."

"That sounds great!" Officer Charles beamed. "We really appreciate your firm's help. Oh…on that note…can we all get your card or something? None of us know if we'll get defunded soon. And our old co-workers seem to be really happy with their new jobs."

"Absolutely!" Jason opened his briefcase, and fetched a small stack of business cards, handing them to Charles. "Feel free to hand these out to whomever you like." He grabbed a larger fistful of cards and handed those over too. "Including anyone that isn't here tonight."

"I'd be glad to!" Officer Charles looked around. "So, are we done here? I think all the tenants have been dealt with, and the movers and cleaners have already gotten to work."

"We sure are. As soon as the tenants get taken to their new home, I'm off to the next raid of the evening."

"Really?" Officer Charles sounded concerned. "You're working awfully late tonight."

"No, I'm like you; I'm part of the night shift," Jason explained. "But a few more successes like this under my belt, and I'll probably be allowed to change to the day shift. No one starts at the top, after all."

"*That's* for sure!" Officer Charles laughed. "Hey, do you need police backup for that? I mean, we're already here, and we're *supposed* to get relieved, but given how things are, I never know if anyone is going to show up for the next shift."

"We'd really appreciate that!" Jason concurred. He looked at his phone. "They should be ready for us by the time we arrive."

"Works for me! See you there!" Charles and Jason each headed to their respective vans, and the caravan drove away into the night. A series of flatbed trucks, loaded with steel shipping containers, moved into the vacated space. The first movers emerged from the building with furniture, with spider-bots close on their heels, carrying plastic-wrapped boxes.

The wind slipped through the trees of the bucolic forest; a rustling sound eased itself lazily from the grass. Birds chirped as they went about their inscrutable business. The mid-morning sun soaked the pastoral fields with its gentle glow. Slowly, the chopping sounds of large rotary blades overwhelmed the pristine tranquility. A metal box, the size of a shipping container, slowly lowered itself to the ground, its propellers scattering the leaves and a curious squirrel or two. It touched down with a clumsy thud. Immediately, one side opened, and a few people peered outside, squinting in the sun. Some stepped out, looking around uncertainly. The whine of the rotary blades abruptly raised in pitch, lifting the back of the box, dumping its contents awkwardly on the forest floor. As it slowly rose, two stragglers lost their grip and tumbled onto the others. The door swung closed, and it quickly spirited itself away.

"Where are we, man?" asked one lad. He wore a black Dead Konformists shirt, bearing the classic white DK strokes.

A young lady, wearing a multicolored knit cap, peered into the distance. "I think that's the city over there! But it's so far away..." She reared slightly. "...and there's a fence blocking our way."

A tall youth with medium-length ash-blond hair, wearing a long-sleeved flannel shirt, walked up to the fence and peered closely at it. "This isn't just razor wire...it looks more lethal." He grabbed a nearby stick and brushed the fence with it; the stick disintegrated upon touch. "*What* the...?!"

A callow young man, with short black hair and bottle glasses, leaned in for a closer look. "I've never seen razor wire this shiny! And what it did to the stick...hey, wait a minute..." He grabbed a nearby rock and dropped it into the fence; it shaved thin, wispy flakes of stone. He jolted back. "This is some sort of carbide-steel alloy...maybe even nanoconstructed!" He cocked his head as he looked again. "It's got a bluish-gray tint. If I didn't know better, I'd think...hey, you suppose this contains *cadmium*?" He glanced around, taking in his nervous audience. "That would make it highly toxic."

A pretty ingenue cried and grabbed onto a stout young buck in a sports jersey. "Who would *do* this to us? And *why*?"

Sports Jersey's face glowered. "The last thing I remember, I was *protesting*..."

A tall, lanky adolescent in a golf shirt snorted. "Be honest...you were looting..."

Jersey stared back sullenly. "So? You were too."

"That's probably why we're here." A pimply-faced man-child, still wearing a helmet, smiled grimly.

"Is that a sign down there?" A nubile brunette, wearing a black turtleneck, pointed down the length of the fence. The group indolently trudged towards it.

"There's nothing on this side; I think I can get my arm through here." A pale, gawky teenager with auburn, bristle-brush hair slowly snaked his arm through the fence, holding his cell phone. He read the mirrored image: "Millenniaburg...Wildlife Sanctuary? What the heck does *that* mean?"

"I'd look it up, but my phone gets zero bars out here." A round maiden with pigtails tapped blithely on the screen. The others verified their lack of cell reception.

"Maybe it'll work up there." DK started to climb a tall, straight pine tree. His deft moves between the thick branches made quick work of the height. As the trunk thinned, he braced himself against a sturdy growth and held up his phone. A few tense moments passed. "Hey! I got one bar!" A few others tried to climb other nearby trees, but ungracefully plummeted to the earth.

"So it says here that Millenniaburg is the new name of the city, given to it by...its new *owners*?" DK scoffed. He kept reading. "Apparently, after months of rioting, and so many businesses leaving, the city defaulted on its debt and went bankrupt, then...a group of investors purchased authority over it." He frowned. "Can they *do* that?"

"Hey, this sign faces inwards!" Golf Shirt called from further down the fence. "It says Welcome To Millenniaburg: Permit Required To Enter."

"Permit?" Turtleneck was adamant. "Whatever happened to *freedom*?"

"I've heard of this happening in smaller towns," Bottles gravely intoned. "But nowhere as big as...well, I guess it's Millenniaburg now."

DK's face froze. "Oh, wow...I couldn't possibly read *all* of this...but apparently, living in Millenniaburg is subject to terms and conditions." He looked puzzled for a moment. "Oh, that must have been that huge e-mail I ignored. I thought it was a joke."

A scrappy fledgling, wearing a green t-shirt, had managed to climb another nearby tall tree. "Apparently, the company is called Unlimited Partners. They've incorporated as a city-management firm and...a social-media company? Oh yeah, I remember getting some spam about joining it. I never did."

DK angrily tapped on his phone. "That name just brings up a bunch of glowing press releases. I can't find a single unsympathetic word about them!" He groaned uneasily. "Like any dissent has been wiped clean."

"They can't *do* this to us!" Ingenue insisted. "We have rights! There is recourse!"

"Not necessarily," Bottles lamented. "Social-media companies can ban someone for violating their terms and conditions. They don't have to provide evidence, allowing an appeal is almost unheard of, and the government rarely lifts a finger to stop it."

Bristle-Brush stomped angrily towards a large log. "Come on, guys, help me move this to the fence! I'm going over!" Several others, happy for the chance to do something, helped lift it, carry it, and tip it on its end. With a crash, it split in half at the top of the fence and sunk several inches inside, but appeared to hold.

Bristle-Brush whooped with joy. "I'll bring back help! Wish me luck!" Nimbly, he dashed over the log to the other side; it fell further into the fence, the gleaming ridge now poking out from the splinters.

He had run no more than thirty yards when a furious buzzing sound broke the silence. Something in the air headed towards him. He noticed it and raised his arms, but the drone fired. He shook rigidly; the sickening sound of electricity cut through the stillness. As they gawked, a low thrumming became noticeable as a larger rotorcraft approached Bristle-Brush's motionless form. Large claw pincers wrapped around his body before it gracelessly lifted him into the air. Smoothly flying back over the fence, the rotorcraft tried to put him back.

"Don't let it land! Stand your ground!" Pigtails commanded. They began to crowd underneath, waving their arms and shouting fiercely. After a few indecisive darts, the claw simply opened up and dropped Bristle-Brush on top of them, sending them all sprawling. It then flew away.

"There's no escape!" Knit Cap whined. "What are we going to do?"

A low throbbing shook the air; some distance away, another large metal box was descending. Near the surface, it opened its door, tipped out its contents, and flew away immediately. The group ran over to them, happy for reinforcements, when Flannel suddenly stopped. "Hey...why aren't they moving?" Pimples jumped back, startled. "Because they're *dead*!"

It was another group of youths, looking much like them. They all showed signs of violent ends; some shot, many stabbed, but most of them bludgeoned. They stood and shivered, whimpering to themselves. Pigtails blubbered. "This *can't* be happening!"

They noticed a thicker thrumming sound growing louder. Squinting in the sunlight, they saw three more metal boxes, off in the distance, come in for a landing. Knit Cap groaned. "I hope it's not more dead bodies."

The propellers eased the boxes onto the dirt, and the doors swung open. Through the trees, the disembarking passengers appeared to be dogs. They sniffed the ground uncertainly and looked around.

"Puppies!" squealed Ingenue. The dogs heard her, and began running towards them.

Bottles' face went ashen. "No...those aren't *dogs*...this is a wildlife sanctuary, remember?" The others looked at him hesitantly. He continued to stare straight ahead.

"Timber wolves."

"Good morning, and welcome to the shareholder meeting for Unlimited Partners! We have a lot of new faces in here today, and I'm sure you're eager to ask your questions, so let's get this started!"

Eric Thompson smiled as his eyes took in the panorama of the assembled crowd. Interest had overwhelmed the originally chosen conference room, so the meeting had to be moved to the building's auditorium. He recognized the original investors; they looked happy and confident. But most people in there looked nervous, or unsettled. One older gentleman in particular, seated in the front row, stood out; his elegant suit clashed with his wild, bushy mustache. He sat, arms crossed aggressively, staring hotly. Eric flashed him a winning smile; there was no change in the old man's expression.

Eric shrugged to himself, picked up the remote control, and turned sideways so he could view the projection screen. It showed his firm's name and logo, superimposed over an image of the sun bursting through the clouds. His eyes moved past the screen, to the windows that formed the walls of the auditorium, showing the city from several stories up. Multiple abandoned buildings, crumbling from neglect, sullied the ground. The windows of the nearby skyscrapers hadn't been washed in months; the clean streaks made by recent rain clashed with thick dust. Fires still burned off in the distance, their smoke curling into the sky, dissipating as it reached higher.

He clicked the remote, and the screen now showed a beautifully rendered image of a gleaming, clean, orderly city. A jaunty font proclaimed its name. Eric exulted. "Ladies and gentlemen, welcome to the city of Millenniaburg! So to answer your obvious questions, *yes*, the prior city government has ceded its authority to us, and *yes*, our company now owns the city."

"How is that even *possible*?" A middle-aged lady, wearing a faded powersuit, had stood up.

"In one sense, it's *easily* possible," Eric explained. "The city's tax base has been declining for years. The riots were the breaking point; after being looted repeatedly, most of the city's businesses simply cut their losses, packed up what was left, and moved away. You can't really blame them. And given the rising civil unrest, defunding the police was arguably not the wisest move. That left the city with no way to restore order, crippling debts it could never hope to pay, and a rather bleak outlook. But that's where *our* firm comes in!"

"And they couldn't get a bailout from the state?" A young man with a neck tattoo, garbed in the height of hipster fashion, gaped incredulously.

"Well, the former city government isn't here to explain itself, and it's not really my place to speak for them, but if I may express my *opinion*...the state isn't doing all that well either. Its industrial base decamped for overseas locations a long time ago, and nothing really took its place. Its finances are in even worse shape than the city's!"

"Then the *federal* government!" The young hipster was having none of this. "How is what happened here even *legal*?"

"They have their *own* problems," Eric related sadly. "Their control of their own finances has been getting hollowed out for years. The dollar used to be the world's reserve currency; everything in the world could be bought or sold in terms of dollars. Now, our strategic adversaries have successfully supplanted their own currencies for much of what they buy and sell, and to a large degree, don't participate in the 'dollar system' anymore. With less demand for dollars, there's less demand for anything *denominated* in dollars, including U.S. Treasury bills."

Individual sounds of breathing could be heard over the crowd's stunned silence. Eric continued. "And instead of rolling over their securities, as they did in the past, our nation's adversaries don't believe our nation can *ever* pay off its debts, and are demanding territorial concessions in exchange for what they're owed. Faced with that, the federal government decided it preferred to hand that over to U.S. citizens and domestic companies, as a less terrible second choice." He gripped the podium tightly. "And that's where *our* firm comes in! We *already* own an abundance of small towns whose reach exceeded their grasp, but Millenniaburg is our largest acquisition to date!"

The young hipster gaped wordlessly, then sat down. A young lady in baggy clothing, with a swarm of facial piercings, rose from her seat. "How come I've never heard of any of this?"

Eric shrugged. "It's been all over the financial news for countless months. The failures of the last three T-bill auctions were top headlines in *my* news feed. I don't listen much to the mainstream press; I don't consider what they report to be relevant enough to inform an investment strategy. Still, it seems like they should be covering this. Can *you* tell me what they're reporting?"

The young lady swiped her phone furiously. "The big headlines right now are...the upcoming marriage of two influencers, and...an actress has lost her job because of something she wrote twenty years ago, in a classmate's yearbook."

Eric smirked. "Nero fiddles while Rome burns, I guess."

"Is that from an old book?" The young lady sat down again.

Eric's eyes darkened. "Yeah. Something like that. Anyway...in addition to having complete authority over everything within the city limits, we also own the former city government's debts and obligations, and we intend to turn around this bleak state of affairs. And as with any private-equity turnaround, we have to shed what doesn't work, and expand what *does* work! The direness of the situation, and the ongoing collapse of traditional authority, gives us a wide latitude to respond!"

A troubled murmur stirred from the audience. Eric ploughed ahead. "So, in addition to all the interested parties that are here of their own choosing, we've invited all the holders of the former city's prodigious debts, to explain our plan going forward. The—"

The bushy-mustached old man in the front row stood up and interrupted. "And I'm one of the biggest!" Eric stopped and looked at him impassively. "I run the firm that built your power plants, repaved your roads, and retrofitted your aging bridges! In the last few years, the city resorted to paying us with bonds! And I will be *damned* if I'm going to let you default on those!"

Eric raised his palms in a pleading motion. "Sir, *please*...we have *no* intention of hanging you out to dry. On the contrary; we could really use your help going forward! Your firm has the skill and experience we need to turn this city around. Didn't you read the prospectus we sent you?" Eric covered the microphone and barked a few short orders to his colleagues nearby. They began furiously typing on their laptop computers.

The old man huffed. "Yes, but I didn't understand most of it! It seemed like it was designed to lull me to sleep! I remember when men went into business to *do* things, to *build*, to create works that would withstand the test of time, and belong to the ages! I can't *stand* your style of so-called businessman...you're only good at shuffling paper and spouting words!"

Eric chuckled. "Very pithy, sir. But whether or not you realize it, we're on the same side. Our firm *also* wants to see a city built on solid fundamentals, on old-time values. They're what made our country strong, and they'll do it again! In fact…" Eric watched two of his colleagues approach the old man, showing him figures on their computer screens. "…our firm is willing, *right now*, to invest a significant sum in yours. Consider it seed money for the many tasks ahead."

The old man looked at the screen, and snorted. "Well…it's a start. That'll keep us going for a few months, at least. But this is *my* firm! I'm not going to let you surreptitiously take it over!"

Eric laughed. "I think all the kids in the room are looking up the definition of that word." Scattered chuckles flitted across the audience. "But if you'll let me continue, you'll find out how we're planning the *opposite* of that. Our goal is for *you*, and all the other creditors of the defunct city, to own part of *us*!"

A small swarm of curious murmurs emerged. Eric smiled. "As I'm sure you're all aware, the city's debts became too large to ever be paid back. Even the wisest turnaround specialists in the *world* wouldn't be able to solve *that* problem! At the same time, we need people committed to seeing this city get revitalized, people interested in building a future worth having. And that's why we're proposing… swapping your debt for equity in Unlimited Partners."

The sound from the crowd swelled with disquieted murmurs; Eric pushed ahead. "Keep in mind, in a traditional bankruptcy, the debt holders would get little or nothing. Or maybe you'd get possession of distressed assets, too damaged to be resold, with no one willing to buy them. Instead, you get to be a part of the solution…one with *voting* rights! Your work and dedication will be instrumental in ensuring this city becomes a place of value again!"

There was a pregnant pause. Then a sharp-eyed gentleman in a fine suit stood up. "Well, I'd *love* to believe in this plan, but…what are you going to do with all the citizens that can't, or *won't*, be a part of this?"

Eric sighed happily. "Remember, Millenniaburg is no longer a traditional city…that era is past. It's a corporation. It may be helpful to think of it as the country's largest gated community. We can have rules and regulations that go far above and beyond what was present, or even *allowed*, under the old system. Anyone that wishes to remain living here will be considered an employee of the firm, or for the children and retired, a ward. And as employees and wards, they will have to agree to a code of conduct, one that doesn't allow for laziness or unethical behavior. Anyone that violates these rules will find their right to remain terminated, and will have to find somewhere else to live. It's not fair to the rest of us, the ones trying to build a better future, to have to tolerate criminals and parasites."

"Well, *that's* convenient!" the young lady with the face piercings interrupted. "What about the elderly and handicapped? Are you just going to push them out?"

Eric cleared his throat. "We have analyzed the situation carefully, and our statistics show that less than five percent of this city's inhabitants are *truly* needy. The elderly and the handicapped, as you put it. They are welcome to remain; the cost of caring for them is well within our budget. And productive work can be found for many of them. I'm talking about the people that *choose* to be needy…people that are perfectly capable of contributing to the world around them, but elect not to. They're the only ones that have anything to worry about."

The young lady's face fell. "I see." She sat down again.

Eric hunched over the podium. "And *that* brings me to addressing the rioting and civil unrest of recent months. These people pretended to serve the cause of equality and justice, but their actions demonstrated they were only in it for themselves. Their only *real* activity was to loot, pillage, and terrorize. They treated civilization as if it was something to *plunder*. People like that don't *deserve* the benefits of civilized society. In the end, they caused the destruction of the old order, and allowed for a firm like Unlimited Partners to arise. I and my colleagues are here because *no one* could find a way to solve the problems they caused. In short, they were more stupid than the city leadership was smart." Eric pounded his fist on the podium. "Stupidity and incompetence are *not* a lifestyle choice!" The crowd erupted with laughter, and a few scattered cheers.

Eric beamed as he swept his arm across the assembled audience. "Now, for *you*…the ones that own the enormous amounts of debt owed by the former city…the productive citizens that want a chance to demonstrate your worth…and anyone that wants to help build a world that'll let their children soar to the limits of their skills, talents, and motivation…I ask you…are you with us?"

The crowd overflowed with excited chattering. A din of applause slowly started, then quickly expanded to a thundering roar. Eric extended his arms and held his hands high. Whistles and cheers erupted from a mass of attendees. Only a few sat quietly, their heads hung low.

Finally, the excitement died down. Eric referred to the bushy-mustached old man, his expression now beatific. "And what do *you* think, sir? You are probably owed more than the rest of these people put together. What's *your* opinion?"

The old man grinned excitedly, his flushed skin taking several years off his appearance. "I must say, I'm *deeply* impressed with what I've heard here today. I must commend you young guys for your brilliance! I apologize for what I said earlier; you're not a paper shuffler, you're a *doer*! I'm proud to be a part of what you're creating, and I'll happily remain with your firm." This brought a flood of affirmative shouts and more applause.

Eric ended with a flourish. "You'll all find more information about our path forward, and *your* part in it, on our website. I wish you all much success in the better world to come!" After giving him a standing ovation, the crowd began to break up and leave.

As Eric conferred with his colleagues, he felt a tap on his shoulder. He turned around to find the young lady with the facial piercings. "Hello! I'm Amber."

Eric smiled politely and shook her hand. "Nice to meet you."

Amber cocked her head. "Actually, that's just it. Have we met before? You look so familiar." His colleagues arched their eyebrows and excused themselves.

Eric chortled politely. "With all due respect, ma'am, I don't think our social circles intersect."

Amber giggled. "No, you're probably right. It's just that your face looks…so familiar."

Eric shrugged. "I guess I just have one of those faces."

Amber glanced pensively. "You look a lot like the guy that once granted a large amount of money to my social-protest group; our goal was to defund the police. Except *that* guy had long hair and sideburns."

"*Really*. How very interesting," Eric remarked. "I'm sorry, but you must excuse me. I have plenty to do still; my day is far from over."

Amber snickered and blushed. "Of course. Don't let me stop you. I wish you all the success in the world." She turned to leave.

"Thank you." Eric walked away, following his colleagues through a door. He turned to look at Amber, shooting her an apprehensive glare. Then he closed the door behind him.

4

Dan pulled into the parking lot of one of Full Service Eviction's satellite offices. A manila folder with all the paperwork from his family's eviction lay in the passenger seat. The jingle of the previous advertisement faded, and a strident voice returned to the radio.

"Welcome back to 'Justice Denied'! I'm your host, Malcolm St. David. For those of you just joining us, we're discussing the wave of evictions in the newly-crowned city of Millenniaburg. With us in the studio are Ellsworth DeGuerro, from the U.S. Department of Housing and Urban Development, Vanessa Abrazo, national tenants-rights advocate, and Humphrey Llewela, managing partner of Crake & Gibson, a leading national law firm. On the phone with us is Ted Danbury, representative for Unlimited Partners."

"And I'm pleased to be here," Ted sniped. "You might want to bring some more people into your studio; I still outnumber you."

"Before the commercial break, we were discussing the stunning lack of rights granted these tenants," Malcolm responded angrily. "No due process, no grace periods…in most cases, they didn't even get to pack first! How do you get away with this outrage?!"

"Wow…that was an impressive series of lies by omission," Ted countered. "Their belongings were packed on their behalf; no significant theft or breakage has been reported, or even *insinuated*, by the evictees. They had plenty of grace; each one was, at a minimum, three months behind on rent, and were fully aware of it. And as for due process…everything that happened was in line with our city's terms and conditions."

"Ah yes, the much vaunted social-media inspired contract, forced upon the city without notice," Malcolm accused. "Years of individual rights and freedom, flushed right down the drain."

"It's no worse than what you deal with, on a daily basis, on any social-media site you care to mention," Ted countered. "Even the Big Tech companies you rely on have similar contracts. You can buy *thousands* of dollars worth of their content, but violate their rules and it's taken from you in a heartbeat, with no explanation or recourse. You're no doubt aware of the class-action lawsuit I'm talking about, right, Humphrey?"

"I think I heard about it somewhere," Humphrey dismissed.

"So you can't tell me there's no precedent for this," Ted crowed. "This has literally been happening for *years*. Do you have a problem with what they're doing? When do you plan to confront *them* on your radio show? Oh, that's right, they *sponsor* your show. I guess your silence can be bought."

There was a pregnant pause, punctuated by shrill breathing. "I'm more concerned with the lives of these evicted tenants," Vanessa interrupted. "I've heard reports they end up in abandoned college dormitories. What happens after *that*?"

"Another skillful lie by omission," Ted retorted. "I expect nothing less. They're *unused* college dormitories. And that's only the last resort. Most people are given a plan to pay off their debt, and offered housing they can afford. Full Service Evictions lives up to its name."

"Answer the question, Mr. Danbury," Ellsworth piped up. "They can't stay in the dorms forever. Are you planning to dump them on the street?"

"I'm *so* glad you're concerned for their well-being," Ted snarked. "I take it that means you're willing to assume custody of them. Or do your strident beliefs end the instant you have to make an effort?"

"I...no, we can help them," Ellsworth promised. "That's what our agency does, after all. We help the less fortunate."

"So," Ted pounced, "does that mean you'll send us some addresses, and we can put these people on the next bus out of town?"

"I...er..." Ellsworth stammered.

"Of *course* we will!" Vanessa interjected. "There are *plenty* of cities that would be *happy* to take them! I could arrange that *myself*, through my own contacts. We're not *heartless* and *cruel*, like *you*."

"And there it is," Ted cheered. "The perceived moral superiority. I never get tired of it." There was a pregnant pause. "So, what do *you* think, Malcolm?" Ted continued. "It sounds to me like we're all in agreement."

"Uh...yeah. Yes, it does," Malcolm managed to say.

"Thank you for having me on your show today," Ted finished. "Once again, you've made the world a better place. No wonder you do this for a living."

Malcolm inhaled sharply. "We'll be back with our next guest, right after this."

Dan scowled as he turned off the radio. He pinched the bridge of his nose with his hand, and sobbed quietly for several moments. Morosely, he turned to look at his phone, which continued to remain silent. It also showed he had ten minutes before his meeting with Full Service Evictions. He blanched at the thought of his wife and two kids living in a dormitory. Jessie would never forgive him for that... if she even forgave him for losing the house.

Abruptly, his phone rang. He didn't recognize the number, but it was local. Hesitantly, he picked up his phone and answered the call. "This is Dan."

"Hi, I'm returning a call from Dan Ranger?"

"This is Dan McGranger."

"Oh, great! Nice to meet you! Alf Bozinski, attorney at law, at your service! You said something about being evicted?"

"That already happened," Dan clarified. "Last night. I was hoping to hear from you sooner."

"Wow, sorry. We all need a night off every *once* in a while... you know?"

Dan sighed. "Sure. Is there anything you can do for me?"

"Of course, brah! I can file a counterclaim today. It probably won't go before a judge for another month, though; the courts are *really* backlogged. But the sooner you get in line, the sooner you can get your house back. Can you give me the address?"

Dan told him.

"OK, let me look it up." Dan could only hear typing and mouse-clicking for several seconds. "Ah, see, that's why I couldn't find you; I spelled your name wrong. Says here that...oh. Bad news: the house has already been sold."

"Wow," Dan exclaimed. "They *said* they were fast, but that's gotta be a record."

"Not in *this* housing market," Alf explained. "It's tighter than a floozy's skirt. And the problem is, anything I file is going to be useless. I only had a chance to get you back into your old house; I can't force the landlord to rent you a different house. At this point, you're just a prospective tenant, like any other." More furious typing. "Whoa! And not a very choice one. You are *really* behind on rent. I doubt anyone else will rent to you, either."

"Well, aren't *you* a lot of help," Dan grumbled.

"Not if you can't pay me," Alf deadpanned. "How can you afford me, if you're *this* deeply in debt? I don't do this for free, you know. It's either moolah, or move along."

"What are you, some sort of surfer dude?" Dan snapped. "I'm trying to imagine how you could be any *less* professional."

"Oh yeah, tough words from the homeless guy," Alf snarked. "You can't even keep a roof over your wife's — hey, I just found a picture of her. *Damn!* She's got it goin' on! You'd better chain her to the stove, or she's gonna run off with the first guy she finds with a fat wallet."

Dan cursed unintelligibly as he stabbed angrily at his phone's hangup button. It fell limply from his hand onto the passenger seat as he let out a long breath and slumped. He felt tears well up in his eyes again.

When he finally thought to look, he realized he only had three minutes to get to his meeting. Quickly, he grabbed his phone and manila folder, locked his car, and trudged toward the gleaming foyer of Full Service Eviction's office.

Sam sat at the workbench, a magnifying visor strapped to his head. His eyes pored over the details of the most-recently assembled spider-bot. All the welds looked solid, all the circuits appeared to be in place. He moved the legs around to test their range; they pulled back uncertainly, seemingly miffed by the imposition. He gazed uneasily at the brain; the oblong lump of neural tissue sat in a fluid-filled glassine tank, a trunk of fiber-optic cables trailing to the external interface. He closed all the access hatches and looked into its optical sensors; they returned his gaze impassively.

Sam smiled sadly and placed the newly-born spider-bot on the ground, facing it towards more of its kind. It seemed to recognize them instantly, and moved to join them. It lumbered unsteadily over the floor, reacting with surprise to its own footsteps. Before long, it had reached the outskirts of the bot's play area, and stood there to watch the others.

Sam turned to pick up the next bot from the assembly line, but a flashing red light distracted him. He sighed, removed his visor, and stood up. "I gotta take this call," he told Gary, seated closer to the end of the automated factory. "Just let the bots through; I don't even remember the last time I found a flaw in one."

"Yeah, me either," Gary concurred. "It's a little unsettling, isn't it?"

"What do you mean?"

"They're advancing awfully quickly. Are we ready for *this* much progress?"

"*I* sure am!" Sam laughed. "I've been rotting on the vine for *way* too long. It's nice to see some real advances! Besides, this is better than languishing in that poor excuse for a university lab, isn't it?"

"Can't refute that, I suppose," Gary sighed.

Sam noticed Gary's troubled look. "What is it? Are you worried about the impending robot rebellion? Or are you just not used to accomplishing this much?"

Gary shrugged. "I don't know. A little of both."

Sam smiled. "Well, you can head off the *first* one easily!" He motioned towards the play area, their whimsical term for where the bots worked out the basic physical laws and their effects on themselves. "Why don't you join them? They could use a mentor."

Gary smiled. "Sounds like a great idea." He looked at the three new bots, fresh off the assembly line. They looked up at him uncertainly. Gary waved them closer. "Well, what are you waiting for? Come with me!" He turned to walk to the play area; the bots followed clumsily.

Sam exited the workshop and found himself in the office area; two rows of cubicles ran the length of the room. He heard Stacy call out to him. "Your nephew's on line one."

"You mean our boss," Sam corrected.

Stacy peeked over the cubicle wall. "Sorry, didn't mean anything by that."

"You're fine," Sam assured. "Just don't let *him* hear you say that."

"Well, duh!" Stacy guffawed.

Sam smiled as he grabbed the receiver from the retro-style office phone and punched line one. "This is Sam."

"Hey, uncle!" piped up the voice. "How are things?"

"Just fine, nephew." Sam looked towards Stacy and winked; she returned a beaming smile before sitting down again. "You should come by the lab some time! I think you'll be impressed with our progress."

"If only I had time for a *tenth* of what I'd like to do," Eric lamented. "I'm sure a visit would blow my mind. What you've produced so far has already done that!"

Sam sat down on the nearby couch. "We didn't produce that so much as find it. Nearly all of it was existing technology."

"Really?" Eric sounded surprised. "I know you told me about suppressed science and technology, but...I don't know...part of me wasn't willing to believe it."

"Nearly everything you've seen so far is stuff we pulled off the shelf, so to speak," Sam explained. "We may have tweaked it a little to make it fit for service, but most of it was ready to go."

"Quite impressive, for your set of personal contacts," Eric complimented.

"Hardly just *my* contacts," Sam corrected. "My team's contacts, and their contacts, and so on. Plus, a lot of it was found just by reading tech-oriented news sites such as TildeNerd. We scanned through several months' worth of back articles, looking for new advances, and contacted the inventors directly. Nearly all their work was languishing, and most of them signed on to join us."

"Signed on?" Eric asked. "Are we paying them? I couldn't help but notice that you're staying well within your budget."

"We don't sign them on directly, not in the way you're thinking," Sam explained. "We pay them for working demonstrations of their inventions, then for their help integrating them into devices. That weeds out a lot of pretenders. I've hired several of them, and have spun up many satellite research groups. But they operate autonomously, and mostly earn their own way."

"Sounds like a lot of investment opportunities for me," Eric trilled.

Sam laughed. "Yeah, you *would* look at it that way. You see them as potential streams of recurring income. I see them as something I can help get started, get back my original investment with a small bonus, and then let them go their own way. Heck, I've even funded a few that *compete* with each other. I don't have the time or inclination to micromanage them; I have my own work. And as long as they can fund themselves, they don't need investors. Sorry to break this to you, Eric, but...they don't need you."

Eric laughed. "You're right...I just instinctively look for revenue streams. I need to stay focused on the big picture."

"Don't fret, I get it," Sam assured. "There's a lot of money, and a lot of neat tech, happening out there. We can't possibly be involved with all of it."

"Fair enough," Eric agreed. "And you found a lot of them on

public web sites? What'd you call it? TildeNerd?"

"That's one of the oldest tech-oriented news sites around," Sam explained. "Most places only cover something once it becomes commercially viable. TildeNerd reports stuff as soon as it's barely working in the lab. A lot of the articles link to research institutions, university laboratories, or in some cases, just someone's personal blog. It's a treasure trove for people in a position to make use of it... much of it *way* too raw for professional investors, or the rest of the mainstream. But once I had a budget...I felt like a kid in a candy store."

"Well, you've certainly proven your point!" Eric laughed. "Is that where you found the eviction droids?"

"No, that was even easier," Sam related. "They're from a bankrupt warehouse-robot company. The problem was their technology worked *too* well; there was a groundswell of opposition from the workers they were intended to replace. The public outcry ruined their business; it also made them easy to find. The story behind the construction, demolition, and security droids is similar; most of that tech was mature, proven, and ready to ship, but got shut down by bad publicity."

"Which is code for people unwilling to work and unable to change," Eric commiserated.

"Exactly," Sam agreed. "People that just want to sit on the couch all day and watch TV." Sam let out a hollow laugh. "I genuinely don't understand such people. To me, the world is a mad science laboratory, just waiting for me to unveil its secrets! But I don't have the time or energy to do a tenth of what I'd like to do. And somehow *I'm* the oddball."

"You and me both," Eric concurred. "I don't understand people like that, people that lack vision and motivation. It's like they're a different species."

"Homo minitherium?" Sam quipped.

"Wow, that takes me back," Eric reminisced. "I barely remember that would mean little sloth-people." They shared a laugh.

"Your air-mobile security drones were ready to go, too," Sam explained. "Their bad press came from the people that got tased, as if they were innocent and the bots had run amok or something. We bought that company out of bankruptcy for pennies on the dollar, too."

"Certainly good fortune for *us!*" Eric guffawed. "Did you hear they've created an open-air prison in a derelict college dorm? No fences, no bars, just droids securing the perimeter."

"I think I heard something about that," Sam sighed. "But I didn't read up on it. There's too much happening; I can't keep up with the firehose."

"Well, they're doing an incredible job," Eric related. "The droids are impressive enough, but the surveillance A.I. that ties it together is really out of this world. I can't believe they went bankrupt; seems like they should have made a fortune."

"Actually, no...that's one area where we made improvements. You've seen the cats with the neural implants; they're fighting the rat and pigeon infestations in the older parts of the city. But we've also perfected neural implants in humans."

"Really?" Eric exclaimed. "Where do you find your volunteers?"

Sam smiled as he leaned back in his chair. "The coma wards of nearby hospitals. We get consent from the families; most are only too happy to try. We've confirmed a lot of them are unrecoverable; that news makes the family unhappy, but they still thank us for the clarity. The rest, we find, are highly mentally active, though bored out of their gourds. Their neural implants allow them to communicate with the outside world, and even to drive their own motorized wheelchairs, even if they remain comatose outwardly. To make a long story short, the surveillance A.I. is being supplemented by so-called invalids, who are happy for the chance to work, and far from being a drain on resources, now earn their own paychecks."

"That makes more sense," Eric conceded. "I had a hard time believing artificial intelligence could be that good. And these people don't mind being put to work like this?"

"Quite the contrary," Sam assured. "They describe the neural implant to be like giving them a much larger body, one consisting of buildings and machines. They find it incredibly liberating. And...that isn't even the full story."

"I can't imagine how much bigger this can get," Eric quipped.

"The neural implants help us recover minds, but in some cases, we can recover the rest of them," Sam related. "Nearly a third of recipients, with some directed therapy, have woken up, and are regaining the ability to control their bodies. We're confident many of them will *fully* recover!"

"Wow," Eric exclaimed. "Talk about making full use of

available resources!"

"You gave us that direction," Sam reminded. "We're following it as well as we can."

"And you're doing a great job!" Eric gushed. "It *already* looks like the future on the city streets. Legions of gleaming droids, wresting the city back from chaos."

Sam slowly sat up, and leaned over slightly in his chair. "If I haven't done this recently…I want to thank you again for providing this opportunity. I'm sure I speak for all the other mad scientists working for us, too."

"I'm glad to have you all on the team!" Eric cheered. "And speaking of mad science…how are *your* experiments going? I look forward to seeing some biologically-sourced machine intelligence on the streets!"

"Much better than we had hoped," Sam explained. "We're still using depatterned cat brains, but we're having a lot less of the trouble Angie and I encountered in our early experiments. Maybe that's the difference between using suburban strays versus urban strays; the latter seem more prone to appreciating their improved condition."

"Any idea when we can field them?" Eric asked.

"They're still learning," Sam conceded. "We build spider bodies for them, and let them explore their new abilities and surroundings. The older ones show promise, and some might be capable of becoming service droids, but I'm not sure how many. It seems that once a cat, always a cat."

"That's too bad," Eric sighed. "We can't have droids that get distracted by a dust mote."

"Having said that, though, I have some good news," Sam continued. "Our lab-grown neural material is showing great promise; right now, they're developing in a software-simulated virtual world. But we plan to transplant some of them to spider-bots, possibly as soon as tomorrow."

"Nice!" Eric gushed. "Keep me posted!"

"I'll let you know as soon as we can field a bio-brained bot," Sam promised.

"I'm sure you will," Eric agreed. "Hope to hear from you soon."

They said their goodbyes and hung up.

Sam heard metallic clinking, getting closer. "Stacy?" Sam

called out. "Do you hear that?"

"Yeah, it's just a stray," Stacy answered. Sam saw her stand up behind the cubicle wall, then disappear; he walked over to where she sat. Stacy looked down at a spider bot, who was staring back up at her. "Are you lost, little one?" she cooed. "Let's get you back home."

The spider-bot lifted its two front legs and pointed them upwards; Stacy smiled and picked him up. She stroked its head as she walked towards the play area; the bot clung to her gently. Sam followed both of them back. "I wonder how it got loose? Gary is supposed to be keeping an eye on them."

"I guess we'll find out," Stacy offered.

They found Gary seated on the floor in the play area, surrounded by spider bots, smiling beatifically. Stacy put the bot down; it scurried back to its mates. "We found this one in the cubicle area," Sam announced.

Gary turned slowly to face Sam, his smile unchanged. "Do you see what they're doing?"

Sam looked; his jaw dropped. "How long has *that* been there?"

"A while," Stacy answered. "But it was a lot less elaborate the last time I saw it! They've been *busy*!"

A sprawling jungle gym filled the northern portion of the cavernous room. The lower rungs were wrapped in carpet; the upper reaches showed bare wood. A line of bots continued to carry in new building materials, left over from the lab's renovation. Other bots attached new wood to existing structures, maneuvering their handless legs to grip screwdrivers, laboriously but nimbly driving in new screws.

"It looks like a…a giant…" Sam began.

"Cat tree," Stacy finished.

"That's it!" Sam exclaimed, snapping his fingers.

"Isn't it beautiful?" Gary purred, a dreamy look in his eyes.

"I wonder why they stopped carpeting it?" Sam asked.

"I've been watching them for a while, and I think I've figured that out," Gary related. "The younger bots need the extra traction when they start climbing. The older bots don't need that crutch. Also, the lack of carpet lets them do other things." Gary pointed toward a darkened area. "For instance, that fellow up there."

Their gazes followed Gary's gesture. As their eyes adjusted to the darkness, they spotted a spider bot engaged in freeform gymnastics. It skillfully hooked its legs around a wooden beam, swinging around it, using its weight to propel itself to another beam, which it caught deftly, continuing its routine.

"*There's* something you don't see every day!" Stacy laughed.

"More importantly," Gary pointed out, "it's something you wouldn't see a cat doing. Cat bodies aren't made for swinging."

"So they're finally getting over not being cats anymore," Sam noticed.

"I'm glad to see them growing into their new bodies!" Stacy trilled.

"I know I obsess a lot over the possibility of an uprising," Gary conceded. "But sitting here, watching them play…I'm a lot less worried now. I mean, there still might be one…but it won't be *our* bots." He raised his hands to gesture toward the jungle gym as a whole. "They're much more interested in building than destroying."

"I wish I had known this earlier," Sam pined. "I could have given some more good news to Mr. Thompson."

"Don't you mean your nephew?" Stacy quipped.

"Let's not get into *that* again!" Sam guffawed. "I just wanted to give him the best update I could. For instance," he said as he gestured to the bots adding to the structure, "some of them are probably ready to become construction droids."

"Or lab assistants," Gary suggested. "We need all the help we can get building the assembly lines. We have no end of other machine-building projects, either." Gary looked up and smiled. "I'll get them started with some mounting hardware for the ends of their legs, something to let them wield tools better."

"I'm sure they'll appreciate that," Stacy chimed. "Can't wait to see what they come up with!"

◊ — ◊ — ◊

Eric Thompson entered the large conference room; the television on the wall displayed the Unlimited Partners logo. He found the board of directors already there, seated. They glared at him as he arrived.

Eric smiled and touched his hand to his chest. "Now, I know you're *all* wondering why I called you here today…"

"Enough of the japes, Mr. Thompson," shot back Mrs. Verhage. "Your irreverent attitude might score points with your subordinates, but it has *no* place here."

Eric coughed politely. "Of course." He found his chair and sat down. "I always enjoy these in-person board meetings."

"Some news is simply better delivered in-person," Mrs. Verhage opined.

"I couldn't agree more," Eric replied, a twinkle in his eyes. Mrs. Verhage didn't respond; Eric continued. "So, shall we get to it?"

"We have a number of pointed questions about your style of governance," chairman Carl Beaumont opened.

"Before we get into that," Eric interrupted, "can I clarify whether you have any problems with the financial results?"

"I—" Carl began.

"After all, under the profit-sharing deal we worked out in the beginning, Unlimited Partners has paid back its initial seed money, plus given the investors a tidy profit, all while eliminating your delinquent-tenant problem. I assume this is to your liking?" Eric tilted his head expectantly.

"We...yes, of course, we're fine with that," Carl declared. "We have no financial complaints. Our objections concern how you're running the city, the sort of laws you're putting into place."

"I'll happily explain, and defend, any decisions you wish to bring up," Eric asserted.

"Let's start with a smaller issue," Drew spoke up. "What on *Earth* possessed you to make Ted Danbury a spokesman? He may be a tough-as-nails executive, but you've put him in the public eye, speaking for you during hostile interviews and the like. How is this a good idea?"

"I believe you answered your own question," Eric pointed out. "The key word is *hostile*. You can't throw a positive thinker, or an agreeable type, into a hostile situation. And you certainly don't want someone whose instinct is to form consensus! Ted was fully forewarned of the situations I asked him to involve himself, and he readily agreed. Personally, I think he's done a *great* job! You have to fight hostility *with* hostility, otherwise one looks weak."

"I just don't think that's the sort of public image we want in this company," Drew asserted.

"I don't think it's fair for you to criticize Mr. Danbury's work in his absence," Eric countered. "He should be here to defend himself."

"No, I...I'm not criticizing Ted," Drew stammered. "I just don't think it's fair you put him in this position."

"It was by mutual agreement," Eric explained. "He was under

no illusions. He knew what he was getting himself into. And he looked positively *pumped* after each of his public appearances! It's clear he enjoyed them greatly, and I think he accomplished what he set out to do." Eric's brow furrowed. "What is your complaint, exactly?"

Drew appeared to be at a loss for words. "Never mind. Let's move on."

"So, your complaint was that I somehow forced him into this, against his will?" Eric asked. "That couldn't be further from the truth. You certainly didn't ask *him* about it. Where did you get this idea?"

"Let's discuss your policy on recreational drugs," Drew interrupted. "This is a *huge* change from existing practices. How do you defend it?"

"Actually, it's *completely* in line with existing practices," Eric corrected. "The laws on alcohol and tobacco are that you're allowed to use them, but you're liable for any consequences. You can't use drug-addled states of mind as an excuse for violating the law. And your health insurance isn't going to pay endlessly for the damage you caused yourself with drug use. So, although they're legal, they're naturally discouraged. I've just extended that to all the other recreational drugs."

"Including heroin? Fentanyl? Cocaine? Acid?!" Drew barked.

"Yes, all of them. But before you jump to conclusions, I want to make it clear that we don't condone the use of *any* of them. It's my understanding that most users of opiates set themselves up for deportation; if there *are* functional users of those substances, they're pretty rare. And the dangers of cocaine seem to be mostly a consequence of how it was prepared for illicit transport, by distilling the essence from the plants using gasoline and whatnot. Now that it's legal, powdered and crystallized cocaine have nearly vanished, in favor of coca leaf tea."

"Really?" Drew snorted. "Coke addicts turned into tea drinkers overnight?"

"Of course not," Eric explained. "The coke addicts generally do something to get themselves deported. Keep in mind that coca has been used for centuries, in its native countries, without the horrible problems we have here. That has to do with the way it's used. Consuming coca leaf involves a lot of other compounds that, taken together, produce a profoundly different effect than concentrated cocaine powder." Eric smiled. "You may have noticed that coca leaf tea bags are available in our break rooms, though it costs quite a bit more than regular tea. Have you tried it?"

"Of course not!" Drew huffed.

"Well, *I* have...but only once," Eric offered. "Mostly, I just stick to caffeine. But there was a particularly bad night recently, where I had to stay up late to deal with a minor disaster. One bag of that tea at the end of my normal day, and I was bright and awake for the next four hours! I managed to solve the problem, and then had the deepest sleep I've had in a long time. So I can't say I'll ever do that again, but I certainly didn't get addicted after one use. And from what I hear, most users of coca leaf tea report similar experiences." He fixed Drew with his gaze. "Have you heard differently?"

"I...well, no," Drew confessed.

Eric leaned in. "Did you simply assume that *any* use of drugs somehow equaled the *worst* possible use of them?" Drew didn't reply; Eric sighed. "I'm fine with being challenged, but I have to admit, I was hoping for better-sourced counterarguments. All I've heard so far are strident emotions."

"Well, *I* believe I have a less emotional argument," Mrs. Verhage interjected. "I have *big* questions about the city's foray into cryptocurrency. The conventional wisdom is that they're merely speculative investments, but you intend to base the city's finances on them. And why does it take an increasingly large number of dollars to buy them?"

"Wow...there's a lot to unpack here," Eric protested. "First, I agree, most cryptocurrencies have no inherent value, beyond what one is willing to pay for them; they're fiat currencies, not backed by anything. Our city's cryptocurrency isn't like that; it's backed by the full faith and credit of the city, its holdings, and its prospects for future success."

"Isn't the *dollar* backed by the 'full faith and credit' of the United States?" Mrs. Verhage declared.

"Indeed it is," Eric countered. "And how is *that* doing these days?"

Mrs. Verhage didn't answer; Eric continued. "That answers your second question, by the way — the dollar is losing value compared to our city's currency."

"Why did you go with a cryptocurrency?" Carl asked.

"Because it neatly solves our problem," Eric explained. "One of the big limitations of creating corporation-run autonomous zones in the past has been money; in other words, how would they meaningfully issue their own currency? Cryptocurrency has solved that problem. And ours is backed by our city's full faith and credit, which involves our extensive asset holdings."

"Why not something more traditional, like gold and silver coins?" Carl asked. "That wouldn't depend on the city's reputation."

"We're more than happy to; we exchange our currency for gold and silver all the time," Eric replied. "But using them as coins brings up the possibility of forgery. There are some high quality fakes out there, using metals such as tungsten to mimic the weight and density of gold. Although there are ways to spot fakes, they're still beyond the ability of everyday people just trying to use them for currency. Besides, most people these days don't pay cash; they use a credit card. Our cryptocurrency works like that, so nothing changes for them. In short," Eric quipped, "it's mostly the older generation that wants to pay with cash."

"I see," Carl mumbled.

"It's not like merchants don't take cash anymore," Eric continued. "You can still pay with dollars anywhere in the city. But merchants seem to prefer our city's currency, if for no other reason than it's a better store of value."

The room responded with silence. "Any other questions about our currency?" Eric probed.

"Let's pivot to your policies on surveillance," Carl brought up. "I, for one, have a big problem with that."

"I'm not sure why you would," Eric countered. "The city already had an extensive public surveillance system; we're simply making full use of it. And the 'global surveillance disclosures' are old news now; everyone knows the world governments are watching *all* of us, *all* the time, and *not* with our best interests in mind. That's the big difference here; the city isn't interested in enforcing conformity, or collecting blackmail. We only care about genuine crimes against others, and when at all possible, only for the purposes of restitution."

"How can I be sure of that?" Carl protested.

"Well, why don't we take a look?" Eric offered as he stood up. Carl's eyes grew wide. "Don't worry, sir, we'll do this with your laptop. Only you will see it." Eric brought with him a portable retina scanner; he plugged it into Carl's computer. "If you'll allow me, sir, I need to log in to the central surveillance site with my credentials."

"Be my guest," Carl mumbled feebly.

Eric typed for a short while, then stared into the retina scanner. It brought up a new page with lots of red banners and strident warnings. "OK, now you log in with *your* credentials. I don't have the authority to do that, but you're allowed to look at your own records." Eric turned his body, facing away from Carl. "So follow the instructions and then let it scan your retina."

Carl did so; a few moment later, he let out a gasp. Eric raised his eyebrows. "I take it you found them?"

"Oh my…" Carl trilled.

"Some of it may be embarrassing, but the important part is on the 'criminal summary' tab. You can click on it if you want to read it, but before you do that…what color is it?"

"Green," Carl answered.

Eric smiled. "I expected nothing less. That means nothing you've done is considered even *vaguely* criminal. Most people warrant a yellow, but not you."

Carl chuckled as he found the contents of the criminal summary to be blank. "I guess I'm less off-put about this now."

"I'm sure it gets better!" Eric piped up. "Click on the rightmost tab, labeled 'rating'. What does it say?"

Carl clicked. "It says '24'. Is that good?"

"It's excellent!" Eric exulted. "The median score is 50; higher numbers are worse. Anyone with a score over 90 tends to get deported immediately. And finally, click on the tab to the left of 'rating'; it should be labeled 'views'. What does it say?"

Carl clicked. "It has one line…dated a few minutes ago, with my name."

Eric smiled. "That means you're the only one that's looked at your record. Anyone else would require probable cause, and as you just saw, there hasn't been any. In addition, even *looking* at someone's record leaves an audit trail. These logs are collectively signed and accrued cryptographically, just like transactions in our currency. It's not possible to retract those log entries without invalidating a lot of other, unrelated records, which of course would get noticed quickly. So you can be confident that no one is snooping around."

Carl let out a sigh of relief. "That's great news. I never would have expected it to be set up like this."

"I would demand nothing less!" Eric exulted. "Go ahead and close the window when you're done."

"I'm done," Carl reported as he clicked. "I feel much better now."

Eric turned back. "Think about what this means. The surveillance A.I. may see everything, but doesn't act on it without cause. And with all the information it's collected on you, it has determined that you're an upstanding citizen. So, unlike every other surveillance state in the world, good people genuinely have nothing to fear from ours. It's not meant for control; its job truly is fairness and restitution." Eric looked across the table. "And the rest of you can look at your own records at any time. I can help you, or you can find a high-ranking security officer on your own."

"I would prefer *no* surveillance," one board member piped up.

"*That* ship has sailed." Eric walked back to his seat and sat down. "Once it was technologically possible, the surveillance panopticon quickly became a reality. All I can do is try to minimize the evil consequences."

"Is that the reasoning behind your surprisingly lax employment policies?" another board member asked. "Like your fanatical opposition to overtime?"

"A little, I suppose," Eric confessed, "but mostly, I think it's just common sense."

"Mandatory overtime is the rule in most parts of the world," the board member countered.

"Maybe, but that's not a good thing, and Millenniaburg's not like most parts of the world," Eric pointed out. "This isn't just another city; it's a demonstration of a new way of life."

"Here comes the messianic part again," someone quipped. Arrogant chuckles washed over the room.

"With all due respect," Eric asserted, "the court of public opinion is judging our effort here. We have to demonstrate that this is a better way to live than what's offered elsewhere. One way we ingratiate ourselves to our employees is to not require overtime, or any *other* excessive commitment to their jobs. We realize people need to be able to live their lives. That's not only a good way to avoid burnout, but it allows people to create value in other ways, such as raising good children, coming up with innovative ideas, or starting a sideline business that might end up creating additional value."

"You *want* to lose good employees to their own ventures?" Mrs. Verhage dismissed.

Eric didn't budge. "We consider this a small price to pay to ensure future stability."

"You may be surprised to find it a very *big* price," Mrs. Verhage snapped.

"On the contrary," Eric defended. "It's a huge draw for people tired of working themselves to death. Many are sick of running themselves ragged in government-run cities, and are grateful for the alternative. We may be deporting a lot of people, but our immigrants more than make up for that loss, and they're much more hard-working, and of much higher quality, than the ones we lose."

"What happens when that pipeline dries up?" Drew asked.

"That would only happen if the government starts running their cities better," Eric answered. "Frankly, I like our odds."

"But your ideas are so speculative," a board member countered. "Nothing like this has ever been tried before."

"Actually," Eric replied, "they're pretty standard libertarian ideas."

"*Really*." Mrs. Verhage's icy voice dripped with venom. "I'm surprised you admitted that. Libertarianism has never run a government before."

"I'm not sure why you would say that," Eric protested. "The United States was effectively libertarian until around the 1930s, with ever-increasing regulation ever since. Sure, the 1929 stock market crash was a traumatic event, but the cure has become *far* worse than the disease, as one can see by the increasing chaos and signs of collapse all around us." Eric stood up and leaned on the table, planting his hands firmly on the surface. "I hardly need to point out how the Federal Reserve has systematically destroyed the purchasing power of the dollar."

No one responded; Eric continued, casting his glance over the assembled board members. "It's long past time to throw out the old system…and do something that *works*."

"You're asking us to take a huge leap of faith," another board member countered. "Libertarianism has failed every time it's been tried."

"You're subscribing to a false binary fallacy," Eric insinuated. "The choice is *not* between heavy regulation or no regulation; the truth, as always, is several shades of gray in between." Eric leveled his gaze at the board member. "I put it to you that most of your counterarguments involve false strawmen."

"Watch yourself," the board member hissed. "You don't know your place."

Eric continued, undeterred. "Libertarianism, in its essence, is people interacting with each other by *choice*, setting up their own systems, formal *and* informal, to handle what would normally be done by a government. Technology has only made that *more* practical. Much of what governments had to regulate in the past can be handled by individual choice and widespread democratic communication, such as social media. The remainder can be handled by a vastly reduced government." Eric relaxed and smiled. "And in the end, any excesses can be handled arbitrarily by application of the original 'terms and conditions'. So there's a ready-made escape hatch for anything you wish to impose."

"I couldn't have said it better myself," Mrs. Verhage snarked. She looked around the room. "I think this is as good a time as any, wouldn't you agree?" The board members all nodded, sly smiles on their faces. Eric's brow furrowed as he perused them uncertainly.

"Mr. Thompson, despite your spirited presentation today, the board feels that too many of the consequences of your policies are unknown, and so we've drawn up a plan that favors a more traditional approach to governance. We'll take a vote on it now, and then send you the details."

Eric smiled cryptically. "I guess this is as good of a time as any to announce *this*."

Mrs. Verhage reared, unsettled. "*Excuse* me…?"

Eric smiled as he raised a clicker to the television on the wall; it now displayed a labeled pie graph. "As you can see here, I and my supporters now control *well* over fifty percent of the shares, and we're primed to vote in a *new* board of directors."

"You can't do that!" one board member protested.

"Of course I can," Eric quipped. "It wasn't my decision to make this a separate corporation, but this takeover is a natural consequence of that."

He leaned in and leveled his gaze at his gawking audience. "Also, it wasn't my idea to only provide *half* the seed money I asked for. But that *did* make it twice as easy to reach this milestone." His only answer was a sea of gaping stares.

The laptop computers of all in attendance beeped; each turned to view their own screen. "The new board has been elected," Eric announced. "Our first meeting is at the top of the hour, in this room. Those of you no longer on the board are welcome to attend it…as observers."

Eric noticed Mrs. Verhage's fuming glare. "Don't be so surprised," Eric consoled. "After all, it's not like I personally own the company now. The majority owners are the city's former debtholders. But they're on *my* side, because they believe I'll deliver a return on their investment. And together, we've elected a board that's more in tune with *their* desires—" Eric pounded the table once. "—instead of the, shall we say, *limited* vision we've had to put up with until now."

The sullen silence was almost deafening.

Eric turned to Carl. "So what do you think, sir?"

Carl's chuckle soon grew into rolling laughter. "Well *done*, young man! I'm truly impressed!"

Eric smiled. "Thank you. I *knew* you'd understand. And that's why I hope you consent to remaining the CEO on the *new* Unlimited Partners board."

Carl beamed. "I'd be honored."

5

The "applause" signs lit up; the audience dutifully clapped for them. In front of the hosts, the stage manager counted down with his fingers, and got out of the way. At the moment the countdown would have reached zero, the familiar theme music blared, the spotlights waved across the room randomly, and the hosts — Megan, Pamela, Julie, and Amy — smiled gushingly at each other. Finally, the music died down.

Megan, the lead host, looked into the camera. "Hello, and welcome back to 'Our Views', the show where we tell you what we think! Our next guest's company has been in the news quite a bit lately, and we have *plenty* of questions for her. From the self-crowned city of Millenniaburg, please welcome Danielle Strohmeier from Unlimited Partners!"

The peppy theme music played again as a young lady with long auburn hair, dressed in business formal, elegantly walked towards the stage. Loud boos and shouts from the audience threatened to drown out the music. Danielle arrived on stage and was greeted perfunctorily by the hosts, who couldn't hide the nonplussed looks on their faces. As the noise quieted down, Danielle turned sharply towards the audience. "I'm glad you're booing me! If the audience of *this* show approved of me, I'd think I was doing something wrong!" The crowd quickly went silent, and the few that remained standing meekly sat down.

Megan smirked. "Well, wasn't *that* a perfect demonstration of Millenniaburg authoritarianism."

"Hardly," Danielle retorted. "I gave them a choice. I didn't tell them what to do."

"And you shouldn't!" piped up Pamela. "This show is called '*Our* Views', not yours."

"Really?" Danielle observed. "*That* sounds pretty authoritarian."

The hosts went silent; a small gasp could be heard from a member of the audience. "Well, why don't we get down to it," Megan declared, looking Danielle in the eye. "You're a top executive at Unlimited Partners, the firm that *somehow* gained control of a major American city."

"Bankruptcy," Danielle interjected.

"*I'll* ask the questions here!" Megan declared hotly.

"Was that a question?" Danielle asked.

Megan glared at Danielle furiously for a few seconds. "Your company threw away all of the city's existing laws and regulations, replacing them with your nebulous 'terms and conditions', allowing you to rule any way you see fit." She turned to the audience, holding her arms wide. "In *this* great nation of our, on *our* hallowed territory, democracy *itself* has been subverted." The crowd started to boo.

"Oh, please…you can't *possibly* be that naive," Danielle dismissed. "Democracy was subverted long before *we* arrived." The booing quickly came to a stop.

"Oh really? Care to explain *that*?" Pamela taunted.

"I'd be happy to," Danielle claimed. "But before I do, I just wanted to point out that your previous three guests today made it clear they thought this country's history was nothing but oppression and slavery. And I watched you four agree with everything they said. So suddenly it's a *great* nation, and *hallowed* territory, when it suits your purposes? Pardon me for getting whiplash." The hosts didn't respond; Danielle simply smiled. "Democracy was subverted the moment more than half of the people voted their hands into the wallets of less than half of the people. That's the moment it became a tyranny of the majority."

"Oh, really?" Julie interrupted, leaning in front of Pamela. "Sounds like a right-wing conspiracy theory to me."

"Actually," Danielle intoned, "it's from Plato's *Republic*. The descent into strong-man tyranny is a long-understood weakness of democracy. The point of a republic is to act as a check against unfettered democracy. But you wouldn't know that from looking at *our* country."

"But the alternative offered by Millenniaburg is *neither*," Amy countered. "It's a straight-up oligarchy."

"As is the American government, if you hadn't noticed," Danielle pointed out.

The hosts' faces froze as several gasps erupted from the audience. Megan's face boiled over with fury. "What? How dare you!"

Danielle looked Megan squarely in the eye. "Really? So you haven't noticed that, no matter how we vote, things don't really seem to change? Sure, the *talk* changes, but the actions remain remarkably the same. Every four years, the powers-that-be put up two bland, mediocre, focus-grouped, poll-tested 'compromise' candidates, whose only differences lie in words. And once in office, nothing fundamental changes."

The hosts didn't respond. Danielle continued. "Cambridge University did a study on the influence of voting on policy. You can look it up." She turned to the audience. "Search for 'Cambridge Theories of American Politics'; it should be the first link." Several heads that weren't already tilted toward their phones did so. "You can make time to read it later, but the punch line is, when it comes to actual policy making, the preferences of ordinary citizens — your democratic voters — have *much* less effect than economic elites. In short, the oligarchy rules this country, and voting is a sideshow."

"Well…it doesn't mean it *has* to be that way!" Megan retorted. "You can go along with a broken system if you like, but *we*, and our *viewers*, choose to fight the power! *We* don't give in to convenience!" A few heartfelt cheers flitted from the audience; applause started to rise.

"That's because you can *afford* to!" Danielle interjected. The weak applause died down quickly. "You may be willing, and able, to engage in some sort of march against the system, but the people in your audience can't do that. They want peace, stability, and good governance, because they actually *get* something out of it. If things get too bad here, you can board your yacht and sail to another country. Your audience can't."

"*You* could do that, too," Pamela sniped.

"But I don't, and neither does anyone else at Unlimited Partners," Danielle corrected. "Instead, we stay here, in the middle of the mess, and try to make things better. You claim to 'fight the good fight', but what do you actually *do*? All I see coming from you are lofty words. You get outraged, your audience gets outraged, and nothing happens, nothing changes. My firm is *physically* reclaiming the decay of a once-proud city, working every day to make it more of a place people would actually want to live."

"So they *want* to live under a fascist surveillance state?" Julie scathed.

"Again, not a new development," Danielle pointed out. "I'm sure you all remember the 'global surveillance disclosures' of several years ago. That's still in place; nothing has changed since then. It's actually gotten quite a bit worse. And it *directly* serves the interests of the oligarchy that you're pretending isn't in charge. Ours, on the other hand, strives to apply the lightest hand possible, and is mostly concerned with restitution. If someone commits a crime, they must make up the damage they caused. At worst, it leads to deportation. We don't use it to control how people think; we wish to encourage a diversity of views." Danielle smirked. "Not just *our* views."

Danielle could see Megan's face turn red. Amy finally spoke. "Let's talk about your deportation for a moment. So that's how you solve your problems? You pack them on a bus, and pass them off to some other poor city?"

"Not at all," Danielle explained. "We get permission from their new hosts. *More* than permission, actually; all have seemed positively enthusiastic about taking in these people. They're practically overflowing with some sort of perceived moral superiority, to be frank. Finding new homes for our deportees has been a lot easier than we ever expected."

"Really?" Amy murmured, looking down at what she held in her hands. "That wasn't in my notes."

"And it's a far cry from what the federal government does," Danielle continued. "People from other countries cross our southern border, and the authorities literally bus them to destinations unknown. Their new hosts cities are never even informed! It's a long-running scandal, and nothing seems to change—" Danielle turned back to Megan. "—*despite* the will of the voters." Megan continued to stare angrily.

"At least we still live under the rule of *law*, not your ambiguous 'terms and conditions'," Megan huffed.

"You're perfectly aware that the laws are less important than how they're interpreted," Danielle reminded. "The difference between a principled whistleblower, and criminal charges of espionage, comes down to a matter of opinion…of the *government's* opinion. That opinion is all that separates celebrated journalists from poor sods rotting away in prison. In the end, your laws don't protect you any better than our 'terms and conditions'."

Danielle turned to the audience. "How many of you are posting on social media right now?" Several heads looked up. Danielle continued. "Is it one of the big social-media sites, or a smaller independent site? Seriously, raise your hands if you're posting to an independent site right now." No one raised their hands. "So you are *literally* supporting the oligarchy that runs this country." She turned back to face the hosts. "Your complaint against Unlimited Partners can't be that we're an oligarchy. You also can't fault our rule of law, or our deportation policy. So what *is* it, then?"

No one spoke for a few seconds. "How about Councilwoman Karen?" Pamela blurted. "She ran afoul of your 'new order', and got deported for what she believed. How do you explain *that*?"

"I'm sorry, but your story isn't even *remotely* true," Danielle laughed. "She was offered a position without our company, but it was clear within a few weeks that it wasn't going to work. She then voluntarily left the city to go live somewhere else."

"Yeah, right," Pamela snorted. "You expect us to believe that?"

Danielle smirked. "Why don't we ask her?"

Pamela's face fell. "Wait, what?"

"I'd love to know where you get your information," Danielle deadpanned, "but until then, we can settle this debate very easily. I'm pretty sure I still have her phone number." Danielle fished around her chair for an audio wire and plugged it into her phone. "This'll let everyone listen in on the call, right?" As the hosts gaped at her, she calmly scrolled to a phone number and selected it. The phone's audio played over the studio's public-address system, and for the home audience; the call was answered after the first ring.

"Danielle! Great to hear from you!" Karen gushed. The hosts became pale.

"Karen! It's been a long time. Have a few minutes?"

"Of course!" Karen chimed. "I'm watching the show right now. I heard you were going to be on; I wouldn't miss this for the world!"

"Then you know there's some debate over how you left Millenniaburg," Danielle explained. "Would you like to tell your side?"

"You pretty much already did, but I'd be happy to," Karen clarified. "And I admit, I was really surprised when you called me into your office the first time. Your offer to employ me — or, as you put it, 'make full use of my passion and motivation' — caught me off guard. But after a few weeks, it became clear to both of us that, while I might have identified the problem correctly, my solutions all involved force. I literally had no idea how to solve any of these problems without forcing people to believe a certain way. I was crestfallen, but I agreed it was time for me to go."

Danielle glanced at the hosts; they continued to stew. "So how have you been since then?"

"Oh, you know, it's an adjustment," Karen admitted. "I've been trying to teach myself different ways to resolve problems. It's not easy to overcome a lifetime of thinking. But at least I've taken the first few steps in that direction."

"Glad to hear it!" Danielle piped up. "I don't want to keep you on the spot, so I'll let you go, but first…is there anything you'd like to say about their specific charges? Of running 'afoul' of us and getting 'deported'?"

"Yes," Karen affirmed. "That's not at *all* how it happened. I have *no* idea where they got that. They certainly didn't talk to *me*."

"Thanks, Karen," Danielle ended. "Have a good day!"

"You too!" Karen trilled. "Give 'em hell!"

Danielle hung up and disconnected the cable. She turned to face the hosts, all of whom looked ashen. "Well? What do you have to say for yourselves? Where exactly did you get your information on Councilwoman Karen?"

The hosts began speaking over each other; the words came out in confused jumbles. "Errors in research"…"differences of opinion"…"we're not on trial here"…finally, Amy stood up and spoke loudly, cutting them all off. "We made it up." The other three hosts glared at her, aghast.

Danielle blinked. "Care to explain that?" Megan made a "cut it off" motion with her hand, but Amy ignored it. "We never even looked into it. We simply jumped to conclusions once we heard she didn't live there anymore." She turned to face her fellow hosts. "Megan, you assured me we were fighting the good fight. But lying isn't part of that. What the heck's going on here?"

Megan didn't respond; she continued to stare hotly at Amy. Danielle broke the silence. "Karen didn't leave because of her criticism, but because her solutions involved excessive force. We regularly hire critics to solve the problem they're criticizing; the passion they bring to their work is highly valued. But it's on *them* to demonstrate how to solve the problem. If their solution works, that's wonderful, since there are now less problems. But if their solution *doesn't* work, then they forfeit their right to criticize, since events have proven their ideas to be wrong." Danielle settled back in her chair. "I think that's eminently fair. Don't you?"

Danielle noticed that Megan's collar was soaked with sweat, as was the upper part of her blouse. Megan finally managed to respond. "So what sort of people qualify to live in Millenniaburg, then? You pick and choose among the privileged?"

"Hardly," Danielle responded. "Our criteria are not difficult to meet. If you can hold down a job, go to a restaurant without screaming at the waitstaff, and return your shopping cart to a corral, then you're *more* than qualified to live in our city." An appreciative murmur arose from the audience.

"How many people, do you think, can live under such rules?" Pamela sneered.

"We're not sure," Danielle answered, "but we believe it's a silent majority." More approving noises from the studio audience.

"Do your citizens have *any* voting rights?" Julie asked.

"Yes, like any other shareholders," Danielle explained. "That's one way that universal suffrage fails; the voters don't necessarily have skin in the game, so to speak. But shareholders do. Also, you never know why voters make the decisions they do…for all you know, they could be trying to crash the system deliberately, voting for the most destructive ideas possible. Shareholders are much less likely to do that, since it'll hurt them directly. For this reason, Unlimited Partners' plan is to make *all* citizens stockholders, so that they can share in the profits realized by the peace and prosperity they're creating. This contrasts with the current system, where the rich get richer, the poor stay poor, and the middle class find it increasingly difficult to join the ranks of the rich."

"Still, the majority shareholders are likely to get their way," Julie pointed out.

"Of course," Danielle conceded. "Just as how, in your system of government, special interest money can sway voters. In the end, it's a problem that neither of us have solved. But at least we're not any worse off."

"I heard that company stock is also your currency?" Megan charged. "Your people literally sell their voting rights for their daily needs?"

"We also have non-voting stock," Danielle explained. "That's used as currency."

"And there's no danger of forging them?" Megan griped. "The U.S. Treasury goes through a lot of trouble to make their bills difficult to forge. That takes time and effort. Have you cut corners here?"

"We took an easier way out," Danielle said with a smile. "All classes of our stock are technically cryptocurrencies. The paper versions, when they're used at all, are just tokens representing the electronic versions."

Megan frowned. "Well, it seems like you've thought of *everything*, haven't you. It remains to be seen how many people want to live under such a blatantly right-wing regime."

"Our system is inspired by the terms and conditions of Big Tech companies that publicly profess left-wing values," Danielle reminded. "How does that make us right-wing?"

Megan smoldered as Danielle continued. "Besides, we only have to offer something better than the alternative. Big Government is collapsing. Big Tech wants to impose a totalitarian state where your every online utterance is censored. Frankly, we're a lot better than *either* of those alternatives." A single shout of "Yeah!" erupted from the audience. Danielle turned and smiled. "Hey, thanks for the vote of confidence!"

"I'll still never understand how the government lets you get away with this," Pamela seethed.

"Like I said earlier…bankruptcy!" Danielle reminded. "The government agreed to our terms, and gave us permission." Danielle shifted in her chair and smiled. "It was remarkably easy! Once the city defunded the police, civil order broke down quickly. They eventually tried to rehire some police, but got few takers. The city was literally in danger of collapsing into anarchy. Unlimited Partners put a stop to that."

Megan looked off-camera at the stage manager. "Well, it looks like we have to move on to the next guest," she huffed. "We'll have to take this up again later."

"I'll be glad to come back," Danielle smirked. "I've had a lovely time today." Megan's eyes flared with anger, but before she could respond, Danielle turned to the audience and pointed. "Looks like someone has a question!"

Julie snarled. "Hey, *we're* the only ones allowed to do that!" But the staff member with the roving microphone had already reached the audience member. A quiet voice spoke up. "I'm impressed with what I've heard today. How does one become a citizen of Millenniaburg?"

"You only need to demonstrate that you have something to contribute, and that you won't be a drain on the system," Danielle explained. "That's not too much to ask. There's an application form on our website."

The audience member chuckled. "I guess I'll have to ask my grandchildren about that. I don't know a web site from a garden spider."

"I'm not buying this for one second," Megan retorted. "You're obviously a plant."

"A what?" The staff member holding the microphone explained it to her. She looked irritated. "No, I'm not. I've never met Danielle before."

Megan crossed her arms angrily. "We'll see about that."

Danielle's eyes grew wide. "Wow. So, you're *openly* willing to attack an innocent person, hurling accusations at them, abusing your position…is that not the mark of a corrupt, self-serving oligarchy? And yet you deny it exists."

"Can I say something about this?" came the quiet voice.

Megan turned toward the speaker and glared furiously. "*No!*"

"Go ahead, ma'am," Danielle reassured.

"I'm insulted you think I'm a plant," the audience member lectured. "And until today's show, I opposed what Millenniaburg stood for. But now that I've heard their side of the story, I've changed my mind." She pointed her finger directly at Megan. "So *go ahead* and investigate me; I might just be an old lady, but I'm not afraid of any of you. Do you worst, dearie." She then abruptly sat down, leaving the hosts gaping.

Danielle bemusedly pondered the silent hosts. She then turned to the camera, smirking, and said "We'll be right back." Immediately, the theme music started, the search lights played over the room, and the "applause" signs flashed. She got up to leave.

Megan stood up suddenly. "*Get out!*" she commanded.

"I *was* leaving," Danielle responded flippantly. "Have a great rest of your day! Enjoy being miserable!" As she left the stage, the audience gave her a standing ovation, turning to face her as she walked out.

The doorbell rang. Jessie looked up from her knitting, then set it down and padded over to the front door. Peering through the dingy peephole, she could only see an indistinct, burly shape. A wave of nervous energy washed over her. "Who is it?"

"Handyman. I'm here for the kitchen sink."

She shivered slightly. "How do I know you're who you say you are?"

"You received a one-time pad when you made the appointment. It should be on the receipt."

Jessie walked back into the kitchen, dug though the rental paperwork she still hadn't fully read, and finally found the repair appointment. She returned to the front door and cleared her throat. "OK, it's six—"

"*No*, ma'am. I'm supposed to read that number to *you*. That's how you can tell I'm who I say I am."

"Oh, of course." She closed her eyes and smacked her forehead. "Go ahead."

"Six, one, six, three, five, nine, nine, seven."

Jessie smiled. "That matches!" She moved to open the front door, but the chain stopped her. Through the crack, she could see the handyman. Much taller than her, taller even than Dan, his muscular build was clearly visible through his medium-blue jumpsuit. Despite the heat, he had long sleeves. On top of his head was the same surveillance headgear she remembered being worn by the movers. Involuntarily, she locked eyes with him; the dark shadows in them seemed to accentuate his fierce glare. She froze.

"Ma'am? May I?"

She blinked. "Oh, of course. Sorry." She closed the door, reluctantly disconnected the chain, and after taking a deep breath, opened the door. Now, she could see his name tag — "Henry", with the now familiar U-P logo — and, with more light, she could see that the look in his eyes seemed placid, not fierce. He gave her a friendly smile; she returned it. "The kitchen is this way."

She locked the door behind him as he walked inside. "Have you shut off the water yet?"

She turned to look at him, noticing how easily he hefted the heavy toolbox with one arm. "No...I'm not sure how to do that."

"In apartments like these, it's usually near the water heater. Can you take me there?"

"Of course." He followed her past the master bedroom towards the laundry area; she stopped there. "The water heater is in this closet."

He put down his toolbox with surprising grace, opened the closet, and looked inside. "Yep, the shutoff is right here." He opened his toolbox to retrieve a medium-sized pipe wrench; attaching it to the valve, he began to turn it slowly, holding the pipe with his other hand. Jessie looked around nervously, her eyes darting down the hallway; there was no way to leave the laundry area without getting past him. Finally, he stopped pulling on the wrench. "Just a little sticky from not getting used much," he trilled. "Nothing a soft touch couldn't handle."

As he replaced the pipe wrench in the toolbox, Jessie quickly slid by him. Henry looked up with surprise. "The kitchen is this way," she called as she turned the corner. He shrugged and followed her.

Jessie stood apprehensively by the refrigerator as Henry walked in. He set down his toolbox and looked under the sink. "Oh, wow," he cried out. "This will *all* need to be replaced." He looked up at Jessie. "I wonder if the previous tenant *ever* washed dishes." Jessie didn't answer.

Pulling out his tools, Henry began disassembling the under-sink plumbing. Jessie stared at his head. "I couldn't help but notice your headgear. The movers that packed up our house wore something like that."

Henry snorted slightly. "Yeah, standard issue. Keeps us out of trouble, I guess." He reached deeper under the sink, his head partially disappearing from view.

Jessie's lips drew together. "Does that mean you're also a prisoner?"

"Yes," he answered nonchalantly.

Jessie withdrew into the corner of the kitchen near the refrigerator; her breathing became uneven.

Henry poked his head out. "Hey, no need to worry about me; my headgear keeps me under surveillance. In any case, I wouldn't have been allowed in here if they thought I was any sort of risk."

"And how did they determine *that*?" she huffed.

He shrugged. "I'm not really sure, given the severity of my crime. But I *do* have a history of good behavior since being committed. I'm *really* trying to put my life back together."

"Dare I ask what you did?"

Henry leaned out from under the sink, carrying the first load of damaged pipes. He looked up at Jessie sheepishly, not meeting her gaze. "Triple homicide."

Jessie blanched. "*What*?! And they let someone like you into my *apartment*?!"

Henry didn't answer; he leaned under the sink again, continuing to remove pipes.

Jessie swallowed hard. "Want to tell me what happened?"

Henry let out a short laugh. "Seems only fair. I'm not making any excuses for what I did, but…when I left high school, I didn't have a lot of prospects. Being a sports star didn't count for anything anymore; people wanted to know what I could do for them *now*. And all I had was my strength and agility; I could push people around. So I fell in with a bad crowd."

Suddenly there was a metallic snapping sound. "Crap. Well, it was coming out anyway." Henry emerged with a broken pipe, putting it into his trash pile. "Can I get some spray cleaner and some paper towels? I'd like to wipe out the wall socket before putting in new plumbing. They didn't send me with anything like that."

"Oh…sure." She grabbed a bottle of spray cleaner from the counter, wadded up some paper towels from the roll dispenser, and handed them to him. "Thanks," he said as he smiled agreeably, disappearing again under the sink.

"Anyway," he continued, "before I knew it, I was involved with all sorts of shady stuff. Mostly smuggling, that kind of thing. Lots of intimidation. But nothing involving the general public. Fast forward a few years, and I found myself fighting for my life with members of a rival gang. I killed three of them before the rest ran away. The police *really* didn't like how they were armed and I wasn't; they thought I was lying. But it was true…I killed them with my bare hands. And now I'm serving twelve to fourteen."

"And then you became a plumber?" Jessie asked incredulously.

"I tried several trades inside prison," Henry explained. "I found I was good at this, plus I could heft heavy steel pipes." He emerged with the soiled paper towels; removing the top tray from his toolbox, he began to remove a series of pipes, elbows, valves, and seals, looking occasionally under the sink before adjusting the set of parts.

"How long have you been on work release?"

"A few weeks now." He began deftly assembling the parts together.

"You don't mind being forced to work?"

"Not at all," Henry assured her. "It's much better than rotting away in a cell, and besides, it's no worse than the life of the average member of the working poor. I figure that's fair."

"I'm glad to hear it's not so bad," she replied, smiling.

He returned her smile. "Besides, I find it's a great way to meet women."

"I'm *married*!" Jessie snapped haughtily.

He looked at her apologetically. "I wasn't implying anything, ma'am. I'm sorry for any offense."

Jessie looked down sadly. "No, *I'm* sorry. I'm giving you the third degree, and you don't deserve that."

Henry smirked. "Well, I *do*, actually. You go *right* ahead and hold me to a high standard. I won't protest."

She looked at him for a few moments. "So you're telling me women are interested in *prisoners*?"

He finished assembling the parts and leaned under the sink again. "Well, not as such. But, unlike random guys on the street, my background has been investigated. I've been screened for all communicable diseases. And it's not like I'm *currently* wanted for anything! That actually makes me less of a risk than some random stranger."

"I never thought of this that way," Jessie observed. "I sure wish Dan had admitted we were behind on the rent; the eviction came as a complete surprise. I wish I could have investigated *him* beforehand."

Jessie heard Henry click his tongue. "Wow, that's rough. Still, it looks like things are better for you *now*…for me, too."

She looked at him as he worked. "I hope it works out for you."

Henry momentarily leaned out from under the sink to catch her eye with a sly look, before returning. "It's amazing, isn't it? You went from being terrified of me, to *sympathizing* with me. *That* didn't take long."

Jessie giggled. "I guess you're right." She gazed at his muscular torso briefly. "Somehow, you make it easy."

"That's good to hear," he replied. "I really want to put my life back together; I'm *done* being a criminal. I'm grateful that Unlimited Partners is giving me this chance; the old system just wanted to lock me away, then throw me back onto the streets with no prospects, and no one willing to give me a chance. But they tell me, if I handle the responsibility of my work release, I have a job waiting for me once I'm out."

"I have no doubt you'll make it," Jessie agreed.

Henry emerged from under the sink. "That should be fixed!" He grabbed a small pipe wrench and proffered it to Jessie. "Can you turn the water back on? You saw what I did to turn it off; just do that in reverse. I should stay here and check for leaks."

"Glad to!" She snatched the wrench from his hand and flitted to the water-heater closet. Mimicking his actions, she held the pipe as she slowly turned the valve. It gave way under her strength very easily; finally, it was fully open. She quickly returned to the kitchen to find Henry's head under the sink. "Everything looks good here! Turn the faucet on and off, please."

She leaned over him to do so. It worked fine. "Everything looks good here, too," she answered, a lump rising in her throat.

Henry looked at the pile of debris on the floor. "I don't suppose I could use your—" But Jessie had already moved the trash can closer to him. "Much obliged, ma'am!" It took a few handfuls to dump the whole mess into the can; he wiped up the remainder of the mess with the cleaner portions of the paper towels. Finally, he packed the tools back into his toolbox, and moved to stand up.

Henry smiled. "All done here!"

Jessie pouted. "So soon? I'm sorry to see you go."

Henry gave her a demure smile. "It was a pleasure to meet you, ma'am."

"My name is Jessie," she fluttered. "I should have told you that earlier." She smiled at him coquettishly. "I wish you didn't have to leave so soon…Henry."

"Everyone calls me Hank," he offered.

"Of *course* they do." Their eyes locked, each staring comfortably at the other.

Hank broke into a wide grin, then looked up at his headgear. "Well, overlord? Any problems here?"

The headgear emitted a few noncommittal machine sounds before replying in a synthesized voice. "I see no rule violations. She initiated the contact. Permission granted. But it'll be deducted from your lunch time."

"I think I can handle that," Hank said coyly. He looked at Jessie again. "Well, I hate to romp and run, but it's all I'm allowed to do."

She grabbed him by his shirt and dragged him out of the kitchen. "I prefer it that way."

They disappeared into the master bedroom. His last words for some time were "I love my job!"

Ron watched Hank as he scarfed down his food. "What's *with* you today?"

Hank gripped his soda tighter as the truck hit a bump in the road; he momentarily stopped shoving his cheeseburger into his mouth and swallowed. "No big deal; I had to eat and run today. I'll clean up any mess I make, obviously; I don't want it to count against me. *I* know I'm being watched."

Ron shook his head, staring levelly at Hank. "That's not what I meant. I was talking about your ear-to-ear grin." The other guys, sitting on the bench seats in the back of the box truck, leered as they listened to the conversation.

Hank looked up as he chewed his next bite, his eyes gleaming.

Ron laughed. "Really, *again*? What *is* it with you?" Hank continued to chew. "So who was it this time?"

Hank swallowed. "A bored, put-upon housewife. Cute, in a nerdy librarian sort of way. My arm tattoos startled her at first, but she quickly got over it." He looked away dreamily for a moment. "She had *lots* of enthusiasm."

Ron gestured incredulously. "I can't believe the overlord lets you do that. Seems like there'd be a rule against it."

"I guess the A.I. looks at it logically, not emotionally. It doesn't understand what the problem would be. And it only cost me some free time during my lunch break."

The voice in Hank's headgear came to life. "Upon further consideration, you won't be penalized for the time spent delivering enhanced customer service; you just received a five-star rating and a glowing review. The overlord considers this a strong contribution to the positive image of the firm."

Hank smirked before taking a big gulp of soda. "What *he* said." He sighed happily. "Just one *more* reason why I love this job!"

"And what if the husband finds out?" one of the guys jeered.

Hank's headgear spoke again. "The overlord considers this experience to be statistically likely to strengthen their marriage, due to the female partner working through her stress, plus it's statistically unlikely the male partner will ever find out."

Ron laughed as he shook his head. "Gotta love cold logic."

Hank shrugged. "Hey, it's collating a huge number of real-world experiences to come up with that decision. Who am *I* to say that it's wrong? I'm just one person and one viewpoint."

"You're more than just *that*," another guy interjected. "You're a *lucky dog!*"

The guys cheered as Hank smiled broadly, trying to finish his lunch.

6

The two gladiators stood on the ground, facing each other. Surrounding them on all sides were cage walls; various platforms and obstacles hung from chains, connected to the bars that formed the ceiling. Any of these could be used as help or hindrances, possibly even weapons. The chains suspending them in the air might serve as cover, or with sufficient skill, a type of bolas or konpei, useful to entangle an opponent. Various objects, of a wide variety of shapes and sizes, also littered the arena, some arranged in racks, others haphazardly spilled onto the floor. The possibilities were as limitless as their imaginations, and too complex to solve with any reasonable confidence in real time. Chess has nothing on combat.

Each of them rested quietly, taking in the details of their environment, and each other, with every sense available to them. Their nerves surged with life, and awareness. The call to battle could happen at any moment. The quiet murmur from the spectators bled off the impending surge of excitement, as the supporters of the red team and the blue team speculated on the imminent success or failure of their champion.

Finally, the klaxon sounded. Quickly, their blades folded out from where they had been stored, and each one leaped into the air, their propellers whirring ferociously. The murmuring gave way to cheering; each combatant fought to separate the noise of the crowd from the far more pertinent sounds of battle.

The first projectiles soared through the air, aerodynamic darts with their own rudders and flaps, used to steer them after launch. Each employed this tactic, as well as expecting it. With a combination of predictive motion tracking, aerodynamic knowledge, and tactical wisdom, the darts sought out their targets; through a combination of inertial changes, deft flying, and judicious use of cover, the deadly missiles were avoided.

Soon, the underwhelming success of this tactic was acknowledged by both, and it was discarded in favor of something resembling jousting. Pondering the delicate subtleties of momentum, each tried to ram his opponent; although the propellers were an obvious target, sudden changes in rotational speed made it easy to move them out of the way. The true target lay in the thorax, the host of all the most important organs, including the brain. At times, the jousting gave way to swordplay, as each tried to swat the other's weapon, attempting to gain even a moment of advantage.

The red duelist found itself knocked backwards by a fortuitous blow from its opponent; the blue supporters cheered. Almost too fast for the naked eye, it bounced off the cage wall, flipped itself around, and caught the blue swashbuckler with a devastating transverse whack. The blue trooper momentarily spun out of control, colliding with an obstacle before righting itself; in a flash, it ducked for shelter. Team Red erupted in jubilation.

The red scrapper immediately charged its lance into its adversary's sanctuary, sending it swinging. The poor blue militant took the full force of its refuge's betrayal, caroming artlessly off a hung platform and spiraling clumsily to the ground. Seeing this, the red knight stopped in mid-air, and merely pointed its weapon upwards, in a respectful gesture. The wounded blue tussler tried to limp into a better position, preparing for another round.

Sam arrived at the arena; he banged on the bars to get everyone's attention. "People! Playtime is over!" They responded with a sea of juvenile groans and whines. Sam was unfazed. "No! I just got word from Mr. Thompson! He's going to be here with an investor in ten minutes!" Quickly, their faces assumed serious expressions as they ran back to their stations.

Gary unlocked his computer; the usual barrage of in-progress software assailed his eyes. "Couldn't he have given us more warning?"

Dwight shrugged as he straightened out the jumbled papers on his desk, before putting them into a drawer. "Well, that's what we deserve for getting too familiar with him. Never forget, he's a suit!"

Isabel peered over the cubicle wall. "Oh, come on, he's not *that* bad."

Gary shrugged. "Yeah…by the standards of suits, he's really not a bad guy. He certainly supports our work!"

Dwight's desk now looked more organized. "I know, I was just venting. But still…ten minutes?"

Irwin was standing behind them. "You know how it is for suits. If an important customer, or investor, wants something, they have to do it immediately. And shi—" He caught himself; Sam was glaring at him. "Well, you-know-what rolls downhill."

Stacy chimed in. "And since when has he ever been on time? I think we have plenty of slack."

Her words proved prescient; they had a full twenty minutes to prepare for his arrival, far more than they needed. The door opened, and Eric Thompson, the youngest of the high-ranking executives in Unlimited Partners, entered the lab's foyer, grinning widely. Behind him was the tall, lanky, and increasingly familiar form of Brian McTierney, the president of a legacy civic-engineering firm, and one of their newest investors. Even the engineers were aware his opinion could sway a lot of well-heeled captains of traditional industry to join their side. Dwight wished he had dressed more conservatively today.

Eric spoke up. "And so we come to the nerve center of our company's future. How we pay for our operations is of course important, but without a firm grasp on what's coming next, there's very little that's *worth* paying for! Let me introduce to you our premier research-and-development wing…16otaku!" The assembled scientists and engineers beamed happily.

Confusion washed over Brian's face. "Ota…what now?"

"Otaku!" Stacy piped up. "It's Japanese for 'nerd'. We felt it described us well. As for the 16…it's something of an inside joke."

Brian chuckled to himself. "I have a feeling this is only the *beginning* of things I won't understand today."

"Don't worry, they'll do their best to explain it to you," Eric remarked. "They're surprisingly good at that. Even *I* feel I have a decent grasp on this place!"

"Well, I have *one* question right off the bat," chided Brian. "I was expecting more of a pigsty. How do you all keep this place so *clean*?"

Sam smiled. "What a great segue into our research direction!" Scattered snickers flitted from the assembled engineers. "We're focused on using the latest advances in artificial intelligence to create consumer products that give people back their most precious commodities…time and energy!" As he spoke, a few of their robotic cleaning devices glided to where he stood, surrounding his feet and looking up at him. "A big part of that is household maintenance. We've had dishwashers, clothes washers/dryers, and automatic sprinkler systems for years. Robotic vacuums are a recent addition, but they were unable to handle complex tasks. But our current generation of maid-bots can handle real-world conditions!"

He looked down at his gleaming metal minions. "OK, gang!

Show him what you can do!"

They immediately scattered, searching out signs of disorder. One of them burst forth with hoses and brushes, and cleaned a nearby office chair. One protrusion paused momentarily over a spot; it withdrew, and a different hose emerged, which promptly began steam-cleaning a stain. Several seconds later, the stain was gone, and the appendage retreated into the base. Another robot scurried under the desk, vacuuming up dust and debris. As it left, it neatly placed a pen it had found onto the desk, after sanitizing it. They continued down the line of workstations.

"How did it know the pen wasn't garbage?" Brian wondered brightly.

"They learn over time," Dwight explained. "Their artificial intelligence is leaps and bounds over anything else available today." He reached down to a bot that was scurrying by. "Good boy!" The bot paused to receive the scratch on its carapace, then continued on its way.

Brian smirked. "You treat them like your pets! It's as if you believe they're really alive."

"Actually, sir, they sort of are," Sam declared. "A large portion of their intelligence is derived from biological material."

Brian frowned. "Then is it really artificial? I once heard you use cat brains from strays."

Sam raised his palms in a pleading motion. "You're talking *ancient* history. Our machine intelligence is a sophisticated combination of computers and lab-grown organic material, merged fluidly to create near-sentience. No one has to die any more."

"Really?" Brian marveled. "And they work better than what nature produces?"

"For our purposes, they do," Irwin conveyed. "When we used animal brains, we had to induce the neurons to unpattern themselves; they would expand in the tank, looking like a cloud of fibers floating in the fluid. Then we would train them to do what we wanted, and they would contract again. But it was very time-consuming, the results were never as intelligent as the original animal, and there would be leftover traces of negative personality characteristics. But once we could grow our own neurons, all of these problems vanished."

Brian blinked his eyes. "I'm not going to pretend I understand all of that." That elicited a few laughs. "What I heard was you don't kill animals anymore, and the results are better."

"Indeed, you're grasping it perfectly!" Sam grinned. "Besides, we couldn't bear to keep killing stray cats. Our hearts went out to all of them! Bruno, over there, has quite a bit to do with that."

Brian turned to look at a nearby couch. There lay a large tomcat, well-groomed and perfectly relaxed. At the sound of his name, he raised his head and contemplated them with a disinterested look. Isabel joined in. "At one point, he was just another stray, picked up by the animal-control robots. But we were immediately struck by the look in his eyes; more than any of the other cats we'd encountered, his eyes seemed to glow with intelligence. So we kept him as a pet, and he motivated us to strive for a better solution. And now we have one!"

Sam raised his finger. "Actually, this brings up something I wanted to show you. Maid-bot!" One of them stopped what it was doing and wheeled toward Sam, pausing in front of him. "Go clean up Bruno."

The bot rolled towards Bruno, slowing as it approached. A cable extended from the robot's base, but at the end was a hand-like attachment with articulated fingers. It slowly approached Bruno's head, and began lightly scratching him behind the ears. Bruno blinked his eyes a few times, then started moving his head around, pushing into the hand, enjoying the attention. After several seconds of this, two more attachments extended from the robot, gently lifting Bruno's body into the air; he stood up and stretched in the classic feline way, still completely calm. One attachment slowly ramped up the vacuum pressure, and removed the fur from under where Bruno lay; another one began grooming him, also slowly increasing the rate of airflow. Bruno stood there sedately, letting them brush and vacuum him all over. Several seconds passed, then finally most of the attachments withdrew. The one with the hand-like tool remained, to give Bruno one final scratch on the head; he pushed into it affectionately, then settled back down on the couch and resumed his nap.

Brian was astonished. "Every cat I've ever seen is terrified of the vacuum! That was really incredible!"

"Even Bruno had to learn to accept that, but we approached it gently," Stacy remarked. "It helps that he's always seemed OK with technology. It's not for nothing that he's our lab cat! He's our little *aibo*! That's Japanese for 'buddy'."

"I was going to ask about that," Brian interjected. "I don't think I've seen so many Japanese posters in my life." Plastered over the walls were several depictions of Japanese animation; most of it appeared to be action-oriented or superhero-related, all the women with short skirts and impossibly long legs.

"Scientists and engineers have traditionally drawn a lot of inspiration from science fiction," Sam related. "Most of *us* just happen to be fans of anime and manga. That even shows up on the robotic cables!"

"It...what?" Brian seemed confused.

"Maid-bot!" One of them interrupted its cleaning duties to move near Sam. He smiled coyly and gestured to Brian. "Show him your tentacles!"

The maid-bot slid up to Brian; in a flash, all of its cables flailed upwards. Brian jumped back, but the cables didn't go near him; instead, they simply undulated in the air as the maid-bot made a silly monster sound. Brian could now see that the cables had minute depictions of squid-tentacle suckers all over them; he guffawed loudly. The maid-bot stopped its roaring, retracted its cables, and went back to work. Brian's eyes teared up with mirth. "And you did that just for fun?"

"Not completely," Sam pointed out. "It actually increases their grip traction, when they need to hold onto something. The cables are completely prehensile anyway, so the patterns are actually practical!"

Brian threw up his hands. "This is amazing. Just amazing. I've seen the robots rebuilding the city, cleaning up the debris and patching up structures, but I hadn't seen them up close. I had *no* idea they were so sophisticated. I've never seen *anything* like this!" He arched his eyes. "How come no one else has done this before? How did you get so far ahead of the curve?"

Dwight sighed. "Well...it's a combination of things. We get a lot of support here from the company. They truly wish to push the envelope, and we're happy to do it! And we have a fantastic team of engineers here, with skills we can trust. Whereas before..." He trailed off. "How should I put this?"

Stacy leveled her eyes at Dwight. "If you don't want to say it, I will!"

Dwight gestured to her with a flourish. "Be my guest."

Stacy fixed Brian with an intense gaze. "All of us have had to work with a lot of lazy morons in the past. By the standards of traditional companies, each of us has a 'spotty' work record. But it's completely unfair! We were all high performers with true vision and the skills to back them up; most of our co-workers, sadly, have been apathetic clock-punchers. We found ourselves marginalized for our supposed inability to get along with our so-called peers. The *real* story, as far as we're concerned, is that we don't suffer fools well, and have little tolerance for slackers and phonies."

Brian smiled broadly. "Gee, miss, why don't you just come out and say what you *really* think?" The room filled with polite chuckles. "She's always like this," Gary beamed. "It's why I hope to work with her for the rest of my career."

"Here, we can soar to the height of our skills, talent and motivation!" Isabel gushed. "And all the normal people…well, they can go off and do normal things, somewhere far away from us. I'm sure there's a place for them somewhere. But it's not here."

"We have to find places for a lot of different types of people," Eric added. "It hasn't been easy. Having to run a corporation with the members of an existing population has been no small task. But if they're willing to work, and make an honest effort, we keep them."

"What happens to the ones that don't?" Brian cocked his eyes curiously.

"We can discuss that later with Linda Carlyle. She's one of our directors in Human Resources, in charge of that very problem."

"Fair enough," Brian conceded. "I'd rather hear about what *you* all do, anyway! I still wonder how you can create so many intelligent devices. It seems like magic!"

"It *is* magic!" Isabel trilled. "The magic…of family."

Brian chortled politely. "*Now* I know you're putting me on."

"Hardly, sir," Gary filled in. "We can only program them so much. And instructions for neural tissue are notoriously difficult to upload directly. So instead of being programmed…our devices are *raised*!"

Sam waved towards a door. "This sounds like an excellent time to explore the next part of our facility." They moved through the door to an adjacent room, lit eerily with a bluish-green glow. "Welcome to the nursery!"

Brian gasped. It looked to him like a set from a 1950s sci-fi B-movie, except it was in color. Fibrous material grew in translucent vats; small robots that looked like giant ants fished out clumps of it and put them into glass orbs. Other ants grabbed assortments of spare parts from conveniently-placed racks and laboriously assembled new spherical bodies. A later stage attached legs and sense-organ packages. The new robots walked off the assembly line, looking much like giant spiders.

Brian gestured helplessly. "Now *this* is really too much. I'm overwhelmed. I've never seen such glorious mad-science in all my *life*! I half-expect some…oh, what are those things called, that throw off all the sparks?"

"Tesla coils?" Irwin pointed to a few darkened devices in the corners. "We have those. But they had a bad effect on neural tissue quality. So we had to turn them off." His eyes gleamed. "It's not like we didn't try!"

Brian straightened his jacket. "Well, *now* I feel everything's in place." A few joined him in light laughter. "But where do all the spiders go?"

Gary stood near another door; all around him, the spider-bots moved through flap-covered holes near the floor, like a row of demented doggie doors. "Sir, if you thought *this* room was mad-science…wait 'till you see what's next."

Casting his gravitas to the wind, Brian gleefully strolled through the door. After only a few steps, he stopped and covered his mouth with his hands, gaping at what he saw. The others politely walked around him and moved further into the room.

Much of the cavernous hangar space in this area was filled with what looked like a jungle gym from another planet. It wasn't just ladders and girders; there were a multitude of self-contained areas, small open-walled rooms and arenas, each seemingly with their own theme. In one area, spider-bots wrestled each other as ant-bots looked on. In another, ant-bots apparently performed repairs and upgrades on other bots. Yet another appeared to be a circus, with bots flying from trapezes and catching other ones in mid-air. The play area stretched out into the distance, the details lost in the heights and depths.

"What are they *doing*?" Brian could hardly contain himself.

Stacy slid up beside him and whispered. "They're *learning*."

Sam beheld the wonderment like a proud parent. "Here you see the bots going through their training. The first step is to understand the concepts of spatial perception, inertia, and gravity. None of them possess that knowledge inherently; it must be learned. Afterwards, they're put through a battery of tests, to determine their abilities and skills. The way neural tissue arranges itself is still something of a mystery, and there's even less data on lab-grown tissue. But these bots are surprisingly like newborn infants; their environment and experiences affect them greatly. So we have to evaluate how they develop."

"What happens to them after that?" Brian continued to gape at his surroundings.

"It's much like people," Dwight stated. "After they finish basic training…they go to college! Spread throughout this complex is a nearly unlimited variety of higher education. Most bots pick up several certifications, qualifying them to do different types of jobs. And some choose to be teachers, and stay in here to mentor the newbies!"

Brian turned to Dwight suddenly. "Did you say…choose?"

Dwight's eyes twinkled. "I did indeed! As Sam mentioned earlier, these bots show near-sentience. They're not capable of higher reasoning; the quality of our lab-grown neural tissue isn't good enough for that. But we estimate their intelligence is a little past crows, but not quite up to cats. They're pretty good at grunt work. You've seen them doing construction and demolition work out in the city. You saw some of our more sophisticated ones today, keeping the lab tidy. We hope to field those in a couple of weeks. We expect our next project to be robot butlers, able to do more for you than just clean."

Brian looked wistful. "Your bots could already put my domestic help out of business. I'd hate to do that to them."

"But don't you see?" Eric interjected. "That would free them up to do something more productive! As long as they're willing to work, and make an honest effort, they're welcome to stay in our city. And we'd rather let them rise to their full potential, instead of trap them in a job that can be done by robots!"

Brian sighed. "That *does* sound better for them, doesn't it."

"The court of public opinion is still judging our effort," Eric reminded. "We have to demonstrate that this is a better way of living, and governing, than what's happening in the rest of the country. There, automation puts people out of work all the time, quite often permanently. They lose their income, they lose their self-respect, and worst of all, they lose their hope for the future. Unlimited Partners is all about freeing people from the trap of dependency and desperation, not just because it's the human thing to do, but because the alternative is a terrible waste of valuable resources! It's just good *business*!"

Brian shook his head. "This is *such* a nice change of pace from the old ways. I remember when the titans of industry simply chewed people up and spit them out."

Eric smiled wanly. "That's exactly what caused the problem that the rest of the country is dealing with. We're here to try something different…something more sustainable."

Brian beamed. "I'm sure glad I joined *this* on the ground floor!" He looked past Eric to an open door. "What's down there? Is that a cage?"

Stacy blushed. "Oops, I guess we left that door open." The others chuckled. "Well, may as well show you some of our more *advanced* research!" All began walking towards the door. "In here is our battle arena, where our latest prototypes fight each other," Stacy chimed. "Combat has always been the ultimate competition, and there's certainly no shortage of need for crowd control and pacification, so…"

They entered the room. Stacy looked around uncertainly. "Where are they?" The cage door was open.

Sam was aghast. "They can jimmy *locks* now?!"

Eric turned to Sam. "You mean to tell me we have two highly-armed, near-sentient robots on the loose?"

Sam tapped on his phone. "Let's not panic yet. I should be able to find them." Two dots appeared on his screen. "Ah, here they are. They're just around the corner, in our workbench area."

"Doing what?" Eric peered at Sam's screen.

"Not sure, but they're not moving," Sam replied. "Let's go take a look."

"Is it safe?" Brian worried. "Somehow, killer bots don't sound all that safe."

"How's this," Eric offered. "Sam and I will go up ahead, and see what they're doing. Does that work for you?"

"Way ahead of you, boss!" Eric caught up with Sam just as he disappeared around a corner.

◊ — ◊ — ◊

Most people sat quietly on their chairs in the cavernous meeting room; it was what they had been told to do. Others stood in groups, having animated conversations. A few chose to move from person to person, harassing and threatening them; no one stood up to them, but several exchanged uncomfortable glances.

Without warning, a klaxon sounded, followed by a voice blaring from a loudspeaker: "Please take your seats. The forum will begin shortly." Most people ended their conversations and returned to where they should be, but a small number retorted angrily and made rude gestures to the loudspeakers before resuming their bullying. Thirty seconds later, the klaxon sounded twice; the voice on the loudspeaker became more strident. "Return to your seats *now*." More defiant shouts and obnoxious laughter.

The faint buzzing sound was mostly drowned out by the collective murmuring; no one noticed the small doors opening in the ceiling. The sharp sound made by the projectile as it sliced through the air was much more noticeable. One of the bullies screamed as the dart discharged its electricity, causing him to shake uncontrollably and then collapse. The victim he had been holding suffered the same fate indirectly, but his inert body cushioned her fall. With wide eyes, the remaining stragglers quickly found their seats. The ceiling-mounted taser gun stayed where it was, mounted between the two small open doors to its cavity. The murmuring quickly died down; the sound of breathing was not much louder than the room tone created by the bustling city traffic outside.

With a nearly simultaneous crack, all four entrance doors opened; in walked some burly guards and a few people in suits. The crowd watched them uneasily as they strode to the front of the room and onto the elevated stage. The projection screen behind them showed the company's name and logo; both were all too familiar to the city dwellers these days. After switching on the microphone, one of the suits, a striking middle-aged woman with platinum hair, began speaking.

"Good afternoon, everyone…my name is Linda Carlyle, and I'm a human-resources director for Unlimited Partners, the corporation that now owns *and* runs this city." She paused briefly; there was no response. "Well…I know you've all been shuffled around quite a bit in the last few days, and you're probably wondering what's going on and where you're headed."

"You're damn *right*!" came a shout from the crowd. It was one of the bullies; he was standing now. "I don't have time for this! I got places to *be*!"

A few of the suits glared at him; Linda was unmoved. "*Please* sit down. All is about to be explained."

He continued being defiant. "I'll sit when I damn well *want* to! You can't—" Another whooshing sound cut through the still air. The sickening sound of electricity moving through flesh filled the room for a brief interval that seemed like an eternity; he dropped to the floor. Linda quickly interrupted their gasping. "If you refuse to control yourself, you will find yourself controlled by others. Do I make myself perfectly clear?" The room responded with stunned silence.

"That's better. *Now*...we have reviewed every one of your cases in detail, and have determined that the correct handling for the problems each of you cause...is deportation." Scattered gasps erupted from the crowd.

A woman in the audience raised her hand. Linda smiled. "Now *that's* a good example of proper behavior. Yes? You have a question?"

She appeared to be middle-aged, somewhat older than Linda, wearing a garish multicolored dress. "How can you *do* this to us?"

"It was *not* an easy decision," Linda replied. "If the company had its way, it would find a place in the new system for *all* current citizens." After capturing the petitioner's image on her phone, she began tapping on the screen. "But unfortunately, every single person sitting here has repeatedly demonstrated that they can't contribute to the common good. You're *all* a drain on valuable resources. And although the decision to expel you from the city is a last resort...it's one we feel we must make." Her screen lit up. "For instance, Gladys Frampton...you've had four sons; one died in gang violence, two are in jail, and your youngest is already in second-chance education."

Gladys hung her head. "I...I've tried my best...but they're such a handful..."

"That's putting it mildly," Linda retorted. "You're not raising productive, law-abiding citizens; your mothering is *not* a value-added activity." Gladys stared at the ground, embarrassed; Linda continued. "You've never been married to any of their fathers, and receive no financial support for any of them." One of the other suits showed Linda something on his phone; she nodded.

Gladys looked up, indignant. "Those flaky bastards! Bunch of lowlifes!"

Linda fixed Gladys with a steely gaze. "And yet you chose to bear their children?"

"I—" Gladys began. Her lips curled into a surly expression. "I wish I could find those deadbeats."

Linda pointed to someone in the room. "We've been able to find *one* of them." Gladys whirled around to look, her eyes burning with venom. Linda sneered. "Well, Terry? What do you have to say to Gladys?"

Terry froze, unable to make eye contact with Gladys. "Baby," he stammered. "...I always meant to come back."

"It's a little late *now*!" Gladys screeched.

"Not necessarily," Linda glowered. "You can always make good on your promise...when you end up where you're going."

Terry swallowed. "Where *are* we going?"

"To a different city," Linda explained. "One still run by the government. We asked if they would take you, and they readily accepted; they seemed to exult in some sort of perceived moral superiority." She smirked. "So we didn't ask too many questions after that."

Linda called on another raised hand. "I demand to see the evidence you have against me!" Another woman's voice called from the crowd: "Leroy? Is that you? You worthless bum!" Linda smiled. "Well, there's *some* of the evidence! But if you're brave, why don't you come up here on stage, so we can go over your record?" After a hesitant start, he slowly began walking to the front of the room.

By the time he got there, the projection screen showed his name and age, along with his most recent mug shot. His pleasant expression in the photos belied the seriousness of the charge he had been arrested for at the time. Linda glared icily at him. "Is this how you *normally* look after gunning down two people?"

"But...it was in self-defense!" Leroy stuttered. "I didn't *want* to do it!"

Linda sighed as the projection screen switched to a surveillance video. It showed Leroy in an alleyway, with two unknown males; it was clear they were buying drugs from him. "Turns out the old city government had an incredible amount of recorded security-camera footage; they just didn't have the resources to do much with it." Her eyes twinkled. "But *we* do." The screen showed a heated argument between Leroy and his customers; without warning, he drew a firearm and shot them both in the torso. Both uselessly raised their arms for protection, but fell to the ground, clutching their wounded bellies.

Leroy vanished from the frame a second afterwards; stitched-together video showed him running down the street for about two blocks, before looking around, relaxing, and pumping his fist in the air. The crowd murmured with astonishment. Linda shook her head. "You seem awfully happy about something you didn't want to do. Just be grateful they both lived." Leroy just stood there, gaping uselessly. Linda waved him away. "Sit down, Leroy." He glumly left the stage, looking around with some alarm as a woman approached him.

Linda leaned into the microphone. "Dwayne Smith? Why don't *you* come up here, too. I think your story would *also* be instructive." After a moment's hesitation, a tall, thickly-built man trudged up to the stage. As he arrived, the projection screen filled with his head shot, as well as his name and age. Linda beheld him. "You also deal drugs for a living, but unlike Leroy, we have no evidence of you shooting anyone."

"Can I ask something?" Dwayne pleaded. "Your new rules allow these drugs to be sold legitimately. Why don't I qualify to work for *you* doing that?"

"Well, several reasons," Linda chimed. "First of all, you *did* beat several people to within an inch of their lives. Granted, they were all lower-level street hustlers; we can almost forgive that. But our evidence shows you supplied many of them. In doing so, you engaged the authorities in *several* dangerous high-speed chases, often reaching speeds that, all by themselves, were felonies." Dwayne frowned sourly.

"But here's the *really* unforgivable part," Linda added. "Not *once* did you pay tax on *any* of this income!"

"Because I didn't want to get *caught*!" Dwayne shot back, incredulous. "Are you saying that would have *helped*?"

"In *our* eyes, yes, it would have," Linda offered. "Some of your peers have been laundering their income, so even though their business was illicit, at least they weren't a drain on public resources. Some of them now run legitimate drug-dealing businesses. Do you remember a Jamal Cooper?"

Dwayne hung his head. "Yeah. He was my competition." He sighed. "Jamal always did more business. It really irked me."

Linda shrugged. "Well, at least he paid his taxes. And he doesn't have your history of violence. That's why we gave *him* a chance. He now runs a series of dispensaries in the central-west district, near the park."

"But that was *my* territory!" Dwayne protested.

"Not any longer," Linda interrupted. "But there's more to his story. Were you aware of his sideline?"

Dwayne raised one eyebrow. "That sucker had *another* hustle?"

"Indeed," Linda smiled. "Are you familiar with the New Beginnings Recovery Center on 116th Street?"

"Yeah, but…" Dwayne's eyes shot open. "You mean that…?!"

"That's right!" Linda gushed. "He has them coming *and* going! *Truly* a visionary entrepreneur!"

Dwayne's mouth hung open. "He…wow. I had no idea."

Linda gave Dwayne a reproving look. "And *that's* why he's working for us, and why *you're* being sent away."

Dwayne's shoulders slumped. "I see." He faltered a moment. "I'd like to go back to my seat."

"Knock yourself out." Linda waved him off the stage.

She returned to the microphone. "But not *all* of you are out-and-out criminals. Some of you are just indolent." She looked at her phone. "Darrell Criek? Would you like to join us up here?"

A few seconds passed. Then a quiet voice floated through the air. "I…I can't rightly do that. I'll need some help."

Linda looked in the direction the voice had come from. There sat a morbidly obese man, so large that he had to sit across two of the seats. Somehow, he had managed to sequester himself in the center of a row.

Linda winced. "Then you can just stay there. So tell me, Darrell…you've been on welfare your entire life, fifteen of those years as an adult. What do you have to show for it?"

Darrell demurred a moment. "I can't get a job."

Linda stood, arms akimbo. "What skills do you have to offer?"

A long pause followed. "I can't think of any."

Linda looked exasperated. "What do you *do* with your time?"

Darrell looked pensive. "I watch TV, and play the lotto."

"Haven't you tried to do anything else?!"

Darrell looked sad. "I…I have a disability."

Linda looked at her phone. "According to our records, your disability is completely voluntary. You eat junk food, you never exercise, and you drink a lot of hard spirits." She looked at him uncertainly for a moment, then glared fiercely. "Are you drunk right *now*?"

"Yes'm." There was no trace of guile in his voice.

"You've been locked up for two days. Where did you even *get* alcohol?"

Darrell smiled wanly. "The others help me."

Linda pinched the bridge of her nose. "With all the time on your hands...how come you've never tried to learn a skill? Something you can do to support yourself?"

Darrell looked cross. "'Cause I don't *want to*! And *you* can't make me!"

Linda threw up her hands. "And *that* confirms you're a *willing* drain on resources. You're *exactly* the sort of person we can't abide anymore. And *that's* why you're being deported."

Darrell didn't say a word.

Linda leveled her gaze. "Would anyone *else* like to argue their case?" She swept her eyes over the room. "Anyone at all?" No one stirred.

A low rumbling outside could be heard. Linda narrowed her eyes. "Fine. You'll all get on the buses immediately. You're being taken in by Sioux Ridge, a few dozen miles south of the state border. You're *their* responsibility now." The guards opened the exit doors; the noise of the buses was much louder now. The guards moved to herd them outside, but the people simply stood up and walked onto their waiting transportation, to take them to grayer pastures. Darrell managed to waddle there by himself. A few of the deportees carried the unconscious bullies and the one victim.

Rico and Stuart, two of the guards, stood near Linda as the buses drove away. Rico looked sanguine. "There, but for the grace of God, go us, eh Stuart?"

Linda waved dismissively. "Not even close. You two had your issues, but I knew you were recoverable."

Stuart let out a small laugh. "If I'd known guard duty paid better than street hustling, I'd have gone legit a long time ago!"

"But who would have taken you?" Rico pointed out. "With *your* record?"

Stuart let out a long breath. "Yeah. I'm surprised Unlimited Partners gave me a chance at all...gave *either* of us a chance." He turned to Linda. "Why did you? Why did you think we were recoverable?"

"Simple," Linda said with a smile. "I saw your prison records!

You two took advantage of that time to improve yourselves! Both of you finished high school, neither of you had any disciplinary issues, and you even qualified for early release! That convinced me you were worth the effort."

Rico grinned. "Well, we're both grateful! Every day!"

Linda shook her head. "No need for that. It's just good business to make full use of available resources."

She stared off into the distance, as the buses crested a hill and dropped out of sight. "The old system's answer to lawbreaking was jail time. It was like sending people to crime college; amateur criminals would learn from expert criminals. They came out *far* more dangerous than they went in. It's much cheaper to rehabilitate than to throw someone away. And if they can't be rehabilitated…it's best to just get rid of them."

Stuart shrugged. "Harsh, but true." He tapped Rico on the shoulder. "Come on, man, we got other work to do." Rico followed Stuart as he walked away. "Have a good evening, Mrs. Carlyle."

"You too, guys." She watched them walk out of earshot, then muttered to herself. "And if no one will take them off our hands… there are other fates."

7

The members of 16otaku, and their guest, exchanged nervous glances. Several tense moments passed. Then Eric and Sam returned with very self-satisfied smiles. "You *have* to see this," Eric intoned. "It's just precious."

The curious crowd followed them. Once they turned the corner, they could not believe their eyes. The blue bot lay on the workbench counter, completely passive. The red bot hovered over him, its legs extended, fussing over its cohort obsessively. The people watched as the red bot removed broken parts, grabbed spare parts, and performed repairs. It even touched up the paint.

"They can *fix* each other?" Brian was amazed.

"Not only that," Isabel explained, "but in our experience, they appear to *want* to."

"Are you serious?" Brian beheld Isabel, his eyes uncertain.

"So…" Isabel began. "One unexpected development from using real neural tissue is that our so-called devices seem to develop a camaraderie with each other, sometimes bordering on affection. These two may have fought a pitched battle earlier, but here, they're friends again. We've also found that some of our construction bots prefer to work with certain other bots, if given a chance. And at night, when their biological systems are rejuvenating…they nest together, in clusters we've come to refer to as 'families'."

"And this behavior doesn't worry you?" Brian seemed unsettled.

Gary looked uneasy too. "It worries *some* of us."

Isabel looked slightly indignant. "Well, *I* think it's *adorable!*"

Gary smiled. "Some of us think it's adorable."

"At their level of development, it's not really a danger," Sam declared. "Like we said, none of them even rise to the level of cat intelligence. Bruno is an inspiration to us, on *several* different levels! Still, it's something to keep an eye on."

The red bot got off the blue bot; it stood up and moved around a little, testing its repaired systems. The red bot's propellers emerged and powered up; it gave the blue bot a playful-seeming swat, and quickly flew away. The blue bot extended its propellers and gave chase. Isabel sighed. "See? I told you they were friends again."

"Where are they going?" Brian watched them as they flew away.

"Probably back to the jungle gym," Stacy suggested. "That's where they were before we summoned them to the cage. They spend a lot of their time teaching the newer bots how to fight. They each have their own dojo, and their students spar against each other."

"They've organized their own *dojos*?" Brian was incredulous. "And you're not concerned by any of this?"

"We don't leave them *completely* on their own," Sam reassured. "Big Daddy spends most of his time overseeing them."

"Why don't we go visit him?" Eric suggested. "He's not that far away."

Before long, they had entered a room with the same eerie bluish-green glow as the nursery. The room's walls were covered with rack-mounted computers, but its central feature was a fluid-filled tank. In it floated a solitary person, a corpulent young man, clothed minimally, with wires and tubes protruding from him. A single computer console, on a pedestal, stood in front.

Brian was taken aback. Eric gestured towards the tank. "Meet Big Daddy!"

Brian looked alarmed. "What have you *done* to him?"

"We *saved* him!" Isabel chimed. "We found him during our evaluation of long-term care facilities. No one had even given him a name! They thought he had been born retarded and uncommunicative, but we soon learned otherwise. He was one of the first human recipients of our neural-implant technology. Turns out only his body is damaged; his mind had been highly active the whole time. We saved him from a dreary nursing-home life."

The console suddenly burst forth with synthesized speech. "I cannot express to you how much I hate Dabney The Dinosaur."

"Oh, he speaks!" Brian thrilled. "That's great! I was concerned. And yeah, my granddaughter watched that show when she was younger. I couldn't stand it either."

There was a hint of humor in the digital speech. "I could *tell* you were one of the smart ones!" The group roiled with laughter.

"So what do you do here?" Brian stared at Big Daddy, fascinated.

"I have only rudimentary senses outside of the neural implant," Big Daddy explained. "Most of my awareness is cybernetic. I busy myself by communicating with our bots, and helping them to learn and grow. I feel like a father to all of them; they're the ones that named me Big Daddy."

Brian snickered to himself. "That might have surprised me half an hour ago. How quickly things change!" He looked around. "Do the rest of you have neural implants too?"

"No, only me." Irwin pointed to the back of his neck.

Brian looked at the faint scar. "So you're the only brave one, huh?"

"Not exactly," Irwin shuddered. "I started as an invalid too. But they were able to restore full functionality."

"Like I said," Eric reminded, "we want to make full use of valuable resources."

Brian shook his head. "That's really impressive. So do you hate Dabney too?"

"Sure, a little," Irwin related. "But my real wrath is reserved for Yowza Kablooey. High-pitched voices *still* send shivers down my spine!"

Brian arched his eyebrows. "Glad I'm a baritone!"

The electronic voice piped up again. "Sir, if you're done with me...may I get back to work? I was having a spirited conversation with the teacher-bots when you arrived, and I really need to get back to it."

"Not a problem!" Eric belted. "We have much more to see." They exited the room, leaving Big Daddy with his thoughts.

Brian kept looking back with fascination in his eyes. "How long have you been putting neural implants into people?"

Dwight shrugged. "Since soon after we perfected them in animals."

"Oh?" Brian asked wryly. "Do animals have a lot to say?"

"Most of our experience is with cats and dogs," Dwight explained. "Their detectable thoughts consist mostly of images. On the other hand, they have a rich emotional life. When they're networked together, they tend to share their feelings, and it lets them work with each other very effectively."

Brian looked distant for a moment. "So the cats have jobs too? Really?"

"Of course!" Stacy piped up. "They're tackling the city's terrible rodent and pigeon infestations. The animal-control bots used to do that, but cats are so much better at it. We'd pick them up to spay and neuter them, and the healthiest ones received a neural implant. The cats immediately noticed the difference, and began a vibrant conversation among themselves. All fighting between them stopped. After that, it was easy to send them images of rodents and pigeons, and they'd take care of the rest."

"What happened next was *really* fascinating," Sam continued. "They began taking down giant sewer rats, ones big enough to threaten a dog! As soon a cat spotted one, the feeling would radiate to the nearby cats, and they'd coordinate an attack the rat couldn't withstand. They also began simultaneously pouncing on pigeons in groups, tackling several before the rest flew away. *Much* faster than one at a time! And at night, we provide them with a safe, warm place to sleep…or they simply go home."

"That's what my granddaughter said!" Brian remarked. "She insisted her cat had a job. I thought she was just being fanciful; *you* know how kids are!"

"Nope!" Isabel answered. "We literally pick them up in the morning, in standard mass-transit buses, take them to where they're needed, and let them loose!"

Brian shivered slightly. "It's too bad cats don't eat cockroaches."

"Yeah, insect infestations are still a problem," Gary agreed. "Neural implants work in lizards and toads, but we don't have enough to work with. So those are still fought by swarms of small robots, with occasional large robots to seal off well-contained areas and gas them. But if we can ever find an overabundance of problem lizards, we're all ready to turn them into cockroach killers!" He looked thoughtful for a moment. "I wonder if we could import them from Florida?" Gary laughed to himself. "We *do* have tiny robots that can invade anthills and termite nests to find and kill the queens, which is far more efficient than any other strategy we've come up with."

"How about the dogs?" Brian asked. "What do *they* do?"

"Pretty much what they did before," Irwin explained. "A lot of police work, a lot of fire work. It's just easier to communicate with them now. And they can work in packs, independently!"

Brian stopped walking and turned around to face them. "These are all very *practical* applications. Don't get me wrong, I commend you for that. But outside of the amazing accomplishments, it seems like a lot of difficult work, even tedious. Don't you have any *fun* around here too?"

The group smiled knowingly, including Eric. Brian was taken aback. "What…?"

"I guess it's time," Eric gushed, "to show you the rest of the hangar! Lead the way, gang!"

They passed through an immense storage area; some of it was finished parts, but a lot of it was simply raw metal, ready to be cut or forged into desired shapes and sizes. Stacks of barrels held precursor chemicals for different types of plastics. As they moved forward in the dim light, a much larger exit could finally be seen, a roll-up door that led to the rest of the hangar. Nothing could be seen through it as it opened; darkness filled the next area. Sam stepped inside; his footsteps echoed dimly in the cavernous expanse. A few seconds later came the crack of a large knife-switch being thrown into position; rows of lights switched on, the sudden illumination of each row producing its own crackling sound. As the room filled with their glow, the lights revealed several large shapes that left Brian speechless.

"Wha…? Oh my…"

Sam swept the area with his arm. "Presenting…our mechas!"

Tears formed in Brian's eyes. Standing before him were three giant humanoid robots, straight out of science fiction. One wore a sphinx-like headdress, one sported a mohawk, and the last had a rounded head and giant soulful eyes. Their highly-articulated limbs sported several loosely-attached panels of unclear function. Each stood nearly sixty feet high. And of course, they were painted with all the garish colors typical of children's entertainment programs.

Brian could hardly contain himself. "I used to see these at the Saturday matinees when I was a kid! All that wild stuff coming out of Japan. But I never thought I'd see a *real* one!"

"They're as real as they get!" Stacy trilled.

"I want to play with them!" Brian exulted. "Do they actually work?"

"Well, occasionally." Sam looked sanguine. "We don't get as much time to work on them as we'd like. We've been so busy lately with the final development on the maid-bots. Hopefully there'll be some time before the big push on robo-butlers."

"I didn't know that!" Eric interrupted. "I'll make sure you get a few weeks in between projects to spiff these up. Seriously, this department meets all their practical-project deadlines with room to spare. Time for this is the *least* I can give!"

"*And* fuel," Stacy added.

"Of course! I'll make sure this airport gets a fresh delivery." Eric tapped a reminder into his cell phone.

"Aw, you can't even start them up? Show me a little of what they do?" Brian's flushed skin took years off his appearance.

"It wouldn't be safe…not right now," Stacy lamented. "We still need to repair them after the last…test."

"What kind of test was that?" Brian gazed at their thick limbs. "Construction work?"

"No, they're not really suited for that," Sam replied. "I mean, they *could*, but it's much more efficient to use specialized equipment, such as cranes. Our mechas aren't very durable or energy-efficient yet."

"So what *was* the last test?"

Sam looked uncomfortable. "Uh…kung fu battle."

Brian whirled around. "Are you *serious*?"

"Oh yes!" Stacy crowed. "They're not as steady on their feet as we'd like them to be, but that's why they're research projects! Still, last time they withstood damage better than before. There are several classic anime battle scenes in our heads; until we can replicate one of them, we won't feel we've accomplished anything!"

Brian doubled over with laughter. "Oh my…you people are silly, in all the right ways. This makes me wish I was young enough to start a second career."

Eric's eyes gleamed. "Well, when we're ready to ship them, maybe you can be one of our first customers!"

"Count me in!" Brian shouted joyously. "What do the controls look like? Do you have a remote station around here somewhere? I'd love to see it!"

"Um…" Dwight began. "They're not remote-controlled… they're manned."

Brian stared at Dwight, open-mouthed. "*That's* it…I'm never leaving this place." Spirited guffaws spilled from the group and echoed off the walls of the yawning hangar.

"Of *course* we control them from inside!" Isabel gushed. "What fun would it be, otherwise? Actually, keeping us from getting injured during mecha kung-fu battles is one of our primary research directions. There's not a lot of prior work in this area; spaceships and jet fighters don't plan for this very much. But we're just fragile nerds; we need all the protection we can get!"

"And on top of the coolness factor, that's why we fund this project," Eric added. "A lot of what 16otaku develops for them makes its way into more practical projects. But the motivation for those inventions is pure childlike joy. And talk about a valuable resource…you don't find a lot of that sort of joy in adults. I'm glad they were able to hang onto it!"

"I think you're bringing it back in *me*!" Brian's skin glowed pink. "Let me know when these ship. Heck, if you need space to store one, you can park it on my roof! I think it'd look great sitting on the edge, posed like Rodin's 'The Thinker'."

"Like what?" Irwin asked.

"You know, the statue of the guy sitting like this." Eric rested his chin on his fist.

"Ohhh…right." Irwin looked slightly embarrassed. "I didn't know what it was called."

Brian sighed. "It's going to be *so* boring to return to my old company."

Eric smiled. "Hopefully, we've shown you today that your investment is in good hands, and our future is brighter than you ever thought possible."

Brian twitched with joy. "Indeed! And that *alone* will put a spring in my step!"

They made the long trek back to the cubicles. When they got there, they found several of the spider-bots on the couch with Bruno, curled up with him. He snoozed contentedly, completely undisturbed by the cuddling arachnids. Brian pointed to them with curiosity in his eyes. Stacy answered his gaze. "Yes, that happens…pretty often, actually. Like we said, it's a family here."

"Well, I never would have believed *any* of this, if I hadn't seen it with my own eyes. I hope to come back here soon!" He moved to leave.

"Mr. McTierney, can you give me a few minutes?" Eric asked. "I want some parting words with my team."

"Of course! I have a few things to do before we board the jet again."

Eric closed the door behind him, and turned to face 16otaku. His face practically exploded with glee. "Gang, that was *great*! I'm amazed what you pulled together on such short notice!"

"Yeah…about that," Dwight said sardonically. "Couldn't you have given us more warning?"

"Sorry, it was a surprise to me too!" Eric pleaded. "I expected just to review financials with him. I had *no* idea he wanted to geek out to this level! You think you know a guy, and then...something like *this* happens."

"Hey, no big deal," Dwight conceded. "I was just venting."

"No problem, I understand." An impish grin spread over Eric's face. "So what's next for the mechas? Got anything planned?"

"Heck, I don't know," Gary admitted. "What would *you* like to see?"

Eric thought for a moment. "Can they fly yet?"

Gary was taken aback. "No, we haven't even started that. But... there's unused interior space, for fuel tanks...that would make it easy to route turbine exhaust out the arms and legs...we'd need high-flow hinged valves to run through the elbows and knees...or maybe multiple turbines..."

Eric faced his palms forward. "Hey...I don't need to know all the details...I'm sure this team can handle them! All I ask, is...if at all possible...make them fly! That'd be *badass*!"

"You got it, boss!" Sam rejoiced. Eric gave them a thumbs-up and disappeared behind the door.

The team looked at each other for a few moments. "So, where were we?" Stacy asked. "Back to the arena, then?"

Sam tapped on his phone. "Oh, would you look at that...they're both waiting near the cage! They actually *want* to duel!"

The team stampeded out of the room, their shouts of "team red" and "team blue" vying to overpower each other.

Danielle drove her car along the rural highway, passing a fortified fence topped with razor wire. She spotted the entrance to the facility up ahead, and slowed down to turn right into the driveway. After showing her credentials to the guard, the gate opened, and she continued driving along the timeworn paved road leading to the sewage treatment plant. She blanched as she perused the unimaginative industrial architecture. "Don't *I* get the glamorous jobs," she muttered to herself.

Parking her car in a visitor's spot, she gripped the handle and braced herself. She flung the door open and sniffed tentatively. Her brow furrowed as she took a few larger sniffs. Finally, she exited the car and drew in a large lungful of air. Danielle broke out into a smile as two employees approached her from the front entrance.

"I was expecting a much worse stench!" she declared. "Is this really the sewage treatment plant?"

"It is!" proclaimed one of the employees; her badge declared her name to be Suzanne. "But all the smelly parts are contained; otherwise, we wouldn't be able to collect and divert the output."

"Well, *I* for one am grateful," Danielle laughed. "I loathed having to come here today, but I see I didn't need to. Sorry if that sounds insulting."

"Not at all," chimed the other employee, whose badge identified him as Tom. After a round of formal introductions, they all walked into the building.

"We were surprised to hear we had a guest today," remarked Suzanne. "We don't get a lot of visitors, especially not from headquarters."

"Most of the time, our reports, and the occasional phone call, are enough to keep everyone happy," Tom concurred. "While we're grateful for the attention, we don't know what prompted it."

"It was two of your recent requests," explained Danielle. "You wanted funding to stand up another waste treatment plant, closer to the farmlands in the outskirts; anything that expensive has to be approved from high up. But the *real* trigger was your plan to begin industrial-scale mining of existing landfills. An odd request like *that* doesn't go unnoticed."

Suzanne laughed. "We assure you, our reasons are completely sound. But you may have to look at what we do here to understand why." They passed through a set of double-doors and continued walking along the hallway, deeper into the facility.

"And for the first time today, I'm looking forward to that!" Danielle laughed. She sniffed the air again. "I can't believe it smells perfectly normal in here."

"If it didn't, that would mean our gas reclamation wasn't working right," Tom pointed out. "And we wouldn't stand for that. Not only would that mean our tech was faulty, but I doubt any of us would want to work under such conditions."

"I can believe *that*!" Danielle chimed. "But how is it possible?"

Suzanne smiled as they reached a set of thick, metal double doors. "Let us show you."

The doors opened to reveal a sealed catwalk with transparent walls, overlooking a field of large, shallow, cylindrical tanks. The glass roof let in natural sunlight; a series of ventilation ducts crisscrossed the ceiling. In the distance, on the other side of see-through walls, were a series of other structures, their purpose industrial but otherwise unclear.

"Welcome to 'the farm'!" Tom announced.

Danielle marveled as she followed a sealed catwalk over the tanks; Suzanne and Tom hovered behind her. Danielle pointed up ahead. "What are all the bright colors I see in the settlement pools?"

"Those are plastics," Suzanne explained. "We don't just recycle wastewater here; these tanks reclaim garbage too. Depending on the material, there are three stages that the waste can pass through."

"How do you reclaim plastic?" Danielle asked.

"With bacteria!" Tom declared. "We drilled into existing landfills, extracted core samples, and tested what we found against various materials. We found bacteria that had evolved to consume the abundantly available resources. We didn't have to breed them to be so useful; they did the work all by themselves! And now, those same bacteria devour our garbage, and turn it into sludge."

Danielle stared at the tanks with fascination. "What do you produce from it?"

"Several things," Suzanne related. "The bacteria liberate methane and carbon dioxide; we collect those gases for our own use. The broken-down plastic eventually enters the tanks you see at the far end of the facility, where it, and the sludge from wastewater, are subjected to hydrothermal liquefaction."

Tom continued. "That involves pressures around 3000 psi, temperatures near 600 degrees, and up to 30 minutes, but the result is biocrude, which can be refined into all the normal petroleum products."

Danielle's eyes narrowed skeptically. "You're not *really* making gasoline from it, are you?"

"*And* kerosene, and diesel fuel, and aviation fuel," Suzanne revealed. "The heavier plastics that aren't reclaimed by this process can be mixed with the thicker biocrude extracts to produce something similar to asphalt."

Danielle's brow furrowed. "Why isn't that mentioned in any of the reports I've seen?"

"Because it's not a profit item," Tom explained. "We use it to defray costs, so it's not broken out into its own top-level summary.

Our biocrude output isn't competitive with traditional sources yet, but at least it's not losing money. Before we got involved, the waste would just go into a landfill, which not only isn't sustainable, but costs money. What we do is an improvement on that. And we continue to experiment!"

"I see," Danielle acknowledged. "I guess we'll have to change how you report your results."

"We've been asking for that for some time," Suzanne pointed out. "But no one at headquarters seemed to understand why. Hopefully that'll change."

"I'll make it a priority!" Danielle chirped, typing something into her cell phone.

"And yes, we can refile our previous reports with those numbers broken out into their own summary," Tom assured. "We've got them ready to go."

"I'd appreciate that." Danielle stared out over the vast expanse. "You said you produce carbon dioxide too. Where does that go?"

Suzanne pointed into the distance. "You can barely see it from here; it's all sent to that large green building on the far side. What say we check it out?"

As they traversed the crisscrossing catwalks, Tom continued to explain. "Once the plastics are dissolved, anything left behind is removed and sorted; it's mostly metal and glass." Tom smiled. "I don't know who in the company is developing the artificial intelligence, but it's been a godsend! We produce collections of scrap metal, and glass sorted by color, ready for further recycling. Only a small amount must be smelted from scratch, as if it were ore. And as the sorting gets better, so does the value of the scrap! Metal extraction is closer to being a moneymaker than anything else we're producing right now."

They walked for several minutes, finally arriving at the far wall. On the other side was a greenhouse-like structure that appeared to contain an unruly, formless jungle. Suzanne pointed to the pipes leading into the area. "The carbon dioxide gets pumped in here, as does the sterile water left over from hydrothermal liquefaction. Algae grows very well in that environment, as do some cyanobacteria; we pump out the excess and send it straight back into crude oil production."

"The algae certainly seem to be doing really well," Danielle observed. "Why don't you try growing food like this?"

"Garbage contains too many contaminants to make that possible," Tom revealed. "Although heavy metals tend to settle at the bottom of the liquefaction tanks, not all of it does. Many of them are toxic. So anything we grow with that water isn't suitable for food production."

"That's too bad," Danielle lamented. "The algae are *thriving*." She shook her head. "This is all really amazing. Why hasn't it been tried before?"

"It has," Suzanne expounded. "But it couldn't compete with traditional methods. That's not a problem here; we're not trying to make money on it, just defray costs and divert waste."

"The other problem has been government subsidies," Tom continued. "Forty percent of the nation's corn production presently goes to biodiesel and ethanol. It was never an efficient solution; it was simply the one chosen by the politicians, and then a whole corrupt industry grew up around it. What we do doesn't have that kind of arbitrary support, so we went back to work on sustainable fuel, and have come up with much better methods, ones that work on truly renewable and plentiful sources, such as waste."

"The science already existed to make this possible, but it wasn't funded, nor was it popular with the powers that be," Suzanne pined. "But here in Millenniaburg, it finally has a chance."

"I'm glad it does!" Danielle trilled. She narrowed her eyes as she perused the vast field of biocrude production tanks, taking up much of the area outside the back wall, surrounding the greenhouse. "Those machines look really sophisticated. I can't imagine they were cheap."

"Surprisingly, they were," Tom explained. "We were able to get most of it through bankruptcy; Big Oil does a lot to suppress the nascent industry. So oddly, it's lucky for Unlimited Partners that the energy industry employs such relentlessly short-term thinking when trying to protect their business."

"Stupidity is the *true* growth industry," Danielle jested. "We're fortunate to find a way to take advantage of it!" They all shared a laugh.

"Even universities seem to have a blind spot when it comes to this," Suzanne lamented. "The techniques aren't that exotic, so colleges have no interest in researching them further, because they don't think they'll be able to patent any of it. And the *rest* of their reasons, frankly, seem to be condescending and puerile."

"I've heard of this problem from others," Danielle concurred. "It's hard to believe scientists act this way."

"They do," Tom grimaced. "They're human beings too, and can be just as jealous as anyone else. As the old saying goes, science advances one funeral at a time."

Danielle let out a hollow laugh. "That's awful. But at least we can turn it to our advantage here!" She sighed happily. "I wonder just how *many* scientific advances are waiting for us to find, if they weren't being hushed up."

Tom and Suzanne exchanged uncomfortable glances. Danielle noticed. "What...?"

"Well..." Tom began, before sighing heavily.

"We've run into something that defies conventional explanation," Suzanne revealed. "Something big." She looked at Tom hesitantly; he simply winced and shrugged his shoulders. Suzanne continued. "I guess it's time to tell you about it. After all, it's likely you'll approve our grand designs once you hear this."

Danielle looked bemused. "I can't *wait* to find out what you're talking about."

Tom sighed heavily again. "So...remember when we said the metal extraction is close to being a moneymaker? Well...it already is. By a *very* large margin."

"From scrap metal?" Danielle sounded incredulous.

Tom looked down. "No...from what settles to the bottom of the hydrothermal liquefaction tanks. We mentioned heavy metal pollution in the water, but it's not just the usual suspects, like lead, mercury, and cadmium. It's...well...most of it is precious metals. Gold. Silver. Platinum. Even vanadium."

Danielle was taken aback. "Where does it come from?"

"That's just it," Suzanne chimed. "The presence of such things in human waste have been known for a long time. The source, however, has been unclear. The conventional wisdom is that it's coming from body care products, such as shampoos and detergents. But that's always seemed ludicrous."

"Then...?" Danielle began.

Tom threw his hands up in the air. "This is going to sound crazy, and we're not going to defend this if anyone asks, but...given the amounts we're extracting...it has to be coming from living creatures."

"How?" Danielle looked unsettled.

Suzanne shrugged. "We have no idea. And we're not saying the human body somehow produces these metals. Maybe it's really coming from household products, but that seems really unlikely. The sheer amount of material we're collecting, though, suggests some really wild theories. Like…"

"Like alchemy," Tom finished. "As if life itself is inherently capable of this." Tom motioned toward the greenhouse. "The algae seem to produce an unearthly amount of vanadium. Some types of ocean algae are known to incorporate vanadium in their enzymes, but…for reasons we don't understand…it's like they're producing their own."

"Ultimately, we don't know the source," Suzanne conceded. "But the volume of it made us really nervous. So we've been keeping quiet. We were afraid people would think we're crazy. But the numbers have held up, and are too large to ignore."

"What gets us is, every wastewater treatment plant in the world has to know about this," Tom pointed out. "There's no way they couldn't. And yet they all stay quiet about it. That takes some heavy suppression *and* coordination. You must understand, this revelation left us *completely* unnerved."

"I guess I can't blame you," Danielle agreed. "And I think we should stay quiet about this. I'd like corrected reports from you, but only for the eyes of senior management and the board of directors."

Tom let out a relieved sigh. "That sounds perfect."

"So, just how *large* are the numbers we're talking about?" Danielle asked.

Suzanne's smile beamed. "We've actually been profitable for a long time. We can fund our own expansion. We can pay for standing up new waste treatment facilities, and for industrial-scale mining in existing landfills."

"Well, *that'll* make the board happy," Danielle trilled. "And they'll be much more likely to forgive your transgression."

Tom faced his palms forward, in a pleading motion. "No subterfuge was intended, we assure you! We were terrified of stumbling upon such a significant game-changer."

"I don't blame you," Danielle agreed. "*I'm* shaking just thinking about it!"

"And it's not the *only* technological marvel we have to share with you today," Suzanne hinted.

Danielle chuckled. "This visit has turned out *so* different than what I expected. Show me what else you have!"

They headed down the catwalk, toward the opaque side walls. Reaching a door, they went inside. "Welcome to our labs!"

Danielle marveled at the rows of cubicles, filled with busy people. "I was starting to think you were the only two that worked here," she laughed.

"Of course not!" Suzanne chuckled. "It's just that most of us don't spend our days gazing into the settlement pools."

They walked along the main corridor for some time, finally turning down a passage. At the end, they passed through a door leading to a laboratory. Computers and viewscreens filled the two side walls; ahead of them was a thick-looking transparent window, showing a room with smaller cylindrical tanks, and several robots moving between them.

Suzanne and Tom walked up to one of the occupied workstations, Danielle trailing behind. "Hi, Roger," Suzanne greeted. "Why don't you show our guest what we do here?"

Roger turned around and read Danielle's badge. "Oh! My goodness. Yes, *ma'am*." Roger moved the controls on his workstation fluidly; the view grew closer to one of the tanks, then rose in the air to peer over the edge. Now it was clear that several leathery-looking orbs, some as large as a basketball, floated in the murky fluid. Metallic arms extended towards one, then raised the ball out of the swamp and brought it closer.

"We call these 'food eggs'," Suzanne explained. "They're actually pretty brilliant. Can you cut this one open?"

"Sure," Roger agreed. "It looks like it's ripe." The view from the robot left the tank and trundled towards a table set up for washing and dissection.

"These are grown from bacteria, reprogrammed by a synthetic virus to become an egg. Once put into the sterilized soupy biowaste you see in these tanks, they absorb raw biological material and grow, forming a rubbery-skinned orb. That skin can then be peeled, to reveal what's grown inside, keeping it fresh and sterile until then!"

Danielle marveled as Roger carefully split open the orb. Several small, bright yellow spheres poured out. "What *are* those?"

"It's our version of corn," Roger explained. "We've eliminated the cob, so they simply grow inside the egg, making it swell until it's ready to harvest." He looked back at Danielle and smirked. "We call them 'corn peas'."

"And it tastes like corn?" Danielle asked.

Roger shrugged. "We believe so. They have all the chemical signatures of corn, and in theory, should taste and feel like the real thing. We've fed the contents of these eggs to lab animals, and we haven't encountered a bad reaction in a really long time. But we have a *lot* more research to do before we let something like this come into contact the outside world."

"We're messing with some *really* heady laws of nature here," Tom confessed. "Seriously, it's a synthetic virus modifying a bacterium to make it into a completely novel life form. And until we understand *all* of it really well, these *and* the lab animals have to stay inside of a sealed biocontainment chamber. All the eggs, the water, the animals — even the *gases* in this chamber — are sent straight to hydrothermal liquefaction. We don't want to risk *any* of this touching the outside world until a *lot* more study has occurred."

"That's very reassuring," Danielle agreed. "The last thing we need is to set off a pandemic."

"But once this works…can you imagine?" Suzanne gushed, a twinkle in her eyes. "We have eggs that become meat, fruits, vegetables, grains…even dairy! And they grow in biowaste! Once we work out all the issues…you're looking at the farm of the future."

Danielle shook her head. "I never knew biowaste could be so *fascinating*!" That set off a round of laughter across the lab.

The viewscreen showed the robot approach a cage, containing a squirrel, with the corn peas. As they were poured in, the squirrel began to feast on the offered food. Roger pointed to the screen. "We haven't been doing this long enough for *true* long-term toxicity tests, but this squirrel has been with us for three months, and shows no sign of health problems."

Danielle waved at the squirrel on the screen. "Good luck, little guy."

The visitors said their goodbyes and left the lab.

All three strolled down the catwalk, heading back to the main entrance. "I'm *really* impressed by what I've seen here today," Danielle trilled. "Working here must be really rewarding."

They slowly became aware of a thick thrumming sound, growing louder. A small shadow above the see-through roof grew in size, heading towards the other end of the settlement pools. Suzanne grimaced. "It has its days."

Danielle shuddered. "Oh, heck…I've heard of these, but never saw one in person."

"We said there were three stages of waste treatment." Tom sadly pointed to the approaching shadow. "This is the third one."

A multi-propellered drone, the size of a standard shipping container, slowed its descent as it reached a hatch in the roof. It stood up on end; as it became vertical and touched down, the roof retracted to accommodate it. The drone's floor opened, and out fell several indistinct, but clearly humanoid, shapes. They plummeted downwards and hit a settlement pool with a splash.

"We try to find a place for all our exiles," Danielle explained. "But the government-run cities don't take every one…especially if we're up front about their criminal acts."

"Can we talk about this?" lamented Suzanne. "The staff is pretty unified in its extreme discomfort."

"You're seeing the worst of the worst," Danielle divulged. "By and large, these people were caught red-handed doing something vile. Very clear surveillance footage, usually with audio. Trials for them would be time-wasting formalities."

"How can you know that?" Tom grieved. "Do you actually look into this?"

"I have access to conviction records at any time," Danielle revealed. "Why don't we look at a few of them?"

Tom and Suzanne exchanged uneasy glances. "I think we'd really appreciate that," Suzanne piped up.

Danielle continued tapping on her phone. "It shouldn't be difficult to find that drone; there aren't any others in the…yes, there it is. Let me get the prisoner manifest…there were seven. And I was right, all of them come with surveillance footage." She looked at the two scientists grimly. "I'll show this to you, but I warn you, it's likely to be really shocking."

"We want to see it," Tom assured. "We have to know."

The first mug shot dissolved into outdoor surveillance footage, showing an elderly lady suddenly get grabbed by a shadowy figure in an alley. The camera changed to one from inside the alley, showing the assailant beat his victim mercilessly. As she stopped moving, he grabbed her purse, began to walk away, then turned around and gave her one final swift kick; she didn't react to it. He then left.

"The rest are likely to be just as bad," Danielle said grimly. "Want to continue?"

"A few more, I guess," Suzanne demurred.

The next mug shot cut away to a camera inside an apartment, where an older woman appeared to drown a young child in a filthy toilet. "OK, enough of that," Suzanne blanched.

Danielle swiped to a different mug shot; the video showed a hairy, corpulent man repeatedly punching a pregnant woman in the stomach.

Tom turned away; he was pale and sweaty. "OK, OK…no more." Suzanne leaned weakly against the wall, gagging softly. Danielle closed the app and smiled grimly. "Every one I've ever looked at has been that bad, and that blatant. Those drones are truly carrying the worst of the worst."

Tom cleared his throat and tried to stand up straight. "Thank you for that. We'll tell the others what we saw. I'm sure we'll all feel better about this…eventually."

"Unless this is a sore subject," Danielle probed, "why is there a third stage? What happens there?"

"Oh…mostly, separating out personal electronics," Suzanne explained. "Anything with batteries. Those can explode under high temperatures and pressures."

There was an uncomfortable silence for several seconds. "If it helps," Danielle offered, "just recall how the city was only a few months ago. You could literally be beaten to death in the streets by masked thugs, simply for being in the wrong place at the wrong time. And somehow, they never seemed to get caught. That *had* to stop. And good can triumph over evil…but sometimes, good has to be more violent and even nastier than evil."

Tom and Suzanne stared at her with haunted expressions. "I certainly don't envy your job," Tom confessed.

Danielle smiled grimly. "Everyone thinks they want to be the boss. Everyone wants to be in charge." She paused, looking them straight in the eye. "Until they find out what's really involved."

She wistfully stared into the sky. "Don't *I* get the glamorous jobs."

8

The bus slowly came to a stop; it jolted slightly as the air brakes discharged. The door opened as the driver grabbed the mechanical handle and pulled. "End of the line, folks," he announced. "Everybody out."

The passengers peered out of the bus, through the dirty windows. Rural highway surrounded a solitary "city limits" sign in both directions. The scrubby brush and low trees continued unbroken as far as the eye could see. In the hazy distance, there were some hints of outbuildings, but nothing definite.

"Really?" one passenger snorted. "We're in the middle of *nowhere*. You can't take us closer?"

"I have no authorization to cross into the city," the driver declared. "You'll have to walk from here." The driver looked the pudgy complainant up and down. "It'll do you some good," he suggested. "I mean, it'll get your blood flowing again, after that long trip."

Uncertainly, the passengers slowly disembarked. The patina of dust on the windows no longer dulled the sunlight; they blinked at its unexpected ferocity. Nearby, they could see other exiles, from the other two buses in the caravan, milling about.

The doors closed with a crash; the backup alarms squealed their warning. Further down the highway, the buses made a coordinated Y-turn, then drove off, fading into the distance.

Gladys turned angrily to Terry. "Well? You said you wanted to protect your family. What do we do *now*?"

Terry shrugged. "I guess we walk." He turned toward the city; the others began ambling in that direction.

Gladys glared at him. "That's all you have to say?"

Terry glanced back, eyes flaring. "What do you want me to do…*carry* you?" He turned away and picked up his pace.

"I'll walk with you, mama," offered Tremain.

"Thanks, baby," she cooed as she took his hand.

As they drew closer to the city, the outbuildings revealed themselves to be derelict gas stations and strip malls. After a brief search, no signs of life, or items of value, could be found in any of them. Even the faucets were dry. They continued trundling down the highway.

Between two decrepit buildings, in an alleyway, they spotted a lone human figure. The old man had long gray hair, a full bushy beard, leathery sunburnt skin, and filthy, tattered clothing. He sat near a shopping cart, staring forward, his blue eyes piercing the emptiness. "Hey, buddy," Leroy opened. "Do you know where we can get any food? Water? Maybe some shade?"

The old man didn't respond. "Hey, buddy, I'm talking to you," Leroy repeated. "Can you hear me?"

Still no response. Leroy tapped him on the shoulder. "You OK, pal?"

Slowly, the old man listed to the left, gently rolling onto his side, his head slamming firmly against the pavement. His facial expression remained unchanged. Leroy reared back.

He turned around to face the gawking onlookers. "Let's just keep moving."

Before long, they found a few more homeless men, pushing their shopping carts through a decayed parking lot, just off the road. Leroy called out to them. "Hey there! Know where we can get some water?" At the sound of his voice, three of them turned away and picked up their pace.

Leroy frowned, and quickly caught up with one. "Hey! We just want some water! Can you…" The vagrant turned quickly to face Leroy, a burning look in his eyes. In one hand he held a fragment of rusty metal, artlessly scraped to a jagged edge, a tightly-wrapped piece of old cloth serving as a hilt. He began to breathe evenly, baring his nearly-toothless mouth behind cracked lips.

Leroy threw his hands in the air and backed away slowly. "Hey, it's all good, it's all good…sorry I asked." Once Leroy was about ten feet away, the dead-ender turned away and left as quickly as he could.

Leroy slowly approached the only indigent that hadn't run off. He continued to push his cart forward, shuffling toward no discernible destination. "Hi there, pal," Leroy opened. "We're just looking for some water. Know where we can find some?"

The homeless man stopped walking, continuing to stare forward. Leroy crept up alongside him and stopped. The beggar turned slowly to look at him; his eyes were nearly swollen shut, the area mottled in greens and yellows, probable signs of an infection. His lower lip trembled uncontrollably. His raspy voice was almost unintelligible.

"Help me," he pleaded listlessly.

Leroy rejoined the others. "There's nothing here," he announced. "We need to keep going."

"How do these people *live* here?" Sylvia demanded. Her faded clothing and scattering of gray hair heralded the obsolescence of her style and the approach of middle age.

Leroy looked glum. "I'm not sure they do."

The group continued in silence.

The indigents slowly grew in number and variety as the ensemble left the outskirts. Rows of shabby tents lined the sidewalks in front of abandoned businesses. Some may have been dressed in nicer clothes, but there was little difference in the expressions on their faces. Bleary eyes, mouths hanging open, each with skin tones more ashen than the next. The ones trying to walk mostly stumbled, stopping frequently to catch their balance. Most simply lay on the ground, either curled up on their sides, or with their backs against the rigid cinder block walls.

Gladys chose one resident and walked up to him. "Excuse me, sir," she pleaded, "can you tell us where we can get some water?"

The gutter-dweller turned around, and looked Gladys up and down with a leering expression. "Sure, I got some water for you," he catcalled. "But you'll have to close your eyes and drink it out of a hose."

"You sleaze!" Gladys snapped. She looked back at Terry; she caught a glimpse of his uncouth grin before he quickly turned away.

Dwayne spotted a faucet between two tents. He walked up to it, as the occupants of those two tents eyed him warily. "Don't mind me, gents," Dwayne greeted. "I just want to get some water."

"What, for free?" one snorted. The others began guffawing disrespectfully. "No way, man. *We* control this faucet. We want a dollar." He looked at the group of newcomers, who stared back pensively. "*Each.*"

"What?!" Dwayne retorted. "There's *no* way we're paying that much."

The lout swayed menacingly as the others stood up. "Well, then, you ain't gettin' no water!"

"But we were invited here by your city!" Dwayne pleaded. "They agreed to take us!"

The faucet gatekeepers threw their hands in the air in taunting surprise. "*Well*, why didn't you say so?" mocked the lout. "We didn't know we had *royalty* here!" The others laughed as he bowed with overly elaborate hand flourishes. "Pardon *us*, yer *majesties*!" As he rose to eye level, he punctuated the event with a loud fart.

Dwayne shook his head. "Never mind." He rejoined the group of new arrivals on the street, and they moved to leave the area. The guardians of the faucet continued to make rude comments and obscene gestures. None of the other homeless people in the area reacted to this, or otherwise acknowledged the presence of others.

They drew close to an intersection. The sound of a vehicle approached them from behind; a lone patrol car crept by. Sylvia broke out in a beaming smile. "Thank goodness! Please, help us!" The officers returned her gaze with abject fear in their eyes. Suddenly, the motor raced as the car jumped forward, tires peeling briefly. A handful of jaywalkers had to dive out of the way as the police tried to thread their way past the obstacles. Sylvia gaped as the squad car disappeared into the distance.

"What's *with* this place?" Sylvia demanded. "It's like we've been delivered to the mouth of Hell itself."

They reached the intersection and peered down each side street hesitantly. "Don't look like it matters none," Darrell observed. "May as well try one." He started to plod towards the right.

"I wouldn't do that if I were you," called out a voice. They turned to see a smirking lad, lounging on the sidewalk, ballcap worn sideways, clutching a bottle in a brown paper bag. Despite his distressed appearance and the deep lines in his face, his eyes showed the spark of youth; he couldn't have been older than nineteen.

"Why not?" Darrell mumbled.

"Because *that* way lies the territory of 'El Jefe', he whose will must not be defied," the layabout crowed. "If he finds you there without permission, he and his fanatical soldiers will kill you five times before you hit the ground."

"My word." Darrell swallowed nervously. He then turned to point to the other side of the street. "How 'bout *that* way?"

The indolent lad clucked his tongue. "Man, that's even worse. That's the undisputed domain of 'Number One', the lord of the zombie army. They'll infect you and make you one of their own. It's said that the living envy the dead."

"The hell you say," Darrell spat.

The sidewalk potato crossed his arms and looked askance.

"Fine, *don't* listen to me. Go ahead and take your chances. I don't care either way."

Darrell stared morosely for several seconds. "Then where *can* we go?" he whined.

The sluggard pointed into the distance. "The main drag here is one of the few neutral zones in the city. On either side, warlord territory extends as far as the eye can see."

"Warlords?" Tremain whispered, his voice stuck in his throat. "Why don't the police stop them?"

"What *are* you, blind?" the sluggard scoffed. "You just *saw* the police; they only look out for themselves. They just like the free ammo and the functioning cars. They're in it for what they can get out of it. And the less they have to do for it, the *better*, as far as they're concerned."

Tremain said nothing as he trembled. The derelict sourly looked him up and down. "You don't belong here," he declared. "Go try your luck elsewhere. Maybe on the other side of the city government complex."

"Where is *that*?" Gladys suddenly piped up.

The cadger annoyingly gestured down the street. "*That* way. Far away from here. What am I, the tour guide? Go figure it out yourself. I have to get back to work."

"Is *that* what you call this?" Leroy snickered.

The wastrel puffed up his chest. "I'm a street poet! I tell the stories of those who have no one to speak for them! I show city life as it *really* is!"

"To *who*?" Leroy disparaged.

The vagrant was unbowed. "My audience is online! My followers number in the *hundreds*! I bring in enough money from my patrons to live *comfortably*!" He doffed his ballcap and proffered it forward. "And from donations for my advice."

"The hell with you," Leroy snarled as he turned to leave. The others followed him down the street.

"Suit yourself!" screamed the pauper, donning his hat once more. "You ungrateful parasites! Can't even lift a finger for the less fortunate!" He looked at his phone. "I guess I'll have to tell the story of the several dozen super-soft out-of-towners, sauntering blithely into the valley of shadows." His thumbs flailed furiously as he typed. "Oooh, that's a *good* one!"

They continued for half a dozen blocks. They slowly became

aware of noises around them — creaking metal, glass bottles getting kicked, some scattered footsteps. Suddenly, several people jumped out from the darkness and surrounded them. They brandished knives, axes, machetes, spiked baseball bats, and other improvised weapons. They all wore black, though most sported pastel-dyed hair bursting from under their hats and knit caps. The out-of-towners all froze and raised their hands in the air.

One of the attackers pulled away from the others, and began strutting. "Yeah! That's what I'm talking about! Just stand there and *bask* in our mighty presence!" He got in Dwayne's face. "Or else we'll straight-up fillet you!" He backed off and stood proudly. "Welcome to our teppanyaki grill of *death*!"

"Your *what*?" Leroy derided.

The young thug turned to face Leroy. "You know, those big metal tables where they cook food," he answered sullenly.

"Never heard of it," Leroy spat.

"Shut up!" the ruffian screamed. "You will show *respect* to the Ferret, your new lord and master!"

Dwayne burst with laughter. "I'm sorry...*what*?" In a flash, he found someone at his back, holding a knife to his throat.

Ferret was unbowed. "Hey, ferrets can be pretty scary. Ever been bitten by one?"

"My neighbor had a ferret once," Terry remembered. "One of the most playful and adorable creatures I've ever met. Smelled like the devil, though."

"The *hell* with you!" Ferret shot back. "OK, everyone, search them. Whatever they have is *ours*!" Hesitantly, the thugs rifled through the pockets of the newcomers; all reported finding nothing.

"Really?" Ferret snorted. "Not even a cell phone? How do you *live* without a cell phone? You must be the poorest people in the whole city. And what kind of faction goes around *unarmed*?"

"We're not *with* a faction," Sylvia announced. "We're new in town."

Ferret leered at her. "Fresh meat, huh?"

"They didn't give us back any of our stuff," explained Sylvia. "We just got off the bus from Millenniaburg."

"Never heard of it," Ferret spat. He looked around uncertainly. "Well...if you *do* get something...you need to give it to us immediately."

"Some criminals *you* are," Leroy growled.

Ferret reared back. "Is that what you think we are? A bunch of conformist warlord goons or something?" He puffed his chest up. "We are *revolutionaries*! You're looking at the Defenders Of Peaceful Coexistence! And we rule *all* that we survey." He looked up and down the street. "This city is our proudest achievement! People of *all* races and creeds, living together in harmony!"

"Are you *nuts*?" spewed Gladys. "They live in brutal *poverty*!"

Ferret shrugged. "At least they're equal."

Gladys looked the revolutionaries up and down. "You don't look like *you're* doing too badly. Those clothes look pretty new."

Ferret was at a loss of words for a moment. Then one of the other street soldiers spoke up. "Our parents bought us these clothes. Most of us still live at home."

"Are you *kidding* me?" Terry sneered.

"Hey, don't fault us for having brains!" Ferret retorted. "It's not *our* fault everyone else is too dumb to think of that!"

"But I *am* the parent!" Gladys boomed. Tremain clutched her side.

Ferret sneered. "Well, sucks to be you, then."

"I don't believe this," Terry guffawed. "A bunch of spoiled-rotten middle-class kids, play-acting at revolution." No one responded. "If you think you're so tough, why don't you grow up, leave home, and live on your own? Stop bleeding your parents dry."

A lone voice piped up. "Well, we *tried* to start an anarchist commune, but no one would follow the rules, so most of us went home."

"This is stupid," Leroy jeered. "I almost feel sorry for you."

"You mock us at your own peril!" Ferret asserted. "Remember, *we're* the ones with the weapons."

"I'll bet your parents paid for those, too," Leroy insinuated.

"And so what if they *did*?" Ferret blustered. "Living at home is *great*! Our parents let us do our own thing, and don't get on our case about responsibilities, or getting a job, or whatever. We have *all* the time in the world to fight for a better future. And now it's here! Isn't it great?"

No one answered. Ferret's face slowly twisted into a sullen look. "Well? Aren't you going to *thank* us?"

A terrified squeal shattered the silence. All turned to look at Dwayne, who had managed to get the drop on his captor. Now Dwayne held the knife to the youth's throat. "I've had *enough* of your crap!" Dwayne shouted. "All of you, throw down your weapons, or this twerp *gets* it!"

But before the words had even left Dwayne's mouth, the rebels had taken off running, scattering into several doorways and alleyways, quickly disappearing from sight.

Dwayne tightened his grip on the back of his prisoner's shirt and drew his head closer. "How about that?" Dwayne sneered, as the stricken subversive stared back at him, wild-eyed. "Your friends left you here…with *me*…all *alone*."

The juvenile shivered. Dwayne slowly became aware of something warm and wet. He jumped back. "*What* the…?" Looking down, he realized the adolescent had peed his pants.

Disgusted, Dwayne launched the kid forward. "Get the *hell* out of here!" The youth cursed in terror, tripping once to fall flat on his face, then scampered off quickly.

"Freaking kids these days," Dwayne snorted. "At least now we have a weapon." He looked at the knife closely, then frowned. "Seriously? This is barely a knife; it's more like a toy." He turned it over in his hands. "Looks more like a souvenir. Completely useless." He flung it across the street; it hit the wall and shattered into several pieces. Dwayne groaned and then continued walking; the others followed suit.

The scene remained unchanged as they walked for several more blocks. After a while, the street widened into an open area, to what might have been a park at one point. There, the tents were arranged in irregular rows; piles of garbage formed ruinous mountains. To the left was a large building, its facade displaying a faded city logo, the stonework chipped from abuse and weathered by the elements. With great relief, they strode up to entrance and walked inside.

There was no one at the front desk in the spacious foyer; trash and piles of rubble were strewn randomly across the floor. Frequent gaping holes in the walls revealed active rodent infestations. They looked at each other with confusion, then walked as a group through the distressed wooden doors, each hanging clumsily by their one remaining intact hinge.

In the yawning silence, a quiet shuffling sound stirred. They looked around uncertainly; the direction from which the sound came was unclear. Without warning, an older lady appeared in the hallway, staring at her phone. She looked up with a start, gasped loudly, and after a few seconds of fumbling, managed to produce an old revolver pistol. She pointed it at the group, her arms shaking, her fist-like grip entirely wrong.

"Leave me alone!" she screamed.

"Don't shoot!" pleaded Sylvia. "We're not armed!"

The older lady continued to stare at them for several tense seconds. Her name badge read Maribel, and identified her as being with the Department Of Welfare. Finally, her face grew sullen, and she lowered her pistol and put it back into her pocket. The group sighed and relaxed.

"Who are you?" Maribel demanded. "What the hell do you want?"

"We need help," Sylvia begged. "We want to apply for public assistance."

Maribel snorted, and motioned towards the building's gutted interior. "Why don't you help *yourself*? Oh, too late, everyone else already did. And the little that's left is *mine*! Not *yours*!"

Gladys looked around with alarm. "What *happened* here?"

Maribel shot her a surly look. "Where have *you* been? You new here or something?"

Gladys' head drooped. "We just got off the bus from Millenniaburg."

Maribel rolled her eyes. "Oh…*that* place," she jeered. "I heard they rounded up their unwanted and *disposed* of them. So you escaped the shipping-container drones, huh? Lucky you." No one responded; Maribel frowned. "Well, you've served your purpose here, so why don't you go home?"

"We're not allowed to," Darrell blubbered.

Maribel sighed derisively. "Sucks to be you, then." She began to walk away.

"But what *happened* here?" Gladys implored.

Maribel stopped walking, turned around, and stared furiously, arms akimbo. "Isn't it obvious? No one wants to *work* anymore! The few that were willing got tired of being robbed and looted, and moved away. The city ran out of money, and had to pull back." She whipped out her pistol and began waving it around, causing a few to duck. "Do you know how hard it is to get ammo? I had to *scrounge* for what I have! I even found a few of these bullets on the sidewalk!" She suddenly put away her firearm.

"So there's nothing for us here," Darrell murmured.

"You have a firm grasp of the obvious," Maribel retorted. "The city can't afford to do *anything* for the people. You're on your own."

"Can we speak to someone in charge?" Sylvia pleaded.

Maribel winced as she pressed her hand to her forehead. "Good luck with *that*. They're locked up in their compound. No one goes in, no one goes out…not without permission. And don't try to break in…the police will shoot to kill."

"Is *that* where all the police are?" Leroy asked.

"The *lucky* ones," explained Maribel. "Those who have fallen *out* of favor have to patrol the city. Not that they do much of that. *They're* not stupid enough to tangle with the warlords."

"Where is this compound?" Tremain's voice cracked.

Maribel groaned and marched back into the lobby; the others followed. She pointed out through the entrance, to a faraway verdant hillside. "That's their compound. You're not likely to get anything there, either, but knock yourselves out. Now, *good day*." She turned around and went back to the office area. The group meandered toward the entrance.

"Who the…?! What *is* this today, Grand Central? No! Back off!"

They whirled around to see Maribel getting accosted by two thugs. She pulled back quickly, managing to raise her firearm. She fired, hitting one thug. She took aim at the other thug and pulled the trigger; suddenly, the pistol exploded, shrapnel flying in all directions. Maribel screamed and collapsed to the floor. Both thugs, though wounded, managed to lumber away.

The group stared in horror at Maribel. Where her hands had been was nothing more than shredded flesh, blood dripping heavily. Several metallic shards jutted from her torso. She looked at them with wide eyes. "*Help* me!"

Leroy stared at her for several cold, hard seconds. Then he motioned to the others, and they all walked past Maribel, going through the wooden doors into the office. Behind them, they could hear her screaming. "Hey! I said *help* me! I'm hurt! Aren't you even *human*?!" A moment later, they had moved out of her sight. She continued to scream. "You can't *have* any of that! It's *mine*! Are you even *listening* to me?"

Deeper within the building, they finally found a kitchen and a gym, both with working water. They gratefully drank their fill, and showered without getting undressed, washing both themselves and their clothes using some old dish soap found under the kitchen sink.

They split a few packets of dry, stale ramen noodles between them.

Tremain eyed the noodles warily. "What exactly is *shrimp* flavor?" Gladys gave him an angry look. "Just shut up and eat it," she barked. "It might be the only food we see today." Tremain nibbled on the noodles unenthusiastically, washing them down with copious amounts of tap water. "I wonder why these were left behind," he mumbled.

A commotion outside the kitchen caught their attention. The diners left their tables and rushed toward the sound. They found Terry in the hallway, wrestling with Darrell. "Stop it!" he shouted. "No! It's *mine*! I found it!" Darrell barked sullenly. Terry managed to yank a bottle from Darrell's hands; Darrell moved to follow, then slumped.

"What the hell's going on?" Gladys demanded.

"I found him drinking *this*." Terry held up a bottle of hand sanitizer.

Gladys looked horrified. "Oh, Darrell, don't you know? This is no good for you!"

Darrell's head hung low. "But I really wanted a drink. And it's seventy percent alcohol."

"But this stuff will kill you!" Gladys exclaimed. "There are all sorts of toxic ingredients."

Tears started to run from Darrell's eyes. "I was desperate. The tremors are really getting to me."

Gladys held Darrell's hand and looked at him sympathetically. "You could get really sick from drinking that. And we don't even know where a hospital is! Or if there are any left."

Darrell looked up at Gladys with unguarded eyes. "I'm sorry. I promise it won't happen again."

"That—" Gladys began. She paused to behold Darrell, and smiled sadly. "I believe you. I know you didn't mean it." Terry shrugged incredulously.

They finally left the building, exiting through the front entrance. They passed Maribel, lying on the floor, not moving. Blood no longer flowed from her hands.

As they passed the derelict park, Tremain eyed the piles of garbage. "Won't the garbage attract rats?" he asked Gladys. Overhearing him, one of the residents shouted back. "Those are *our* rats! You can't have any! Go find your *own* food!" Tremain gagged slightly, then turned away quickly.

They headed toward the green hillside in the distance. After several blocks, it was clear that the buildings were becoming less distressed. Finally, they began to pass some houses; the yards were either bare dirt or patches of dead plants, but the windows looked intact, and there was no sign of homeless camps. A few kids, riding bicycles in the street, stopped to stare at the slowly-moving caravan, then rode away.

They heard a chugging sound behind them. Turning to look, they spotted a security drone, passing behind them laterally, not moving towards them. They traversed a few more blocks. Without warning, they found themselves surrounded by wheeled security robots; two drones hovered in the air near them. A voice burst from one. "State your business!" It was difficult to make out what it said, over the sound of its internal combustion engine; together with the buzzing of its rotors, it sounded like an angry lawnmower. Also, unlike the security drones they were familiar with, the voice wasn't synthetic: it was obviously coming from a real human.

Dwayne walked forward to face the hovering drone. "We're exiles from Millenniaburg; we were invited here by the mayor. We just want to talk to him."

"To *her*, you mean," blared the drone's overdriven bullhorn-like voice. The robots continued to surround the group. They noticed the wheeled drones sported several types of weapons. Each had a rifle barrel, a tear-gas cannon, and what looked like a water nozzle, though conceivably it could spray any fluid. The weapons continued to wave slowly across the crowd, keeping them all covered. Several dozen tense seconds passed.

The drone's voice finally spoke again. "The mayor has nothing to say to you. Go back where you came from." The flying drones dipped one side and flew away quickly. The wheeled robots spun around and headed off.

Dwayne strode forward. "Let's go, people." After several steps, he turned around to notice that only a few had followed. The rest stood there, moping. "What are you doing?" he called. "If they want to stop us, they can send the drones back. I, for one, am going to confront the mayor! She brought us here, and she has a responsibility to *help* us! Where's your righteous indignation?"

He was met with silence. Then most of the crowd turned around and slowly began walking back toward the city center. Dwayne saw that only six had elected to stay with him.

"Fine!" he yelled. "Where are you going, anyway? You *know* there's nothing there for you! At the compound, we at least have a *chance*!" But they continued to leave.

Dwayne sighed heavily as he beheld the few that chose to join him. "I'm glad *some* of you have guts," he declared. "Let's take our case to the mayor."

As they walked, they encountered a few spectators, standing in their yards, eyeing them cautiously. A few brandished firearms, but didn't point them at the group.

A half dozen blocks later, still far away from the hillside, they spotted a formidable fence, topped with a shielded catwalk, where several police officers watched them approach. As they drew closer, they could see houses on the other side, stretching for several blocks. They appeared to be in much better condition than the houses they'd seen so far. Peering into the distance, they could make out a second fence inside, one closer to the base of the hillside. As they neared the outer fence, they noticed the police officers visibly stiffen.

Suddenly, the police drew their firearms. The one nearest the center of the catwalk held a bullhorn; the metallic voice grated in their ears. "Come no further."

The group stopped walking. "We're exiles from Millenniaburg!" Dwayne called out.

"I know," came the reply. "I was the voice of the drone."

"We just want to speak to the mayor!" Sylvia cried.

"And I told you, she's not taking any visitors," the policeman barked.

"But she *invited* us here!" Sylvia pleaded.

The trooper snorted. "Then consider yourselves welcomed," he sniped. "Now go away. You're on your own."

"But we need help!" Gladys whimpered.

"So?" came the overdriven voice. "Why is that *our* problem?"

"Isn't that what the government does?" Gladys asked.

The police officer let out a hollow laugh. "Really?" He turned to his fellow constables. "These people are like *children*, aren't they." Scattered laughter passed through the guards. The one with the bullhorn shook his head and continued speaking. "The government *used* to help people, back when it needed people to stay in power. Now it can get that through armed guards and security fences." A large drone flew past the small crowd and over the fence, entering the compound; he looked up at it briefly. "And air delivery provides the rest."

"Then why did she invite us here?" demanded Leroy.

The policeman glared. "She got her photo-op and her positive publicity. The mayor doesn't need you anymore. No one is going to follow up to find out what happened to you. You're yesterday's news." He cleared his throat before continuing. "So unless you can afford to live in the secured part of the city, you'd best be moving on."

"You know we can't," admitted Terry.

"And why *is* that?" the officer demanded. He pinched the bridge of his nose before continuing. "It's because you're all drains on resources. You're either criminals or parasites, otherwise you wouldn't have been exiled. Every last one of you believes in tearing the system down, whether out of selfishness, or because you think you're revolutionaries. But the system needs people to build it, and when that doesn't happen, it falls apart. There's nothing magic about this; if you stop creating the system, it will cease to exist. And behind you lays the inevitable result of your own broken thinking." He took a deep breath before continuing. "It's very simple; if something cannot possibly go on…it won't."

No one from the crowd spoke. The trooper continued. "Now, *you* need to go away. Go back to the city center. Live in the hell of your own making." The police officers continued to point their firearms in the small crowd's direction.

Disconsolately, they turn around to leave.

It was a few blocks before anyone spoke. "How can he blame us for this?" complained Darrell. "We didn't cause this problem."

"No, but people *like* us did," admitted Gladys. Darrell didn't respond. "We did the same thing to Millenniaburg," Gladys reminded them. "Remember that? Darrell?"

"I don't feel good," he blubbered. Gladys turned to see him collapse onto the ground.

"Darrell!" Gladys called out as she rushed up to him. "What's wrong?"

Darrell winced as he clutched his sides. "My stomach is on fire."

"That'd be the hand sanitizer," Terry mumbled.

Gladys silenced him with a sharp look, then turned back to Darrell. "We'll help you walk," she offered. She glared at the gawking men. "Well, why are you just standing there? Help him to his feet!"

They sighed and tried to lift Darrell, but the strain was too great. They only managed to move him to the side of the road, where he collapsed onto the curb. With great effort, they got him to sit up. He continued to groan as he doubled over in pain.

Gladys looked up to the nearest house. In the yard stood three children, gawking at them. An older man stood there too, holding a shotgun. Gladys called out to them. "Someone call an ambulance! This man needs medical attention!" They continued to glare sullenly. "Please!" she cried. "He needs help!" The three kids looked up at the older man; he met their gaze, and jerked his head back slightly. All three slowly walked toward the house and went inside. The older man continued to watch them for a few more seconds, then followed the kids.

"Are they gonna call an ambulance?" Darrell pleaded, looking at Gladys with innocent eyes.

No one spoke for several seconds. "They—" Gladys began. She looked at Darrell's guileless expression, and smiled sadly. "Yes, Darrell," she answered, "they are."

"Really?" Darrell trilled.

"Yes, really," Gladys declared. "They're good people, and they care about you very much, just like we do." Darrell smiled vacantly, tears forming in his eyes.

Gladys patted his hand and stood up. "Now you stay right here," she ordered. "We're going to go find the hospital, and tell them to get ready for you. The ambulance will be here as soon as it can."

"Thank you, ma'am," Darrell cried. "God bless you."

Gladys smiled sadly and turned to leave, catching a glimpse of the haunted looks in the others' eyes.

After walking only a few yards, they heard Darrell groan. "I think I need to lie down." They turned in time to see Darrell roll gently onto his side, his pleading eyes looking in their direction.

"You do that," Gladys agreed. "This will all be over very soon." Darrell's vacant smile returned.

They turned away and left him there, tormented expressions on their faces.

Dwayne peered into the distance, toward the chaos of the city center. "You want to know what happened here?" His expression became grim. "*We* happened."

"I couldn't help but notice," Sylvia offered. "The compound inside that fence reminded me of Millenniaburg. So, in the end, it's not that different from other cities. We acted like it was new and unprecedented, but it turns out what they were doing isn't really that unusual."

She stared into the distance. "Except *here*, our death will be much more painful and drawn out. They wouldn't do this to a dog."

The rest of the trip was spent in silence.

9

Eric Thompson scanned over his three computer screens, displaying the high-level dashboard for Unlimited Partners. He smiled as he contemplated the sea of green, with only a few scattered yellow areas. Near him hovered an executive intern, assigned for the day to trail Eric and learn what his job was like.

"So as you can see," Eric began, "our madly daring idea is actually bearing fruit! Overall success depends on team-building; that's one of my specialties. But then the people I choose must carry *that* on to the teams they build, and so on. All of these levels have to work, or the entire project could easily fail with speed." He turned to look at the intern. "There's no magic formula for accomplishing that; you have to be well-learned and thoughtful, you have to make your best judgment, then observe their results and see what needs to be changed, without succumbing to micromanagement. All I can say about my method is, I try to hire good people and then get out of their way. So far, it's working for me."

"Very inspirational, sir," the intern chimed. "I hope to contribute to that as much as possible. I believe this company has a bright future!"

Without warning, a red rectangle pushed its way onto his dashboard. Eric chuckled to himself. "Right on time." He clicked the high-priority emergency notification and began reading. Within moments, his eyes glazed over and his jaw dropped. The intern began to shiver uncontrollably. Blinking rapidly, Eric pondered who in the organization could handle this crisis.

His phone rang. He picked it up quickly; he didn't need to see who it was.

"What can you tell me about the intruder?" Eric said anxiously.

"It's heading for downtown Millenniaburg!" his security chief replied breathlessly. "An old-school jet airliner hijacking. They had no trouble slipping through the porous security of what's left of the government forces."

"Not a big surprise," Eric lamented. "But why are they attacking *us*? What's their motivation?"

"Information is still patchy," the chief related. "But the hijackers claim to be people we banished."

"Then what's the point of attacking us?" Eric pondered. "It's not like they want to return; there's nothing for them here, unless they clean up their act. Which they clearly haven't done."

"I don't think they're acting entirely rationally, sir," the chief offered. "We have to treat this as an existential threat, not as something we can fix."

"But what are our options?" Eric pleaded. But he knew the answer.

"We only have one, sir," the chief replied sanguinely. "We have to shoot it down."

"But that would be a disaster!" Eric objected. "Our credibility is based on demonstrating a better way to run things. If we just kill them indiscriminately, it'll set our cause back, possibly permanently!"

Eric could hear the sorrow in the chief's voice. "They'll be in downtown Millenniaburg in thirty minutes. I don't think we have a choice."

Eric's eyes glowed with sudden revelation. "I think we might." His skin flushed red as he took a deep breath. "OK, you prepare to shoot them down, but don't fire until they're seconds from the city border! I'm going to try something."

"Like *what*?" the chief pleaded. But Eric had already hung up.

At a workbench, deep within the 16otaku complex, Stacy pondered the red robotic gladiator. "OK, buddy," she chirped, "show me what you got!"

In a single fluid motion, it flipped onto its back, extended its legs, and popped open its main access panel. Stacy scratched at the empty air above it. "You want a belly rub? Who wants a *belly rub*?" she cooed.

"Oh, come on," Irwin chided, as the blue robot gladiator did the same thing for him. "They're only *partially* sentient."

"You keep saying that," Stacy countered, "but these two keep doing things we don't understand. That's why we're having this examination, remember?"

Irwin shook his head. "Big Daddy is adamant that it's nothing he's changed. So it has to be a crossed wire, or some undetected damage, somewhere. I'm not buying your theories."

Stacy removed the outer circuit board and gently laid it on the bench. "After everything you've seen them do, how can you really believe that?" She gaped at what she saw. "*What* the—"

"What...?" Irwin replied tersely as he finished removing the blue bot's outer circuit board, revealing what was inside. "Oh...oh my..."

Nothing they were looking at was familiar. There wasn't an inner circuit board; it appeared to be a tightly-constructed melange of custom parts, the function of which they could only guess at. Even the shapes of the components were novel. Were they capacitors? Transistors? Semiconductors? Functions seemed to blur together in a kaleidoscope of odd shapes, running over and under other parts to form a complex, yet strangely regular pattern. Clear tubes intertwined with mechanical parts, conducting neural tissue throughout the volume.

"*We* didn't build this!" Stacy gasped. "*They* must have built it themselves!"

"But what does it do?" Irwin pondered. "I mean, obviously they're running themselves with this, but why this arrangement? It doesn't...oh, wait. Maybe it does."

"What?" Stacy watched Irwin walk over to her bench and look inside the red droid.

"I think I get it," he postulated. "Step back and look at the arrangement as a whole, not as parts. What does it look like?"

"Kind of like..." Stacy's brow furrowed. "I don't know, a sponge?" Suddenly her eyes lit up. "It's a big shock absorber!"

"Exactly!" Irwin trilled. "We attach circuit boards with shock-absorbing mounts, but this takes it to another level!" He pondered the intricate assembly for a moment. "*Several* levels, actually. I've never seen *anything* like this."

"Let's not sell it short," Stacy sniffed. "We've never even *thought* of anything like this."

Irwin continued to remove exterior panels on the blue bot. "I think something like this would drive us mad before we got anywhere close to finishing. Plus, we'd need the design insights of a...a..."

"A supercomputer," Stacy finished. "A really big one. Like what all the bots form at night, when they're left alone. Remember, we're only here eight hours a day; they spend a lot of time by themselves. Looking into everything they get up to when we're away would be its own full-time job. Well, several, at least."

"Wow, would you look at this?" Irwin had finished removing exterior panels, as the blue bot continued to lie there supinely. "Even the exoskeleton is different!"

Stacy leaned in to look. "The beams are thinner, more numerous, and...very finely machined." She pushed on one gently with her finger. "It's metal, but it almost feels rubbery. They've strengthened it with...geometry?" She lowered a magnifier lamp over it, and dialed up the power. "Look at the intricate patterns running along the length! I'm not even sure what they do!"

Irwin shrugged. "Well, we can stop *this* part of the investigation. We've answered our original question; now we know how their fighting skills have improved so much recently. We can do the rest from our desks, querying the database about these new designs and how they work." He turned to the blue bot. "So are you willing to tell us all about it?" The blue bot responded by rotating its primary sensor array towards Irwin and mimicking a salute. Irwin laughed. "I'll take that as a yes!" He turned to Stacy. "Now the *real* discovery begins!"

Stacy sighed. "Just as soon as we finish putting them back together."

They heard a noise behind them. The red bot, carrying its outer circuit board, had crawled up to them. It proffered two of its front legs upwards. "Do you want a boost, little guy?" Stacy cooed. She lifted him up and put him on the workbench. It crawled closer to the blue bot and gently tapped Irwin's hand twice. "Oh, you have this under control?" Irwin laughed. The red bot immediately grabbed an exterior panel and began reconnecting it to the blue bot. Irwin and Stacy both stepped back.

Stacy looked puzzled. "How are they operating with their outer circuit boards disconnected?"

Irwin's expression became thoughtful. "That does mostly diagnostic operations. We need it to see how they're doing, but apparently *they* don't. I guess they have other methods!"

Stacy frowned. "And somehow, this all escaped the notice of Big Daddy?"

Irwin shrugged. "Maybe he didn't ask the right questions. But now *we* have a chance to!" Irwin's eyes shone with wonder. "This is bound to be a mind-blowing experience!"

Stacy looked beatific. "Just one more thing I can't wait to learn about!"

Irwin smiled. "Do you feel like a proud parent as much as I do?"

Stacy giggled. "Yes! Our babies are growing up."

Suddenly, Sam burst into the room. Stacy turned to him, smiling broadly. "Wait until you hear what *we've* learned!"

"Never mind that!" Sam shouted. Stacy and Irwin both froze. Sam tried to catch his breath. "We have a *much* more pressing matter! I need you two at the cubicles, *now*!" He ran off. Stacy and Irwin exchanged worried glances, then ran after him.

They arrived to find a video conference with Eric Thompson, already in progress. "So you see what we're up against? We don't have any good options. Your work, in its present condition, is our only hope!"

Stacy tapped Dwight on the shoulder. "What is he talking about?"

Dwight's eyes seemed to be filled with a sepulchral darkness. "A jet airliner has been hijacked, and is headed our way. Eric wants us to try to stop it with a mecha."

Stacy froze. "Seriously?"

"All I want to know," Eric pleaded, "is if there's a *chance*!"

"The rocket limbs have had a few controlled burns," Gary explained. "They all worked as expected. But we haven't actually tried to fly it yet."

Eric smiled tensely. "Well, today's the day! Are you up for it?"

"We've never even taken it *outside*!" Isabel protested. "In *theory*, it should work. All our tests have come back positive. But it's never been tried in the field!"

Eric wrung his hands. "I'm sorry to ask this of you, but our backs are really up against the wall!" He looked more unnerved than any of them had seen before. "And I'm not going to sugarcoat this; you'll all be risking your lives. But a lot more lives hang in the balance, not to mention the success of our entire company! This is our make-or-break moment!" He hung his head. "I can't ask you to take this chance. You have to *choose* to."

No one spoke. Then Dwight piped up. "Some day, I'll be an old man in a rocking chair on a porch, and I'll look back at this time… and if I don't act now, that old man is going to regret it and kick himself."

"Yeah!" Stacy exhorted. "Let's *do* this!"

Sam could hardly contain himself. "Then…I've always wanted to say this…*mecha pilots, assemble*!"

Gary, Dwight, Stacy, and Irwin, cheering loudly, ran for the hangar, the others close behind.

Eric turned his head; the camera followed to watch them leave. "God speed, my brain-trust warriors."

"How much fuel do we have on board?" Gary asked breathlessly.

"Five hundred and twenty pounds," Dwight replied, gasping for air. "We haven't refueled since our last burn."

"No time now! What's our battery charge?"

"They should be full," Isabel answered. "I left it plugged in."

They arrived in the hangar. The four pilots ran off to their respective flight decks. The rest attended to the remote monitoring and diagnostic stations. "Big Daddy!" Sam shouted into the microphone. "We're taking out the flying mecha. Are all systems go?"

"I heard about the hijacking, and the plan," Big Daddy answered in his usual sedate manner. "All systems are go. My confidence is high. I just wish there was time to add fuel."

Isabel threw a knife switch to raise the hangar door, as the various parts of the mecha powered on. "Oh, heck," she said suddenly, as she ran towards the mecha, which was flexing its joints, doing its final tests. "It's still plugged in!" she yelled. "I need a minute!"

Gary's voice squelched over the radio link. "Uh...Sam? How do we get this thing outside? It's too tall for the hangar door."

Sam stared blankly. "Um...not sure. We've never tried it before."

Isabel finished yanking out the assortment of extension cords, then high-tailed it back to her workstation.

Stacy's voice piped up. "I think we have to crawl."

The mecha lowered itself to the ground, and clumsily put its hands down. After a few false starts, it began crawling towards the hangar door, its pace quickening as the crew got the hang of it. "You know what they say," Dwight quipped. "You have to crawl before you can fly."

They reached the taxiway outside the hangar; unfamiliar sunlight poured into the mecha's sensors. Quickly, it adjusted to the new inputs, and gave its pilots a clear picture of their surroundings. Their mission computers all bleeped; the intercom link surged with Sam's voice. "OK, I've linked you to the radar tracking of the bogey. We've got ten minutes until it reaches the outskirts of the city, and fifteen minutes until it reaches Unlimited Partners HQ."

Gary pondered the trajectory as Dwight fired the rocket limbs, preparing them for flight. "We should be able to intercept it at the city's edge…but we're going to have to use our full thrust. This is going to be *really* rough. Are you all willing?"

All pilots answered affirmatively. "Then off we go!" Gary cheered as he slid all four thrust-power sliders to their maximum. The mecha shuddered uncertainly, slowly lifting off the ground, then wavered a little bit. As all four limbs pointed themselves down, in the same direction, suddenly it began picking up speed. It took off into the morning sky, piercing through the morning fog and vanishing.

"Aaaaah! I can't do this!" Irwin yelled. "I feel like I'm being crushed!"

"One moment!" Gary yelled. "OK, your suit should be extra pressurized now. Any better?"

"This really hurts!" Irwin continued to scream.

"Keep screaming!" Stacy yelled. "It'll help keep you from blacking out!"

"She's right!" Dwight interjected. "Scream, tense up all your muscles, and hold in your stomach! We'll have to deal with maximum G forces until we get there!"

Irwin continued to scream; Gary turned down the volume on his intercom. "As long as we can still hear him, it means he's OK. Some prior training for G forces would have been really helpful, but it's too late now."

"Is this right?" Stacy interrupted. "Only seven minutes to intercept?"

"Sure looks like it," Gary agreed. "The rocket-limbs are working really well. We're burning an awful lot of fuel, though. It'll take four hundred pounds just to reach the intercept point. I just hope Irwin can take it. Irwin, you hanging in there?"

"Aaaaaaaaaugh!" Irwin continued to scream. "I love iiiiiiiit! There's nothing else I'd rather doooooooo!"

Dwight was unconvinced. "Are you being sarcastic?"

"As long as he's still screaming, he's alive," Gary joked.

"He's fine," Isabel radioed. "His vital signs are all good. Keep doing what you're doing, Irwin!"

"Yaaaaaaaaaaaa!" he continued to yell.

"Can you imagine what they must be thinking on the ground?" Stacy wondered.

"The anime fans are probably having a religious experience," Gary offered. "Assuming they can see us."

"That brings up an important issue," Dwight pointed out. "What happens when the *hijackers* see us?"

"That depends," Gary offered. "Are they going to be looking for a giant flying robot?"

"Uh…hmmm…good point. We'll have to hope we surprise them."

The mecha continued to fly across the sky, angling upwards, its rocket-limbs spewing white-hot flames several times longer than its body. The mission computers calculated that, given their current trajectory, that at the intercept point, they'd be five hundred feet above the airliner. "I believe we can drop on them from above," Gary suggested. "I think that's our best plan."

"It's getting hot in here," Stacy observed. "How's our cooling system?"

"Not yet running at full," Gary answered. "I can turn it up. We should have sufficient battery power. Isabel?"

"You sure do," Isabel assured. "You were charged to the top when you left."

"I think I'm finally getting the hang of this," Irwin suddenly added, sounding strained.

"Glad to hear it, buddy!" Gary chimed. "I'm going to need your fine motor skills when we move to intercept. You ready for this?"

"There's nothing else I'd rather be doing," Irwin gushed.

"Just keep up your G-force countermeasures," Isabel reminded. "You're doing good, but don't relax them."

"Not a problem," Irwin assured. "They've become second nature."

The rockets dropped their power slightly; the flight computers had adjusted the autopilot for the intercept. Gliding over the river that formed the northern border of the city, the mecha started to rotate in the air. Gary's voice filled the intercom. "Hold on to your stomachs, people. This is going to feel really weird. Try not to get airsick."

The mecha pivoted in the air, and pointed its limbs down, allowing it to hover. It came to a stop.

"The airliner is thirty seconds away, and we're seven hundred feet above it," Gary announced.

"And they don't *see* us?" Stacy sounded incredulous. "Not even on radar?"

"I'm not picking up any radar from them," Dwight observed. "They must be operating on visual flight rules. Not a surprise if they're amateurs. They're probably just fixated on their target. Fortunately for us."

The aircraft finally became visible on their external cameras. "I'm ready for the intercept thrust," Gary announced. "Irwin, you ready to grapple?"

"I was *born* to do this!" Irwin exulted.

Gary counted down. "Six…five…four…three…two…one…BURN!"

The mecha's limbs flung themselves back, and its rockets fired. The external cameras showed the plane approach; a few seconds before impact, its limbs swung down again, to slow its descent. With a loud, resounding crunch, the mecha impacted with the airliner. Quickly, its arms dove under the wings, and its hands met on the plane's roof, near the first-class section, putting the plane into a full nelson. Its feet pushed backwards, finding their grip on each side of the tail wing. A few tense moments passed.

"We're not stopping them!" Gary shouted frantically. "They've turned up their engines, and we don't have the fuel to use ours to slow them down!"

There were a few moments of silence. "Can we kick our legs, like we're on a swing?" Stacy suggested. "If we can point the airliner upward, maybe we can get control of it."

Gary sounded unsure. "Irwin? Do the arms have a good grip?"

Irwin sounded confident. "They're not going *anywhere*. Start kicking!"

The mecha's feet pulled themselves from the tail wings and began bucking wildly. Slowly, the airliner began to pitch upwards.

"I wonder what *this* looks like on the ground," Stacy asked sardonically.

Sam's voice, over the radio, feigned embarrassment. "Um, well, when an airplane and a giant robot love each other *very* much…"

"It's working!" Irwin suddenly exclaimed. "Stop kicking! The airplane is in an aerodynamic stall. Its engines aren't enough to keep it in the air. Just a little bit of thrust from our legs, and we should be able to bring this unholy union to the ground!"

The mecha and airplane, locked in their hostile embrace, continued to plummet downwards.

"Why do you think the airliner hasn't cut its engines?" Dwight asked. "That would make our job a lot more difficult."

"Maybe they didn't think of it," Gary suggested. "We jolted them pretty hard when we hit; maybe they're unconscious."

"Or maybe they're panicking," Stacy wryly observed.

"Let's just hope our luck doesn't run out!" Gary added. "I think I can guide us to that empty field near the interstate. I'll try to slow down before we hit, but I can't guarantee anything. We're getting dangerously low on fuel. Brace for impact!"

"We're trying to get some security drones near you," Sam cut in. "But a lot depends on where you stop."

On the ground, traffic on the interstate had come to a halt. People had left their cars to gawk at the garishly-colored spectacle plummeting towards them. As the airliner's jet engines continued to strain against its captor, the mecha fired its rockets in a finely-coordinated pattern, trying to steer them to the grassy plain, one of the few areas nearby that wasn't either trees or buildings. A few moments before reaching the ground, the mecha's leg-rockets suddenly flared brightly, slowing their descent and starting a few small brush fires. With a surprisingly gentle crushing noise, the airliner landed on the ground, the mecha still firmly attached to its top.

They continued to slide along the ground. "Their engines are still firing! If we don't stop them, they'll drag us both into the river!"

"How about if I pinch their engines?" Irwin offered. "I'll have to let go with the arms, but I should be able to do this."

"I think that's our best bet," Gary agreed. "Do it!"

The mecha's arms relaxed their hold. Quickly, it slid down the length of the airliner, but suddenly, the legs grappled the aircraft's sides, stopping its motion. Now in position, the arms reached towards the engines and crushed them with its hands. Jet fuel sprayed from the wounded turbines as the airliner and its giant passenger slid along the ground for several hundred more feet, finally coming to a stop.

The external microphones picked up a buzzing sound, growing louder. "I think the drones found us," Stacy observed. "But what can *they* do? They'd need to get inside."

"That's it!" Gary suddenly interjected. "Irwin, rip the roof off the flight deck! Let the drones take care of the hijackers!"

"You got it!" The mecha shimmied up the length of the airliner;

when it got near the front, its giant hands dug its fingers under the sides, peeling the roof back like a giant sardine can. Four hijackers stood in the exposed flight deck, gaping upwards in sheer terror. Quickly, the drones swarmed them; a few precisely-fired taser bolts later, and they all collapsed to the ground.

"YOU DID IT!" a voice on the radio yelled. More cheering could be heard in the background. Stacy reacted with surprise. "Wait, was that Eric Thompson?"

"It's me, and everyone else at headquarters!" Eric answered. "Plus several million more viewers on TV."

"Wow," Stacy stammered. "Way to bury the lede there, boss."

"Are you kidding?" Eric gushed. "We wouldn't have missed this for the world!"

"Uh…" Irwin began. "Glad to be of service?"

The external microphones now picked up the cheers of the passengers. The emergency doors were open, the exit chutes had inflated, and passengers were sliding out of the stricken aircraft as quickly as they could. Most of them gawked at the giant robot, which continued to sit astride the airplane, like a brightly-colored cowboy on a white horse. A few had run off, to stamp out the small brush fires caused by the mecha's rockets.

The external cameras showed the highway, the passengers having left their cars en masse. All were cheering and clapping.

"Did we actually live through that?" Irwin's voice gasped weakly. "The adrenaline is wearing off. I think I'm going to lose it."

"Permission to lose it granted," Sam jokingly intoned. "You've all done a great job."

"You know what would be awesome?" Dwight piped up. "We should fly away from here, back to base, and salute in the air for everyone on the highway."

"Not going to happen," Isabel related over the radio. "You only have thirty pounds of fuel left."

"Can we siphon anything from the airliner?" Stacy asked.

Isabel paused for a moment. "You don't have anything to siphon with," she sighed. "We never thought to add such an attachment."

"Then what do we do?" Dwight pined. "We can't just lay here and wait for a big flatbed to pick us up. That'd be embarrassing!"

"There's a truck stop about two miles down the highway," Sam offered. "Diesel fuel is close enough to aircraft fuel for the mecha's systems. And between your remaining battery power, and the internal generators, you have enough power to…" Sam paused for a moment. "To walk there."

"Well, I guess that'll still look pretty cool," Dwight agreed reluctantly. "But not what I was hoping for."

Gary's voice crackled over the mecha's loudspeakers. "Citizens, please give me some space. I need to leave." The passengers obediently formed a wide circle around the mecha. Slowly, it moved to stand up and dismount the airliner, to the cheers of everyone nearby. Unsteadily, the mecha walked towards the highway; the circle of people parted to let them through.

"Blast off! Blast off!" the kids yelled, picked up by the external microphones. "See, I knew they'd want that," Dwight sighed. "We need to plan better in the future."

Gary's voice once again blared from the loudspeaker. "Sorry, kids. Not enough fuel. But maybe next time!" All four pilots could hear their disappointed whines. Gary continued. "Hey, c'mon, kids! I'm still a giant flying robot!" The kids quickly began cheering again. The mecha slowly, clumsily walked away.

"OK, I think our autopilot can handle this," Gary declared. "Just watch for sinkholes and loose soil."

As they neared the highway, the disembarked passengers continued to cheer and clap. The mecha stopped and stood there. The loudspeaker crackled once again with Gary's voice. "Citizens, please move your vehicles. I have to get home." They finally stopped cheering, went back into their cars, and got out of the way. The mecha crawled up the embankment, walked across the lanes of traffic, and began trudging down the highway in the slow lane. Cars slowly drove past it, horns honking and passengers whooping, before driving off. The mecha occasionally saluted, to even louder cheers.

The customers at the truck stop could hear the rhythmic clanking noise from quite some distance away. As the mecha approached, most of them just stood and stared, their mouths gaping. The mecha walked into the parking lot, picked a row of interior pumps, and stood there, waiting. The loudspeaker flared again. "Don't mind me, citizens. I just need fuel. I'll wait in line."

The two truckers that were next in line made several animated arm gestures, then each got into their trucks, started them up, and moved to back up. The mecha backed up too, getting out of their way. Deftly, the trucks slithered past each side of the mecha, smoothly arriving back in their lanes. "Thank you, citizens!" the loudspeaker blared.

Slowly, the mecha lowered itself onto its hands and knees. From there, it shifted to a prone position, and began to army-crawl between the rows of gas pumps. The clanking and scraping made a ferocious noise that caused many onlookers to cover their ears. Finally, the mecha was in position, and the steady hum of its power shut down, leaving behind a ghostly silence.

A few moments passed. Then the sides of each limb opened, and the pilots exited, lowering themselves gingerly to the ground. As the onlookers continued to gawk, the pilots nonchalantly pulled out their company credit cards, swiped them at the pumps, then each removed a gas cap and put the diesel spouts into the exposed fuel filler.

The trucker opposite Dwight stammered. "Uh...er...um...what kind of mileage do you get in that thing?"

"I'm not sure," Dwight answered. "We just burned about five hundred pounds; that got us a total of about fifteen miles. We used a lot less fuel during free-fall, though."

"Free-fall?" the trucker replied weakly. "Buddy, you must have horseshoes in *both* pockets."

A few families crowded around Irwin. "How do you become a giant-robot pilot?" one kid asked.

"First, you have to invent it," Irwin answered. "I'm part of the team that built this. We have two more back at our lab."

"Do they fly too?" The kid's eyes burned with adoration.

"Not yet, but after today, I'm sure we'll add it soon!" The kid looked disappointed. Irwin continued. "But...you know what they *can* do? Kung fu battle! Just like in the movies!" The kid gaped wordlessly.

"What company do you work for?" a man asked. "Who is in the giant-robot business?"

"I'm with a research-and-development division of Unlimited Partners," Irwin answered. "And we do a lot more than just giant robots."

"Well, I'm sure glad you do!" the man exulted. "That was fine work, stopping that hijacking. Can you believe the government hasn't even released a statement on it? I think they're too humiliated."

"I haven't had time to catch up on the news," Irwin explained.

"I'm sure I will…once I fly back to the office."

"That's right, ladies — you *too* can become a giant-robot pilot!" Stacy happily explained to a throng of Girl Scouts, hanging on her every word. "And I don't just fly it; I helped *design* and *build* it! But you'll need to stay in school, study hard, and keep out of trouble! Jobs like these only go to the best! And *you* can make it this far, if you just apply yourselves!"

"We will!" they cheered as they ran off to get back in their vans.

"Thank you, I really appreciate that," the den mother told Stacy.

"No problem, I get it," Stacy answered. "I know the Girl Scouts are for at-risk children. Hopefully they stay inspired."

The den mother glanced at the mecha, her eyes filled with wonder. "If *that* doesn't inspire them…*nothing* will."

A thin, gangly man in business-casual left the shop and approached Gary, a stunned look on his face. Gary turned and smiled. "Are you the manager?" He tried to answer, but couldn't find his voice; finally, he just nodded vigorously.

"What's the pre-authorization limit on these pumps?" Gary asked nonchalantly.

"Uh…ummm…seventy five gallons," the manager stammered.

"Can we all get authorized for about a thousand gallons each? We have a long flight home."

"I…um…yes. I'll…go do…that." The manager walked off, looking behind him one last time before disappearing inside the shop.

As the mecha continued to fuel, Dwight walked up to Stacy. "So…before the next time…*rubber shoes*."

Stacy laughed. "I know, right? I though the *flight* was bad…the walk was easily *twice* as bad! I think my bones are still shaking."

"And rubber knee pads and elbow pads, too."

"Yeah…I'm not looking forward to fixing all those scrapes. But can you imagine it? The mecha will look like a roller-derby player! How awesome would *that* be?" Stacy looked at the mecha, grinning impishly. "How about retractable inline skates? The *heck* with all this walking!"

"Oh yeah, huh?" Dwight agreed. "I guess there are some ideas that don't occur to you unless you try the thing in the real world." Dwight looked at the mecha's back. "And why the heck don't we have a giant flaming sword?"

The four pilots continued to field questions, and receive

congratulations, as the pumps slowly filled up the mecha. Finally, they put the spouts back, replaced the gas caps, and climbed back inside their respective flight decks, giving the crowds one last thumb's up before disappearing inside, to the din of their hails and cheers.

The mecha powered up, its electric hum making the air shake. This brought on another round of applause and whooping. It slowly army-crawled from under the canopy, back to unobstructed space. The metallic screeching and scraping sound silenced the crowd quickly as they covered their ears and winced.

"*Oh* my God," Irwin began. "I haven't dealt with so much of the public in my *life*!"

"I heard *that*!" Stacy added. "This was fun once, but if there are any more public appearances, I think we need to use gregarious pilot types. I thought the *battle* was tough…having to deal with people was *much* more draining!"

"Hey Gary, once we're out, can we launch with only three of the rockets?" Dwight asked. "I really want to try a salute as we leave."

"I think that'll be safe," Gary answered. "But don't try anything fancy. Just one salute and we're done."

"Not a problem," Dwight laughed. "I'm willing to start small."

The mecha walked to the far end of the complex's parking lot, away from the people, trucks, and anything flammable. After turning to face the crowd, its leg rockets ignited, along with one arm. As the mecha launched into the sky, its free arm moved to salute, before dropping that arm down and firing the last rocket. The exterior cameras showed the crowd cheering wildly, but the rockets made too much noise to hear them.

The flight back to their airport was uneventful and leisurely. There was no need to use full rocket power; all the pilots had had enough of high G forces for one day.

The mecha neared the airport. The exterior cameras showed that huge crowds had formed on either side of the runway. The radio suddenly crackled to life. "Welcome back, robo-nauts!" Eric Thompson's voice gushed. "You're all heroes!"

"Oh, man," Gary answered. "I hope you don't expect us to deal with any more people. All we want to do is collapse." The mecha moved to land upright.

"Not a problem," Eric assured them. "You just need to land and crawl back inside. We'll deal with the press."

"Thanks, boss," Gary replied, with great relief in his voice. "The truck stop was agonizing, but we didn't know what else to do." The mecha landed gently on the ground; the exterior cameras showed the crowd cheering wildly, but they couldn't be heard over the roar of the rockets.

"I understand completely," Eric commiserated. "And rest assured, you all get the rest of the day off. Well, after a full medical exam. We want to make sure you're intact."

The mecha got down on its hands and knees. "So do we," Gary agreed. "We're just glad we survived."

"So am I," Eric answered sanguinely. "And tomorrow, I'll tell you all about the reaction. Lots of nonpublic stuff. You all did more good today than you can possibly imagine."

The mecha crawled through the hangar door. "That's fine…but *tomorrow*. We need a break."

"You've earned it," Eric agreed. "Have a good evening."

The hangar door closed behind the mecha, the loud clang reverberating across the runway.

10

Sam and his team spent the morning getting their fill of the previous day's news. The universal exuberance was pretty overwhelming. There was so much amateur footage of their flight, remixes set to music had already started to appear. Video shot from the highway showed the crash landing in all too vivid detail, giving them the shivers. Evidence of the in-air battle was limited to a single shaky, highly-zoomed-in clip until the U.S. government graciously released what one of their own aircraft had recorded. Discreetly, they had edited out the suggestive leg-kicking portion by zooming in during that period and panning the frame upwards.

More gratifying were the headlines. The somber news agencies described it in terms like "Potential Suicide Hijacking Thwarted with High Technology". The click-bait oriented sites screamed "9/11 Wannabes Stopped in Most Awesome Way Possible". Several rapid analyses declared the world had entered a new era, one with a promising future. Even the cable-news channels, usually a reliable source of the most unfavorable viewpoints possible, couldn't find a cross word to say about it.

The drive to work that day was uneventful, until arriving at the small airport where 16otaku made their headquarters. A throng of well-wishers swarmed the entrance, cheering and clapping. They left the driveway unblocked, and the approaching cars entered unmolested. Only a few security personnel, standing relaxed near their motorcycles, kept order; the crowd remained well-behaved.

Irwin arrived to find the rest were already there, in a teleconference with Eric Thompson and several more senior executives. Brian McTierney, the investor who had been so smitten with the mechas, occupied a small rectangle in the upper-left corner of their screen; even at the reduced resolution, his beatific expression was clear. Eric smiled as Irwin walked in. "Hey, *there's* the wrestler of the hour!"

Irwin seemed nonplussed. "I half-expected a cheering crowd at the gate today. It's OK; I had my fill of public interaction yesterday. But still."

Stacy looked at him, puzzled. "What do you mean? *We* had a crowd!" She held Bruno in her arms; the lab cat curled up to her, content. "I was a little worried they were going to storm the airport."

Irwin's face fell. "Really? I missed it? The gate was quiet when I went through."

"I guess that's a sign of the new type of citizen we have," Eric Thompson crowed. "Able to control themselves without a heavy hand forcing them to."

"Guess I picked the wrong day to be late for work." Irwin sat down slowly. "I wasn't moving quickly this morning. They may have deemed me medically fit, but I still ache all over!"

Dwight's expression became pained. "*I'll* say! I have a newfound respect for Air Force pilots. I had *no* idea G-forces hurt so much."

Isabel looked joyful. "The good news is, we gathered enough data during that flight to redesign the pressure suits in several different ways! Before you know it, high-G flights will be possible for all sorts of people, not just trained experts!"

"I'm glad you all had fun saving the world," Eric piped up. "But your success comes at a cost."

Sam raised an eyebrow. "Like what?"

Eric replied stoically. "Now that you've demonstrated such an incredible capability, the company is going to put a lot more resources into the mecha project, and way more oversight! We want to place at least one in every major hub of our operation. Military and law-enforcement personnel will train to operate them. Just their presence *alone* will be a deterrent! Not to mention a huge public-relations boost."

Gary sighed. "Well, we have a lot of design work to do before they're ready to mass-produce. But I'm glad we'll finally have time to do so."

"If I may…one thing still puzzles me." The members of 16otaku turned to look at the rectangle that had lit up. They weren't familiar with the name, but the chyron identified him as the Chairman of the Board. A nervous pride shot through all of them; they had the attention of the big boss!

"What's that, sir?" Sam asked, a lump in his throat.

"It's my understanding that your team considered the mecha project not ready for real-world deployment. And yes, I realize that actual rocket flight hadn't been tested until yesterday's dramatic demonstration. But given how admirably it, and all of you, performed in the field…I can't figure out why you thought it wasn't ready."

"Uh…" Sam demurred. "Well…"

Gary cut in. "We have our own criteria for 'ready', and our mechas don't quite meet that yet."

"*What* criteria?" The chairman had leaned forward in his chair, his staid expression unchanging.

"Well…they're not able to fight hand-to-hand yet. We have a lot to do to improve their balance, and they're too easily damaged by typical martial-arts moves."

The chairman's jaw dropped. "You mean…your criteria is… *kung fu battle*?"

Stacy smiled. "Hey, we gotta have our *standards*!"

An entire screenful of high-ranking suits erupted in laughter. As it died down, Brian cut in. "You see, Carl? I *told* you they were silly in all the right ways!"

The chairman shook his head. "You weren't kidding!"

"Our mechas can easily handle unarmed targets," Irwin chortled. "We lucked out yesterday; the airliner couldn't fight back."

"Well, despite that *glaring* omission," the chairman bantered, "you've really captured the imagination of the public, including the ones normally hostile to us, like the government."

"It seems a giant flying robot is all it took to bring everyone together," Isabel quipped.

"Well, we don't mind the increased scrutiny, or the added responsibility," Sam assured. "We've all had to deal with it in our careers. The extra eyes won't slow us down."

"Actually, it's more than that," Eric warned. "A *lot* more."

"How do you mean, boss?" Sam inquired.

"Remember how I told you yesterday that I had some nonpublic information to share with you? Well, things evolved heavily overnight, and I have even more to tell you now."

The team went silent, staring apprehensively at the screen.

"The federal government finally contacted us directly last night," Eric related. "And I don't mean the usual set of nitpicky bureaucrats. I'm talking about…" He pointed upwards. "…the big boss."

"Wow," Irwin managed to say.

"They're of course going to compensate us for their lapse in security. But the President made a startling admission last night. This has to stay company confidential until we and they make a joint public announcement. But since it affects all of you, and your mecha project, I thought you should hear about it now."

The only noise any of them made was Dwight swallowing hard.

"He admitted that the government is close to collapse," Eric revealed. "The relative peace we've been enjoying in Millenniaburg, and the smattering of smaller towns that we run, is *not* reflected in the rest of the country. The rioting has become endemic, the police and National Guard spend most of their time defending *themselves*, not citizens, and every business that can is closing up shop and heading for the exits." Eric looked around himself, as if to address everyone participating in the teleconference. "The President tried to blame us for drawing away the talent they need to survive and thrive. But I pointed out to him that we didn't actively recruit them; they sought *us* out. Retaining them was squarely on the government's shoulders. And he conceded that too!"

"My God," Gary stammered. "Where do we go from here?"

"Put simply," Eric continued, "we've hit the big time, people, whether we're ready for it or not." He paused a moment. "The government has given us the authority to take over any city we like, to expand our operation across the country."

"Incredible," Stacy peeped.

"I, and the other executives, have a huge task ahead of us," Eric intoned somberly. "The success we've pulled off in Millenniaburg will have to be replicated quickly in other cities. We need to find people that can lead those local efforts, we have to screen law-enforcement personnel, and most important, we'll need to mass-produce the bot armies that have made such a difference here — security drones, construction droids, maid-bots, all of them. I know you've set up several assembly lines within Millenniaburg, but how quickly can you spin them up in other cities?"

"Remarkably quickly," Sam promised. "We just have to pack up a nucleus, and drop it off in any suitable building, and the rest will take care of itself."

"How?" Eric probed.

"Let us handle it," Sam assured. "You always told us you wanted to focus on the big details. We have it all under control."

Eric laughed. "Fair enough. I can't argue with success! OK, we'll give you the names of cities and locations, as soon as we have them, along with some suitable sites."

"If we may," Sam proffered, *"we'll* screen the sites. Our

assembly lines have a lot of…idiosyncratic…requirements that are difficult to explain easily."

"You're right," Eric agreed, facing his palms forward. "We won't micromanage. A list of cities will be enough. We'll tell you as soon as we've negotiated for the authority."

"Now I see why you want to mass-produce mechas," Isabel observed. "You'll want at least one per city. We'll get that working as quickly as we can!"

"Maybe, as a start, you can retrofit the other two mechas to fly," Eric suggested.

"Given their design constraints, it'd be easier to build new ones," Sam explained. "Like we said, yesterday's flight has given us a lot of data on how to proceed. Starting over will be faster."

"You're right, you're right," Eric conceded. "I'm trying to micromanage again." He grinned impishly. "What can I say, I've caught giant-robot fever too. At least we have *one* that can fly."

"We sustained a lot of damage in yesterday's battle," Irwin explained. "A lot more than we've admitted publicly. We're really lucky we were even able to get home. It's not likely to be ready for duty for some time."

"Aw, no fair!" Brian piped up. "I wanted to pose it on my headquarters building!"

"It'll probably work well enough for that," Stacy chimed. "Oh, we meant to ask you…does that building have a heliport?"

Brian's brow furrowed. "Actually, it does. Why?"

Stacy exchanged knowing smiles with the rest of the team. "Then all we can say is…*keep watching the skies*!"

"Yes!" Brian yelped, throwing decorum out the window. He quickly settled himself. "I caught giant-robot fever a long time ago."

"And those large pedestals in front of Unlimited Partners headquarters," Isabel added. "Have any statues been put there?"

"No, not yet," Eric informed them. "We've never come to any agreement what we should do with them."

"Then," Isabel chirped, "two large packages of some value will come to you, shortly."

"*That*," Eric sighed, "would be awesome." Suddenly, he leaned forward. "Well, what are you all waiting for?" he joshed. "Get to it! I and the rest of the suits can handle all the banal details."

"Yes, *sir*!" Sam cheered, throwing an irreverent salute. "We're *off*!"

"*All* of us!" Stacy added, moving Bruno's paw into a salute. He meowed, annoyed. The entire screen burst forth with laughter as Sam shut off the feed.

Sam looked around at his team. "Well…*we* certainly have a full plate. But I know we're up for the challenge!"

They began walking toward the mecha hangar, first entering the robot nursery. Bruno jumped out of Stacy's arms and headed straight for the newborn spider-bot babies. "We just have to ask the bots to put together a large enough team to build their own assembly line and start producing offspring. They'll need time to prepare for that, though."

They passed through the bot's jungle-gym training area. "We should probably send an instructor along with each nucleus. I'm sure some of them will volunteer."

They visited Big Daddy's room. Surrounding him, in smaller vats, were other cybernetically-enhanced former invalids. Gary addressed them. "Hey, Big Daddy! Did you hear the news?"

"Indeed, I did," came the synthesized reply. "Fortunately, I've been training several Little Daddies for some time. I'll get them ready to be on their own, in their new cities." A chorus of synthesized cheers declared their confidence. Gary smiled and gave them a thumb's-up.

They walked through the storage warehouse. Bots thronged all over, opening crates, moving barrels, and helping themselves to the supplies. "Well, *they've* certainly been busy," Stacy chimed. Isabel looked confused. "But what are they doing?"

"Isn't it obvious?" Sam answered, his eyes twinkling, as he opened the door to the mecha hangar. The lights were already on; as the door rose, it revealed four new mechas; the three older models stood some distance to the rear. Bots swarmed over them as others flocked in the air nearby, all busily fabricating parts and assembling them.

Sam smiled. "They pored over the flight-test data last night, and are now applying all their advanced engineering and design knowledge to our new mechas!"

Even in the bright lights, the new designs seemed incomprehensibly complicated. Gone were the rigid lines and flat plates of the original mechas; in their place stood surprisingly lithe and flowing forms, almost lifelike.

Gary seemed incredulous. "All *this* from bordering-on-crows?

I'm not buying it."

"The bots form a hive mind at night," Irwin pointed out. "So these were designed by The Big Crow, as it were. With no small amount of help from Big Daddy, I'm sure."

Isabel seemed unsettled. "How does any of this work?"

"Why don't you ask them?" Irwin waved Isabel toward a nearby diagnostics console. "*I* already have!" Nervous, she approached it and began typing in queries.

In response to a question about the skeleton, the screen displayed an intricate pattern of multi-jointed bones in the center, surrounded by thin metal strips to form the exoskeleton. Active areas could be clicked for deeper dives, revealing the intricate geometry that gave each piece its preternatural strength and flexibility.

"Ask about the electronics," Stacy suggested. "That'll *really* blow your mind."

Hesitantly, Isabel punched up the next query. She was presented with a sponge-like diagram that apparently explained the electronic layout. Larger components blurred together with smaller components in an intricate pattern that delivered high redundancy in the event of damage. In place of plastic, it used a novel polymer composite. "The superstructure conducts heat and…absorbs shock?"

"Every shock except the one *you're* having!" Irwin quipped.

"But what about the limb rockets?" Isabel mumbled. Her query presented her with the expected large fuel tanks, broken into separate volumes, together with a mesh of redundant copper-alloy lines for feeding the fuel to the combustion chamber. A series of tiny dots along the lines showed where micro-valves could divert, or cut off, the flow of fuel. This made it possible to deliver high volumes, or adapt to physical damage, vastly reducing the risk of fire or fuel loss.

A pop-up suggestion box invited her to click it for a related explanation; she did so, and the details of the fire-suppression system took over the screen. Also formed as an intricate mesh of tubes, it was able to reach all parts of the mecha. A different system, armed with more human-friendly chemicals, was in place to extinguish fires in the flight deck.

"Just *one* flight deck?" Isabel's question was met with a diagram of the new flight deck, situated in the head. There was no chair, or command console; all functions and physical support had been integrated into the pressure suit, which was able to open and close at the side, allowing the pilot to enter or exit. The controls had been streamlined, allowing all the mecha's functions to be operated more easily — no more need for multiple pilots.

Isabel was at a loss for words. "Oh...I...it seems like they've used all available space. I have no idea how we're supposed to maintain these."

"We won't," Dwight agreed. "The bots will. We don't have the fine motor skills, much less the attention to detail."

Isabel noticed a countdown on the screen. "And they'll really be ready to use in less than two days?"

"Just this batch," Stacy explained, pointing to a different part of the screen. "But from what they've learned by doing these, they expect the new ones to be constructed in six hours each."

Isabel chuckled cathartically. "Then we *already* have a mecha assembly line."

"Well, as far as the executives are concerned, we do," Sam brought up. "As soon as the bots are well-practiced enough with their designs, we'll ask them to make a true assembly line. Who knows, maybe one day soon, we can crank out mechas as quickly as cars!"

Isabel sighed. "The days of human design are coming to an end."

"Hardly," Sam disclaimed. "We'll just move up the food chain. There's no point in people getting involved in something that bots can do better. This frees us up to do far more interesting work, stuff that bots aren't capable of yet."

Isabel smiled. "I guess you're right." She looked at the rendering of the finished product on the screen, the smooth lines and supple curves sweeping along their height. "But I can't help but notice that the new mechas look less like giant robots, and more like...like..."

"Like a person in a costume," Stacy jested.

Isabel laughed. "I guess that's a more classic shape than the one *we* made!"

"The bots are following their directions a little *too* well!" Dwight guffawed. "But I think the mechas look better this way."

Isabel smiled sadly at the original prototypes. "It's too bad they're obsolete."

"Not at all!" Stacy squeaked. "The controls have already been retrofitted so the bots can pilot them, and they're going on public display. *Those* two can do public exhibitions of kung-fu battle. The console says they're ready for demonstration. Want to check it out?"

"Of course!" Isabel yelped.

Immediately following Stacy's well-placed button presses on the console, the three original mechas hummed to life. Irwin threw the knife switch to open the outer hangar door. All three mechas got down on their hands and knees, but instead of assuming a crawling position, they folded themselves up tightly. Without warning, wheels popped out of the bottom! All three quickly scooted over the concrete floor and drove themselves outside.

Sam's brow furrowed. "Did *you* tell them to install wheels?"

"No," Irwin confessed. "The bots must have come up with that themselves."

"It's a good idea, though," Stacy conceded. "And now they're members of a *different* category of classic giant-robot!"

The team ran outside. The flying mecha had already fired its rockets; they shielded their eyes from the bright light. It rose slowly in the air, then streaked upwards, vanishing quickly from sight.

"Where is it going?" Irwin gaped.

"To its first public display, probably," Gary suggested. "It already had its instructions. The other two should depart shortly, once we get our martial-arts demonstration."

The two mechas assumed kung-fu starting poses. Quickly, they began to punch, kick, and dodge, their bodies and limbs flailing dexterously in fluid motions. Without warning, one jumped into the air! The other one caught it, and quickly spun it around. As one landed on its feet, it began to whirl the other one around in the air.

"Acrobatics, too?" Isabel gasped.

"Oops," Stacy demurred. "I guess the bots took me seriously. I don't suppose they also…"

In an instant, the bots separated themselves and began a synchronized dancing routine, ending by spinning on their backs, then their heads, then flipping up to their feet and striking poses. The team turned to look at Stacy, staring uncertainly at her.

Stacy covered her mouth and giggled. "I guess that answers *that* question. Oh well, too late now."

Flashing lights suddenly poured forth from their heads, as wheels arranged like inline skates erupted from their feet. With fluid strokes, they began skating toward the front gate. The guard began opening the gate, to let them out, but they simply sprung skillfully over it, landing gracefully, and turning right smoothly to skate down the street, merging with traffic.

Brian McTierney heard a roaring noise; he looked up from his desk in the corner office to see the mecha streaking towards his building. With a giddy yelp, he bounded out of his office, neglecting the elevator to race up the stairs to the roof. As he arrived at the door, the roar became deafening; he found two of the younger employees there, covering their ears. He did likewise, and then let out a long, joyous whoop, causing the two juveniles to break out in wide grins. Finally, the noise died down, and they opened the door to the roof.

Brian and his junior team members watched in awe as the mecha strode from the heliport to the corner of the building. Slowly, it put one leg over the side, coming to rest on its thigh. Gingerly, it moved the other leg to dangle over the edge. As Brian covered his mouth with his hands and watched with glee, the mecha slowly adjusted its position so that it was sitting stably on the building's edge. It placed its left arm down, gripping the corner with its hand. Slowly, it raised its right arm to line up with its upper chest, curling its fingers into a fist, as its head descended. With a clank, the head and fist came together, making a perfect mimic of the "Thinker" statue. The electrical hum died down, and the robot's lights turned off. Moments later, four spider-bots emerged and crawled expertly down the side of the building.

Brian continued to gape. Finally, he dropped his hands from his mouth, and looked at his two junior charges. "I feel as young as you two right now."

One grinned broadly. "And I feel like I'm back in kindergarten." The other couldn't speak, but tears of joy streamed down her face.

The drivers in the mid-morning traffic could hear the klaxons of an emergency vehicle, but couldn't see where it was coming from. Without warning, two roller-blading mechas, taller than some of the buildings they were passing, skated towards them. Cars obediently pulled over for the flashing lights and the blaring klaxon. Some people left their cars to gape at the spectacle as they glided out of sight.

Eric Thompson spoke on the phone. "I really think we should get together, in person, for this next meeting. Video conferences are fine for internal use, but when we're dealing with the outside world...especially *these* people...we should present more of a unified front. As in, *physically* unified." He paused a few moments. "Excellent. See you all soon."

Without warning, the door to his office opened. Eric looked up from his desk to see Danielle, his protege and long-time second in command, enter. She could hardly contain herself. "We have visitors. Very *big* visitors." A wide, silly grin erupted from his face, and he vaulted from his desk and out of his office, Danielle not far ahead of him.

By the time he reached the building's front door, a large crowd of employees had thronged to gape at the wonderment. The two mechas had climbed to the top of the vacant statue pedestals in front of the building, and were now turning gingerly to face outwards. When they had done so, each struck a dignified salute.

Eric reached the edge of the crowd and looked back at the mechas. "Aw, c'mon," he pleaded. "You can do better than *that!*"

After a short delay, the mechas moved their arms, so that one hand was on their chest, and the other extended upwards to the side, mimicking the pose of a famous movie duo. Eric smiled as he pumped his fists. "*Excellent!*" The crowd burst into applause.

◊ — ◊ — ◊

Eric Thompson watched the other executives file into the large meeting room, taking their places around the long oval table. Danielle, his long-time second-in-command, sat nearby.

He smiled. "What are you thinking about?" Danielle asked.

Eric sighed. "I remember being seated at the far end of this same conference room, raising my hand to propose my audacious plan, the one that became Unlimited Partners. It seems like only yesterday, and somehow at the same time, an eternity ago. And now I sit at the head of the table."

"You've earned it," Danielle assured him. "I've seen it every step of the way. You deserve to be there."

Eric looked sanguine. "And now I'm about to lead the most important meeting of this company's short existence." He turned to look at Danielle. "This job never gets any easier. But at least it's *occasionally* rewarding."

"Don't fret," she cooed. "You've *got* this!"

He smiled confidently. "You're right, I do. This'll be fun *and* terrifying, like a roller coaster ride."

"The best ride in the *world!*" she quipped. "I wouldn't want to be anywhere else."

The conference room was finally full. The television on the wall stopped displaying the "Unlimited Partners" logo, and showed a live video feed from the Oval Office in the White House. The President sat there, flanked by the Vice President, a highly medaled military officer, and a large man in a dark suit and sunglasses. Behind him, through the windows, was the usual view of the White House greens, though it had largely turned brown. In the distance, columns of smoke rose in the air.

"Good morning, Mr. President," Eric Thompson began. "How are things?"

The President nervously looked behind him, then at the camera. "Oh…you know…the usual. How's the mood in Millenniaburg?"

"Electric!" Eric crowed. "We're the toast of the country."

"While the country is simply *toast*," the President grumbled. "Seems fitting."

"We hope to turn that around," Eric declared. "But we need to know how much leeway you're willing to give us. We've all read the proposed joint statement, and parsed it as thoroughly as we can. And we *like* it…don't get us wrong…it's very diplomatic. But it was our understanding that our authority was to go further than you propose."

"That statement is just an outline," the President explained. "One for public consumption. We're going to send your full authorization after this meeting, under the previously-established nondisclosure agreement. Just as soon as we hash out the final details with you, right now."

"Can you summarize our true authorization, then?" Eric inquired.

The President exhaled sharply as his shoulders slumped. "Remember…*nondisclosure*."

"We'll keep our end of the deal, sir," Eric assured. "What are you trying to tell us?"

The President hung his head, and didn't speak for several seconds. When he finally looked up again, his eyes were filled with tears.

"Total capitulation."

"What now?" Eric sounded alarmed.

"If this was wartime, we'd call it unconditional surrender," the President continued. "Right now, the only thing holding the country together is ignorance of just how bad the real situation is. The federal government no longer has any real control. Our treasury can't fund anything; the central bank can't inflate the currency anymore. I can't remember the last time we sold a T-bill. The military has gone unpaid for weeks and, at this point, has largely deserted; its members have joined the ranks of state militias, taking military hardware with them, and anything else that isn't nailed down. That is, if we're *lucky*. Some of them have joined up with out-and-out criminal gangs."

The conference room was silent. Eric's mouth hung open slightly.

The President leaned in. "All that's preventing total chaos is the *idea* of the federal government. Our only plan is to project an image of strength until a new authority can unify the nation again." He swallowed hard before continuing. "And we hope that's you."

Eric took a deep breath. "Well, we hope it can be, too. Though we've never taken on a project of this size. But let me assure you, we're preparing for it as well as we can." He clicked a button; a diagram appeared on part of the TV screen. "Our plan is to take control of the major cities, concentrating on the bulk of the population. Also, that's where most of the chaos is. The smaller cities and rural areas have mostly avoided the trouble. It seems they already know how to behave, with or *without* our direct involvement."

"And God bless them for that," the President benedicted.

"One order from you, in particular, could drastically improve things," Eric continued. "One that can't be made public. But the law-enforcement community, and the military, are already accustomed to nonpublic orders, so hopefully this won't be a problem."

"I think I know where this is going," the President acknowledged, sounding very tired.

"We realize our banishment policies made your problem worse," Eric admitted. "There was no place in our system for people that simply refused to be part of the solution, so we deported them. And they took their sickness with them…to the rest of the country." Eric leaned in. "Though you must admit, you welcomed them with open arms, out of some misplaced sense of moral superiority. Add to that your policy of not filing charges against rioters, simply releasing them, and the problem became much worse."

"I readily admit that," the President conceded. "I'd be remiss not to."

"So…" Eric clasped his hands together, and rested his chin on his fists. "You need to instruct all riot-control personnel to restore order…by any means necessary."

The President's eyes shot open, alarmed. "It has to come from you, Mr. President," Eric intoned. "It can't come from us. For one thing, they don't know us yet. But more importantly…if anyone looks to blame someone for this in the future, that responsibility needs to rest with an entity that no longer exists."

The President looked stricken. "I understand. I agree." He made a gesture to the military officer; he nodded somberly and walked off camera.

"This should solve a lot of your problems at once," Eric explained. "Once you make a show of force, those on the fence about rioting are likely to stop. When the looting dries up, there'll be food and supplies available to law-abiding citizens. And of course, there's no point in feeding people that have no intention of contributing to the world around them. Sad as it is to say…they've chosen to be parasites, and we need to maximize the survival of contributing members of society, if we're to have a future."

The President buried his face in his hands. "How did it come to this? I know these people aren't the majority, but they cause an outsized amount of damage. Still…how are there so many of them?"

Eric grimaced uncomfortably. "Well, I don't pretend to have all the answers, but I talk to some very smart people, and I've heard some pretty solid explanations…what's happening in the country is in line with what evolutionary biology calls 'r-selection' versus 'K-selection'."

The President looked up, his tears flowing. "I'm not familiar with that. Can you give me an executive summary?"

Eric sighed. "I can try. So, r-strategy and K-strategy are two psychological tendencies that living creatures use to ensure survival. R-strategy assumes infinite resources; K-strategy accepts limited resources. R-strategy encourages quantity of offspring instead of quality, K-strategy focuses on quality, as in survival of the fittest. R-strategy is the mentality of prey species."

"It sounds like the rioters," the President conceded.

"That's my viewpoint too," Eric agreed. "There's a growing acceptance in some circles that welfare policies, and copious illicit income, especially from recreational drugs, lead to people adopting r-selection."

"I see," the President grumbled.

"And obviously," Eric continued, "K-selection is the mentality of predator species. It's a more natural fit for human beings."

"Are you making excuses for human predators?" the Vice President accused.

"With all due respect, Mrs. Vice President, we *are* predators," Eric countered. "Our eyes are in the front of our heads. If we were prey, our eyes would be on the sides, so we could *look* for predators. And we have teeth for grinding, tearing flesh, *and* pinching off; in short, biologically speaking, we're predatory omnivores."

"Well, *I* find your views to be *highly* offensive!" the Vice President protested.

"You can try to deny biological reality, but you're not likely to succeed," Eric quipped.

"What?! *How dare you!*" she screeched.

"For Pete's sake, Hannah, that's *enough!*" the President scolded. She shut her mouth, her eyes burning. "We're here to capitulate, remember? We're hardly in a position to defend our leadership." She didn't reply.

"I have *so* many advisers," the President commiserated. "*So* many academic think tanks, *so* many credentialed experts trying to get my ear. And yet I've never heard of this before, even though it answers so much."

"It's the old struggle between truth and popularity," Eric opined. "When the truth becomes unpopular, society goes straight downhill. Personally, I think social media makes it worse; unpopular truths can literally be shouted down. That doesn't help *anyone*."

"But what could they possibly have to gain from keeping me ignorant of this?" the President pleaded.

"I've long believed it was a Faustian bargain to ensure re-election," Eric answered.

The President looked up. "How do you mean?"

"Generous public-assistance policies created an underclass dependent on the government," Eric explained. "Superficially, that made the government more powerful, more relevant. In order to survive, this underclass had to continue to vote for politicians that would give them what they needed. That encouraged politicians to give them more, taking from the productive and giving to the unproductive, thereby encouraging nonproduction. This created a terrible feedback loop that has destroyed democracies in the past. When more than half of the people vote their hands into the wallets of less than half of the people, society goes straight downhill."

"I thought you said it was when the truth became unpopular," the Vice President interrupted, her voice heavy with sarcasm.

"Either one is sufficient," Eric countered. "In our case…*both* have happened." She didn't reply.

The President buried his face in his hands again. "We were just trying to *help* them!"

"It's like the old saying goes," Eric pointed out. "The road to Hell is paved with good intentions."

"Is that from your Holy Book?" the Vice President mocked.

The President's gaze suddenly became very steely. "That's enough, Hannah." He gestured to the dark-suited gentleman. "It's time. Do it." Without a word, he grabbed the Vice President by the hair and began to drag her away; she shrieked terribly. Just out of frame, the back of the guard could be seen bending quickly toward the ground, followed by a loud thud. The screaming stopped instantly, replaced by pained groans. As the conference room watched in stunned silence, they could hear a door opening and closing, followed by what could have only been the sound of a gunshot. Seconds later, the guard returned and, without saying a word, simply nodded to the President, and returned to where he had been standing, once more glaring into the camera.

"That was a long time coming," the President explained. "She was responsible for a lot of our more disastrous policies. Besides, one more death is hardly going to be noticed, given what's about to happen. But most importantly, I want to make something *perfectly clear*…I'm completely on board with whatever it takes to fix the problem. This country will be put back on the right track…*by any means necessary*."

Eric managed to speak. "I'm glad to hear that, Mr. President. I just wonder how much better off we'd all be if you showed such resolve earlier."

The President smirked. "I don't have to stand for re-election anymore."

That broke the tension; the conference room erupted in laughter, though it died down quickly, replaced one again with a stunned moroseness.

The President sighed; he looked much more relaxed now. "Is there anything else you need from me, at this time?"

"Just one more important issue," Eric answered. "States are not currently allowed to declare bankruptcy. They need to be able to.

And they need to let cities declare bankruptcy. Not all of them allow that. But there's no other way to deal with the massive leveraging."

"Sounds reasonable," the President agreed. "I'm sure you can't afford to bail them all out."

"Actually, Mr. President," Eric corrected, "we don't plan to bail out *any* more."

The President looked up, startled. "What? Why? I thought that was how you worked. You assumed Millenniaburg's debts, and bailed out any number of small towns. You've been very consistent about that."

"That was an incentive, for those that got on the bandwagon early," Eric related. "The holdouts are *not* going to be rewarded for their sloth. At best, they'll get non-voting stock. But that'll only be for assets that are still in good shape. We don't expect there will be many of those."

The President frowned. "I guess that wasn't entirely unexpected." He looked down at his desk briefly. "We'll send out an updated joint statement, for your approval, very shortly. But before we part…is there anything you can do to help *us*? You know we need as much help as we can get, with what's about to go down."

"Actually, there is," Eric shared. He looked up at the conference room. "I think you can all go now," he announced. "The business-oriented portion of this meeting is over." Most of them practically jumped out of their chairs, striding quickly for the exit, a few throwing haunted looks over their shoulder back at Eric, before closing the door behind them. Eric sighed, and turned to Danielle. "Too much truth for one day, I guess."

"The truth is rarely popular," she quipped.

Eric addressed the President. "We had a similar problem in the early days of Millenniaburg, before we opted for banishment. We can send you a series of shipping-container drones; we'll fly each one away as soon as you fill them up with your dead. And for the ones who are still alive…we can retrofit a device into your prisons, which will kill them efficiently *and* place them in a shipping-container drone, in one step!"

The President managed a wan smile. "I'll pass that on to the interested parties. I predict that service will be getting a lot more business in the near future."

"Good business is where you find it!" Eric quipped. "Have a good rest of your day, Mr. President…notwithstanding."

"Indeed." He clicked off the video feed.

Immediately, Eric slumped. "What's wrong?" Danielle asked, concerned.

"We're back in the mass execution business," Eric pined.

"It's only temporary," Danielle reminded. "Also, you had to know that you couldn't just deport your problems away."

Eric turned to Danielle and smiled sadly. "I know…but it was so easy to forget that. Deportation was so *bloodless*. And the cities receiving our exiles were so *arrogant* about it. Somehow, I felt like the problem was solved. But it was just deferred." He buried his face in his hands. "I'm not like the President; I don't have that killer instinct."

"And what happens if you blink?" Danielle asked. "Mass starvation? Fighting for scraps? The parasites dominating the creators by virtue of sheer violence? Until there's nothing left and *everyone* starves? In that scenario, the useless are going to die anyway. This way, not only do the useful get to live, but the useless die in a much more humane way, and valuable resources are preserved. Just remember, you're on the side of good here." Eric looked up at her; she continued. "And good triumphs over evil…but sometimes good has to be more violent and even nastier than evil."

Eric chuckled. "You're right, of course. I just have to suck it up for a while. They only need to be culled to the point where their self-destructive way of life can't dominate anymore." He took a deep breath and exhaled evenly. "And I just need to keep telling myself — it's only temporary."

"Besides, you're missing a very important detail!" Danielle cheered.

Eric's brow wrinkled. "What?"

"Today was an historic day for Unlimited Partners! What do people *normally* do after a major victory?" she asked, smiling coyly.

Eric blinked a few times. "Oh, right. I lost my focus and completely forgot." He slammed his fists to the table. "It's time to *party*!"

"Mass celebration," Danielle corrected, waving her finger.

"Oh, right. Gotta keep it classy. Black-tie affair at the convention center?"

"I was thinking more of the state fairgrounds," Danielle offered. "Concerts, food, games, face painting, that sort of thing. I'm sure I can find a large hall for your formal gathering."

"Sounds perfect," Eric agreed. "Something for everyone!"

11

Eric Thompson knocked on Danielle's ajar office door; she looked up and waved. "Got a minute?" he asked.

"Of course!" she assured. "Come in."

"I just wanted to see how the party preparations were going," he commented as he sat down.

"I've got a hospitality team working on it right now," she disclosed. "It's mostly good news. One hitch is that all the possible locations at the fairgrounds were too pastoral for a formal party. Most of them are made for gardening shows, cattle auctions, stuff like that. Largely dirt floors; concrete if we're lucky. So they've booked a giant ballroom at the convention center downtown for your black-tie event. I assume that's to your liking."

"Of course!" Eric beamed. "I've been to functions there before. Their chefs are top notch!"

"The plans for the public event at the fairgrounds are proceeding quickly," she added. "Once word got out, interest exploded; at this point, we've got a full week of festivities, and we may add a few more days."

Eric seemed taken aback. "Well…I appreciate the popular interest…but now it's going to cost us ten times what I was mentally budgeting."

"Actually, it won't," Danielle corrected. "The people who used to be part of the city's Fair Commission heard what we were doing, and were very interested in helping! It's mostly retired people, elementary school teachers, scout troop leaders, people like that. The civil unrest and budget cuts prevented them from hosting a fair for a really long time; they seem really eager to bring it back! And most of them are volunteers; we'll just reimburse them for some expenses."

"You're right, that *does* sound a lot cheaper," Eric agreed.

"It gets better. Our first plan called for hiring food vendors and ride operators, but that's not how they do things. Now, we're *renting* the space to local businesses. We recoup some expenses, and they get lots of foot traffic!"

Eric laughed and put his hand to his forehead. "That sounds great. I totally had the wrong idea about how to run a fair. This plan sounds a *lot* better." He sat up. "Besides, I'm far more interested in the formal party. How are the plans for *that* going?"

"Mostly well," Danielle began. "As you requested, we have enough space for everyone with a supervisory title, plus key technical personnel. But…16otaku is resisting."

Eric rolled his eyes. "Oh, *them* again. Always a handful. What's *their* complaint?"

"They've begrudgingly accepted your request to fete them on stage, but they would strongly prefer not to be asked to mingle with the crowd. Something about not being good with people, and having had enough of that lately."

"I suppose I can understand that," Eric parried. "But I really wanted to show off our heroes! I think a lot of people are coming just to see them."

"As a concession," Danielle added, "they said around three dozen of the latest-model robo-butlers would be ready by then, to handle serving food and drinks."

Eric blinked. "Wow, that was more than I was expecting. I guess I can cut them some slack." He relaxed in his chair. "Besides, this event is mostly so that *I* can mingle with the crowd. I rarely get to see all the people that make this company work, without the usual hierarchy of intermediaries. It'll be refreshing to hear from the ones down in the trenches, so to speak."

"I sure hope you're ready for that," Danielle cautioned. "You might get an earful."

"I hope I *do*!" Eric gushed. "I look forward to it!" He pondered for a moment. "I wonder what it takes to get power nerds like 16otaku to take an interest in company parties? This was meant to be a reward for them, to celebrate their achievements."

"Oh, I think they're doing quite well on their own," Danielle hinted.

Eric arched one eyebrow. "How so?"

"It varies," Danielle explained. "Stacy is apparently a big music fan; she had very firm opinions about the sort of musical acts she wanted to see. Finally, she took over one of the larger exhibition halls, and plans to have a week-long rave. I and the Fair Commission told her she could, as long as she kept it family-friendly. She assured us she would."

Eric gestured with his hands. "Why do I even doubt them? I should know better. I can't wait to see what she's put together! At least, if I can pull myself away from the midway."

"Gary and Irwin have taken up *that* task," Danielle informed. "I don't have much information on it, but apparently they're working with the ride operators to make sure everything is safe, and to 'soup them up'. I can only imagine what they mean by *that*."

"Sounds like something *else* to look forward to!" Eric grinned.

"And finally," Danielle sighed, "Isabel and Dwight have reserved several time slots in the arena during the day, for…kung-fu battles?"

Eric closed his eyes and pinched the bridge of his nose. "Of *course* they did. I think I've learned my lesson here; I can't believe I was concerned in the first place."

"They're not the black-tie type," Danielle agreed. "But when it comes to the fair, it seems they're in their element!"

The pickup truck came to a stop in front of the tastefully-landscaped suburban house. The truck bore the "Unlimited Partners" logo, and in smaller letters below that, read "home maintenance services". Henry shut off the truck and stepped outside. He gazed at his cell phone, looking confused. "This isn't one of our houses… what am I doing here?"

He walked up the stonework path, which wound its way between several healthy rose bushes, surrounded by a lush, well-kept bluegrass lawn. He stopped for a moment and glanced at his phone again. "Jessica McGranger?" Henry looked up, pondering. "Why does that sound so familiar?"

He approached the front door and knocked. It opened to reveal a piercing set of brown eyes, a lithe form covered in a simple sun dress, and the most man-eating expression he'd seen on a woman in some time.

"Remember me, Hank?" she opened.

Henry's memories flooded back. "It's *you!*" His face broke into a wide grin. "I can't believe you found me."

"It wasn't easy." She beckoned with her finger. "Won't you come in?"

His eyes gleaming, he walked through the front door and shut it behind him.

Hank looked around the opulently-furnished front room. "You certainly look like you've done well for yourself."

"The eviction was the best thing that ever happened to us," Jessie related. "It really lit a fire under Dan's butt. He has a much better job now." She cocked her head coyly. "Looks like *you've* done well for yourself, too. No more headgear!"

He felt the top of his head. "Yeah, those days are long gone. I've paid my debt to society, and am now a trusted member of the work force."

"I knew you had it in you." Their eyes locked; Henry felt a lump in his throat.

"So...what brings me here today, ma'am? Do you need some repairs done?"

Her face became pouty. "Yes. My plumbing is *all* backed up." She threw her arms around his shoulders. "It could stand a *really* thorough reaming."

Hank put his hands around her hips. "I take it you don't mean your house's plumbing." She let out a giggle.

"I've managed to schedule an hour of your time," Jessie purred. "I hope that's enough."

Hank forced himself to make the most serious expression he could bear to muster. "You really shouldn't be doing this. You're a married woman, and your husband clearly cares for you. And I'm finally completely legit."

She drew him closer and stared into his eyes. "Just *one* more hustle...then I'll go straight. I *promise!*"

He broke out in spirited laughter; she joined him. He playfully flicked the tip of her nose. "I see what you did there."

"And I'm sure I can promise you a five-star rating, and a glowing review."

Hank took a deep breath, and exhaled fully. "Oh, you talked me into it!"

She dragged him into the master bedroom; he closed the door behind them.

◊ — ◊ — ◊

The weather on the night of the formal party was clear; only a gentle wind blew. The glass walls of the convention center shone brightly, casting a warm glow on the surrounding streets. Inside the giant ballroom was the pleasant din of clinking glasses and polite small talk. Robo-butlers wheeled slowly between partygoers, offering snacks, taking drink orders, and spiriting away dirty dishes.

Dwight and Gary stood by themselves, out of the way. "I hope we're not the only ones to show up," Dwight fretted. "They promised."

"Hey, guys!" They heard the familiar voice of Stacy as she approached, a tall gentleman on her arm. "Aiden, this is Dwight and Gary. And vice versa."

"It's an honor to meet both of you," Aiden greeted solemnly. "Congratulations are in order."

"Thank you." Gary turned to Stacy. "I think this is the first time I've ever seen you in a dress."

"I own at least one," she offered. "I almost rented one. But I thought I could get away with this."

"And yet, somehow, I can still see an anime logo," Dwight joked.

"Oh...because there *is* one. I'm wearing a t-shirt underneath."

Gary clicked his tongue. "Classic Stacy."

"I knew it'd be too cold in here tonight," she explained. "Why must the thermostat always be set to 'freeze all women to death'?"

"I think it's for the guys who are forced to wear jackets," Dwight offered. "We're cooking in these monkey suits!"

Irwin strode up. "Thank goodness I found you," he opened. "People have been looking at me funny."

Stacy looked him up and down. "Irwin, that's a tuxedo."

"So?" Irwin defended. "Isn't that what black-tie means?"

"Maybe in Las Vegas," Gary joked.

Irwin hung his head. "Nobody tells me anything."

"Don't listen to them," Aiden assured after introducing himself. "I think you look smashing."

"Thanks!" Irwin peered closely at Aiden's suit. "What color is that? Vermilion?"

"Close — it's scarlet," Aiden corrected. "More appropriate for evening wear."

"Well, Stacy," Dwight observed, "either you've been holding out on us, or you two clean up good."

"A little of both," Stacy remarked coyly.

"Hey, *there's* my team!" Sam announced as he arrived with his wife, Angela. "Finally, some people I can *stand*."

"Yeah, we're trying to form an island of sanity in this corner," Irwin quipped.

Angela looked uncomfortably at the robot-butlers. "Are they…?"

"All their neural material is synthetic," Sam pledged. "They've never shown any signs of pain."

"*That's* a relief." Angie continued to look unsettled.

"So you don't have any of these in your—" Stacy began.

"I don't want to talk about it tonight," Angie interrupted. "Let's just try to get through this evening."

"Works for me," Stacy agreed. "I'm counting moments until I can bug out of here."

"Is that who I think it is?" Sam suddenly interjected. They all turned to look.

Isabel walked towards them with a poise worthy of a professional model. Resplendent in a dark-pink cocktail dress, its hemline above the knee, her high heels showed off a degree of femininity they'd never seen in her before. The men continued to look stunned until Angela gently elbowed Sam.

"Wow, Isabel," Irwin stammered. "You look lovely tonight."

"My mother made me go to finishing school," Isabel shrugged. "I guess it comes in handy every once in a while."

"What color is that dress?" Dwight asked. "Pink? Rose?"

"It's amaranth," Aiden corrected. "Very dignified."

"I've always had to dress down at work," Isabel huffed. "Otherwise, no one will take me seriously."

"It's a common problem," Stacy agreed.

"Well, I'm glad you made the extra effort," Sam concurred. "We have to appear on stage tonight, if only just briefly."

Stacy turned to Aiden. "Hon, can you excuse me for a moment? I'll be right back."

"Of course, milady." Their eyes remained locked on each other until their hands finally parted. Aiden watched her leave.

Sam turned to Aiden. "I have to say, you're not what we expected."

"She's a welcome break from what I'm used to," Aiden replied cryptically. "I like how she's so down to Earth."

"Her? Really?" Irwin shook his head. "She really *has* been holding out on us."

"You'd understand if you met my relatives," Aiden explained. "Believe it or not, I'm the most normal one. I'm like the white sheep of the family."

Without notice, the lights dimmed, and a projection screen near the back of the hall lit up. People stopped talking amongst each other and turned to look. The screen showed the Unlimited Partners logo, as a low, dignified crescendo of classical instruments started to build.

"Oh heck, we have to get on stage," Sam announced. "May as well get this over with."

The video shifted to aerial panoramic views of decayed cities. A narrator spoke in deep, elegant tones: "It's no secret that these are troubled times." The video switched between street protests, looting, and violence against civilians by dark-masked irregular forces. The narrator continued. "Many wondered what has happened to our once proud nation." A moving collage of news headlines described skyrocketing crime, plummeting employment, and loss of faith in the future.

The narrator continued. "But average citizens started to take action; they believed their fate was in *their* hands." A news headline announced a small town transforming into the largest gated community at the time, as a time-lapse photo showed the downtown area getting refurbished. Another headline, announcing an apartment complex with a new code of behavior, was superimposed on a video of a crowd cheering, and a time-lapse photo of the same apartment complex transforming from an eyesore into a paragon.

"Then one day, a leading nationwide property-management firm pivoted to the challenge of managing an entire city. And thus began the absolution of urban decay!" As a time-lapse photo showed a slum of skyscrapers changing from gray edifices to gleaming towers of clean glass, a montage of repair activity played. Swarms of cats hunted rodents and pigeons. Construction bots retrofitted dilapidated urban centers. Cylindrical machines moved through pipes, scraping away debris and laying down a thick veneer of new material. Before/after pictures showed distressed, destitute citizens looking healthy and successful. A dark, decayed neighborhood transformed into fixed-up houses with "sold" signs, as the streetlights flared back to life.

"But this was *nothing* compared to what happened next." As bright, energetic anime music played, a dramatic montage of the mecha battling the hijacked plane flooded the screen. The crowd went wild, their noise almost drowning out the music. Complimentary headlines raced across the screen, along with quotes from prominent citizens extolling the new era mankind had, in their opinion, moved into.

Finally, this faded to an amateur video of the mecha lifting away from the truck stop, saluting in mid-air. "Yes!" Dwight exulted. "I *knew* that was a money shot!"

The video faded to a slowly-retreating still shot of the entry to the Unlimited Partners headquarters, the company logo displayed prominently on the front of the building, finally revealing the two mechas standing on pedestals.

"Is that the 'Bill and Ted' pose?" asked Gary.

"Oh, no," Stacy pined, covering her face. "They didn't." She peeked through her hand. "They *did*." Aiden smiled at her comfortingly, lightly embracing her around the shoulders.

The narrator spoke one last time. "Welcome…to our bright future!" The crowd went wild again as the video faded to a still image of the Unlimited Partners logo, in front of a computer-generated image of a gleaming, clean, orderly city.

As the applause died down, the screen showed the profile photo of Carl Beaumont, the Chairman of the Board, as he approached the podium. "Thank you all *so* much for being here tonight. I think we can all agree, Unlimited Partners has finally come of age." More applause. Carl looked to his right. "I remember when a brash young executive first proposed this idea. And I have to admit, I thought he was mad." Scattered laughter. "I also must admit…even though his plan showed us a credible path to profit, half the reason I approved it was just to shut him up." The crowd roared with laughter. Eric Thompson, just off stage, joined the merriment, covering his face in mock embarrassment as his peers playfully punched him on the shoulder.

Carl continued. "This project could have gone *so* many different ways. But fortunately, we had the right person for the job, at the right time. And he deserves a lot of the credit for what we've accomplished." Spirited applause, with several congratulatory shouts. "Eric Thompson, come on up and say a few words!" Uptempo music joined with dancing spotlights as Eric strode onto the stage, all smiles. He and Carl shook hands, then shared a fraternal hug, before Carl left the stage and Eric assumed his place behind the podium.

His wide eyes gleamed as he beheld the crowd. "Wow, what can I say? It's been a whirlwind!" Scattered laughter and applause. "The plan that became Unlimited Partners started in my teenage years, in the mind of a boy that couldn't bring himself to follow the rules if he thought they were terrible." A sudden concurring exclamation from a man in the audience caused Eric to pause. He turned to point in its general direction. "*Yes!*" Polite laughter. Eric turned to look off stage, to address an imaginary lackey. "Get that guy a special test." More jovial laughter.

"I can't count how many times I was told my ideas would never work in the real world. Self-styled experts, that claimed to know more about human nature than me, insisted that people needed a heavy hand, and strict boundaries, or they would simply run amok. But I believed a light touch, and appeal to reason, would work with decent people. And I also believed that most people were decent." Light applause slowly escalated into vigorous cheering, eventually returning to quiet.

"I'm grateful I finally had the chance to try a plan I've labored on for decades. But I couldn't have done it without all of you! All I could do was build the teams that painted the broad swaths. Then they had to build the teams to brush in the finer details. There were *so* many ways this could have gone wrong. But I had faith in the decency of the average person, if they could just be given a *chance* to be decent, instead of overworked and disempowered." He surveyed the crowd in the spacious ballroom. "And all of you have proven to me, and to the world, that you *deserved* to be given that chance!" Heartfelt applause and cheering continued for several seconds before finally quieting down.

"So before we return to the celebration, I want you to meet the people that pushed this victory over the edge." The members of 16otaku quickly strode onto stage, coming to a stop behind Eric. "Giant flying robots don't just invent themselves! That takes people, and talent, and a total disregard for respectable wisdom."

He turned to motion toward the new arrivals. "And these people have enough of that to *spare*! Give them a hand!"

The applause and cheering quickly rose to a near-deafening volume. The members of 16otaku waved shyly, but Isabel stopped that to put her hands over her ears.

As the applause settled down, Eric addressed them. "Would any of you like to say a few words?" No one volunteered. Eric turned back to the crowd and smiled. "That's OK; not everyone has to be good with people." The crowd cheered politely as 16otaku quickly walked off the stage.

"But hey, enough presentations, right? We came here to *celebrate*! So let's do that." He looked at his phone briefly. "Yep, right around three minutes. If I'd talked any longer, I would have gotten bored." Widespread laughter. "Good night!" The applause swelled as Eric left the stage, the dancing spotlights coming back to life.

Eric found the members of 16otaku at the side of the stage, Aiden hovering near Stacy. "You did great, gang!" he exulted.

Sam looked indignant. "Eric! You promised we wouldn't have to say anything!"

"And you didn't!" Eric defended.

"Then why did you ask us to?" Dwight frowned.

"Sorry, I guess I was being too subtle," Eric apologized. "I was making the point that it takes a lot of different types of people to make a company work. Supervisors need to be reminded that not everyone is going to be a suit-wearing, public-facing glad-hander. We all have our skills, and we don't fit into predefined molds. Making full use of available resources involves embracing our differences."

"I guess I can buy that," accepted Isabel.

"Also, it was a spur-of-the moment decision," Eric clarified sheepishly. "Not *everything* I do is well-thought-out and planned. Sometimes I just drift with the tides."

"Now *that* I understand!" chirped Stacy.

"Well, I hope you all find *something* to enjoy about this evening," Eric proffered. "I know it's not your kind of scene."

"The food is decent," Irwin conceded, "but there needs to be more of it."

"Oh…the food-service line should have opened up after the presentation." Eric pointed to the far end of the ballroom. "You can get a more substantial dinner there. And there should be plenty of tables."

"*Now* you're talking!" Sam gushed. As the team walked away, Stacy remarked "I didn't even *recognize* most of that snack food."

As Eric watched them leave, he noticed a young lady some distance away, looking in his direction; when he met her gaze, she smiled at him. A faint twinge of recognition passed through his mind, then it faded. Eric slowly wound his way through the crowd, approaching her. As he got closer, her smile widened and became beaming. She wore a tan mid-length skirt and an understated cream-colored blouse, with a playful-looking pair of medium-height heeled boots.

"Hello," he opened. "Have we met? You look familiar."

"Oh, we've met before," she posed cryptically. "More than once."

"I apologize; I deal with *so* many people," he protested. "Maybe you can help remind me."

"Try to imagine me with facial piercings," she said, her eyes twinkling.

His head reared with a start. "Right! I remember you from the first public forum we held!"

"And a less-public meeting with my social-protest group," she reminded.

Eric blinked nervously. "Oh. Of *course*." He looked around. "Why don't we find somewhere else to talk about this."

Eric moved toward a more deserted area of the ballroom; she gracefully took hold of his arm as she walked aside him.

"So you work for us now, I see," Eric observed.

"That's right!" Amber trilled. "I'm probably the lowest-ranking person that was allowed to attend, but I made it."

"*That's* a story I'd like to hear," Eric piped up.

"I'm more interested in the story of your long hair and sideburns," she teased.

They found a small, empty round table with two barstools, and seated themselves. A robo-butler took their drink orders and scurried away.

"That *was* you, wasn't it?" Amber probed. "I've long thought it was."

"Yeah, you caught me," Eric admitted. "Back in my wild days."

"That was less than a year ago," Amber reminded him.

Eric sighed as he stared into the distance. "It may as well have been a lifetime ago. So much has happened since then."

"It was easy to remember you," Amber revealed. "You wanted your grant to remain anonymous, yet you still wanted a receipt. An odd request like that doesn't go unnoticed."

"I was worried about that," Eric laughed.

"The piercing, visionary look in your eyes was also impossible to forget." Eric simply smiled demurely.

"What I never understood," Amber brought up as she crossed her legs, "was *why* you did it."

"Because we had the same goal," Eric explained. "We just had different opinions of where it would end."

Amber's brow furrowed. "You *meant* to unleash chaos?"

"And you didn't?" Eric pointed out.

"I…" Amber looked down sadly. "Somehow I expected it to turn out differently. I thought defunding the police would cause people to come together and work for peace."

"And they did, after a while," Eric reflected. "Or did you mean immediately?"

"Well…" she started. Then she stared levelly at him. "How exactly did we have the same goal?"

"For me, defunding the police was a force multiplier," Eric explained. "I wanted to take ownership of an entire city, to show what my vision was *really* capable of, but it was still too expensive. Once I heard about the emerging trend of defunding the police, I was certain that would cause crime to skyrocket, and hasten the end of civil order. I found your group as you were soliciting donations. And when you accomplished your goal, that helped me accomplish mine. Once the city crashed and burned, I ended up purchasing authority over it for *far* less than I could have otherwise."

"You *used* us!" Amber protested.

"I helped you get what you believed you wanted!" Eric countered. "You thought it would end one way, I thought it would end a different way. I didn't *create* the chaos; human nature did. Well, the worst instincts of human nature, at least. As the old saying goes, be careful what you wish for."

A robo-butler arrived with their drinks. Eric took his double-shot of single-malt liquor, and Amber eyed the blueberry daiquiri on the table in front of her.

"I…I believed in them," Amber sulked. "Don't you, too? In your speech, you claimed you had faith in the decency of the average person. Were those just empty words?"

"Not at all," Eric pointed out. "You believed in the *wrong* people. Instead of working for peace, they only looked out for themselves." Eric motioned to acknowledge the party-goers in the ballroom. "*These* are the people I believe in. They've come together to work for peace…and prosperity."

"I just don't understand how I could have been so gullible," Amber whimpered as she sipped her drink. "I obviously chose the wrong team to back."

"At least you finally backed the *right* team," Eric comforted. "I'd love to hear how *that* happened."

Amber sighed. "It was soon after the chaos started. The police had been significantly defunded, and our group felt victorious. I told them we should use our remaining donations to fight for a new cause, like repealing the drug laws; I was really surprised when most wanted to take the money for themselves. Then we heard the city had been bought out by a corporation. The next thing I knew, my so-called compadres had emptied our bank accounts."

"Sad, but not surprising," Eric observed.

"I confronted them about it, of course," Amber related. "They dismissed me as a 'true believer'. Apparently they *accepted* the grifting nature of our cause. They said that's why they didn't tell me about draining the accounts; they knew I wouldn't agree to it." She sobbed slightly. "I never felt more hurt and betrayed in my life. And that's when I decided it was time for a change."

"Like the old saying goes," Eric consoled, "a conservative is a progressive who's been mugged."

Amber looked up, smiling. "That's great. I've never heard that before, but yeah, that's exactly how I felt." She took a long drink before continuing. "So I got rid of all the body piercings, dyed my hair back to something close to its original color, started dressing better…and got a low-level management position in Unlimited Partners. I work in Linda Carlyle's organization."

"Oh, yes…they deal with prisoners and criminals." Eric looked at her slyly. "Trying to change the system from within, were you?"

"That was the idea, at first," Amber admitted. "But that's not how it turned out."

"How so?" Eric asked as he sipped his whiskey.

"I quickly learned that most people in police custody were like my faithless compadres — dishonest, disloyal, lazy, self-centered, and just plain evil. It suddenly hit me I had wasted years of my life defending the indefensible." She took another long drink before continuing. "Now, I only seek to treat the incarcerated as well as possible. Fortunately, that's in line with the goals of Unlimited Partners." She smiled as she gestured with her glass. "As everyone keeps telling me, it's all about making full use of available resources!" she laughed.

"Sounds like you found your calling!" Eric trilled.

Amber sighed. "I like what I'm doing, but it doesn't really

make use of my biology degree."

Eric tilted his head. "Really? Somehow I didn't see that in you. Why aren't you working in your field?"

"I wanted to work in a zoo, helping animals," Amber explained. "But so does everyone else, apparently. I eventually ended up in Big Pharma, and getting paid pretty well too. But there are only so many studies you can run, so many conference papers you can write. It got to be pretty mind-numbing. Plus, it really bugged me how they treated the lab animals, and even my reasonable suggestions for better treatment got shot down. So when I met a bunch of like-minded rabble-rousers at a protest, I thought I had found my true calling. But I didn't need a degree for *that*." She sipped her drink. "I assume you have a degree? Do you make use of it?"

"Sort of," Eric disclosed. "I have a business degree, and a minor in political science. But I disagree with practically everything they tried to teach me. Still, I thought it was important to know what the rules were, so that I could break them properly."

Amber's eyes twinkled. "I can see that!"

"My *real* education was self-directed, and began in my teen years," Eric reminisced. "It started with a profound realization about the adult world: *no one knows anything*. All these self-important people running around, spouting off about this and that, claiming to understand how it all works, telling everyone else what to do." Eric took a gulp of his whiskey. "Nothing but pure arrogance."

Amber stared hollowly for a moment before downing the rest of her drink. Moments later, a robo-butler swung by to take her empty glass and ask if she wanted another; Amber ordered a Long Island Iced Tea. The robo-butler acknowledged her and sped off.

"Then maybe you can explain," Amber pined. "The people that work here, and the people I used to try to help, couldn't be any more different. And yet we're all human beings. You can obviously tell them apart, or you wouldn't have accomplished so much. What's your secret?"

"I'm surprised you don't know," Eric said with a small jolt. "It comes straight from evolutionary biology."

"I always liked that subject, but I didn't pay close attention to it," Amber admitted. "I couldn't see it helping me with zoo animals."

"Do you remember the difference between r-selection and K-selection?" Eric finished his drink; a robo-butler arrived with Amber's drink, and to take Eric's empty glass, and asked if Eric wanted another. He ordered a vodka and cranberry juice. The robo-butler wheeled away to fulfill his bidding.

"Yeah, that was fascinating," Amber gushed. "The survival strategies of prey species versus predator species."

"Do you remember the hallmarks of r-strategy?"

"Let's see," she pondered. "It's meant to take advantage of a resource glut. It's characterized by promiscuity, low-investment single parenting, early onset sexual behavior, and producing offspring of quantity instead of quality. There's also little or no group loyalty; everyone is in it for themselves." She looked thoughtful as she stared into the distance.

"Does that sound like anyone you know?"

"Who do you mean?" Amber sipped her drink, then she suddenly stopped as her eyes grew wide. "You mean…oh no…but…but predators in *nature* don't adopt a prey mentality." She was suddenly taken aback. "But predators in an *unnatural* environment might! Like people." She set her drink down. "I can't believe I never made that connection before. Yet I deal with it every day at work!"

"It's a difficult thing to accept," Eric conceded. "But it's the unintended consequences of well-intentioned government policies. For instance, child welfare assistance."

"Right." Amber's eyes shone with revelation. "Mothers are rewarded for having more children, and having to take care of more children precludes employment, so they're *also* rewarded for staying unemployed. The fathers are not needed, nor are they rewarded for staying, so they leave, to sire *other* children." She sipped her drink before continuing. "This is a recipe for large numbers of under-supervised children…quantity over quality. The prey mentality all over again."

"And here's the real kicker," Eric added. "What happens if this is continued for a few generations?"

"Well, natural selection…" Amber started. Then her mouth dropped open, and she reared her head. "You end up with a population that's genetically predisposed to staying stuck in the r-strategy. *Literally*." She turned to Eric. "It's not oppression that keeps people trapped in this cycle…it's *genetics*!"

"Unfortunately, yes," Eric commiserated. "Still, it's not completely bleak. Genetics also allows for outliers — people who can rise above their circumstances. People who have something to offer, despite everything. And that's where *your* department comes in. Don't you see? You find the diamonds in the rough."

"I never saw it that way before," Amber admitted. "It seems so hopeless."

"Not at all," Eric pointed out with a gleam in his eye. "*You* were a diamond in the rough! Look at you *now*!"

Amber giggled and blushed. "Thank you." She sighed. "Still, I wish I could put my biology degree to some use. I'd like to go to veterinary school, but another four years of student debt is just too much to face."

"We have positions for biologists," Eric reminded.

Amber made a disgusted face. "Yeah, if you want to put brain implants into cats. I know they don't seem to mind, but I've had enough of animal vivisection."

"What did you *like* doing in biology?" Eric asked.

Amber's eyes filled with an impish glow. "I was actually really good at neuroscience. The possibilities fascinate me! I showed quite a bit of aptitude repairing spinal injuries in lab animals. And there's *so* much variation between species. Did you know sharks can sense electricity, infrared, *and* water displacement? Even their teeth can sense pressure!"

"You *do* love this subject!" Eric exulted.

"I used to," Amber confided. "Big Pharma abused my knowledge to drill holes in rat skulls, and test drugs that broke the brain/blood barrier. I'd prefer to work in rehabilitation. There's not a lot of call for neuroscience that doesn't involve inflicting pain on animals. At least, not without a *lot* more schooling."

"Don't be so sure of that," Eric responded absentmindedly, tapping a note into his cell phone. "Have you filled out your internal resume with your biology experience?"

"No," Amber confessed. "I didn't think it was relevant. And I wasn't interested in any of the positions I knew about."

"There's more going on in this company than you might think." Eric finished typing his note. "Let me know when you've fleshed out your biology resume. I know of a small group that might be interested in interviewing you."

"No hurting animals?" she inquired.

"No hurting animals," he vowed.

"That'd be great!" she rejoiced. "But what do they work on?"

The robo-butler returned with Eric's vodka and cranberry juice. "Well…this, for one thing."

Amber's jaw dropped. "They're cybernetic? I thought they were just robots."

"Not the latest generation," Eric revealed. "Tonight is their first demonstration outside of the lab."

Amber scanned her eyes over the crowd. The robo-butlers stood out from the people with their thin build and their sensor-packed heads. She marveled as she watched them collectively, darting between partygoers, balancing huge trays of dirty dishes, and deftly handing off their loads to each other. Her eyes welled with tears. "They're *beautiful*."

She downed the rest of her drink. Within moments, a robo-butler arrived to take her glass; she declined ordering another drink. As it sped away, she gave it a wiggly wave. "Bye bye!"

Eric smiled. "You should *definitely* take that interview. I think you'd fit right in."

"I think I will." She looked around. "I really should be going; I didn't mean to take up so much of your time."

"Not at all!" Eric assured her. "This is *exactly* what I wanted to do here."

"To interview people for jobs?" Amber asked.

"Not exactly," Eric explained. "To talk to people directly, without the usual hierarchy of intermediaries, and when they're more relaxed."

"Well, don't spend the *whole* evening working," she chided playfully. "Try to have *some* fun!"

Eric smiled. "I assure you, I am."

Amber blushed again. "Thanks." As she moved to leave, she turned around. "And I think you looked better with long hair. You should try that again."

Eric chuckled. "I don't think that's my style."

"How about a ponytail? That's popular with some executives. I think it'd work for you."

Eric toasted her with his glass. "I'll take it under advisement."

"You do that." She gave him a wiggly wave before leaving. "Hope to see you again."

As he watched her leave, he replied under his breath. "Definitely."

Epilogue

Raymond slowly regained consciousness: all around was darkness. He felt manacles on his hands and arms; though standing, he was pressed onto a rigid, curved surface. A cacophony of metal sounds roared as he was jolted upwards; a few seconds later, it stopped. He heard the echoes die down, then seconds later, it repeated; more loud noises, and another abrupt yank upwards.

As his eyes got used to the dim light, he could see another track to his left. It consisted of manacles and full body-sized seats, like his, but they were empty. Every time his track jerked forward, that one, with a short random delay, would move in the other direction. Raymond groaned; it was like the safety harness on a macabre ride in the world's worst amusement park.

The light intensified slightly as he continued to rise, and the wall to his right ended. Across the way, he could see Carlos, one of the other prisoners. The noise made it difficult to communicate, but after expressing some confusion about how they got here, they both recalled being ordered to hold onto the steel bars of their cell, then feeling a sudden burst of electricity surge through them. Neither had any idea where they were.

The track continued to jolt in fits and starts. Tears welled up in his eyes as he thought of Clara, his lady and love. He vowed, if he could ever get out of this prison, that he would live up to his responsibilities and be a better man for her. He choked up at the thought of his precious son, Julio. It seemed like a lifetime since Raymond last saw him, and he scolded himself for the horrible way he treated his kid. He deserved a better father, and he silently promised he would make up for the years of absence.

Finally, they reached the roof. Raymond could see past the back of the seat in front of him; he realized they were all occupied, as were the ones in Carlos' line. Solar panels covered the vast majority of the roof. It seemed their seats were slowly being taken over the edge of the roof, only to return empty. Raymond swallowed hard and tried to see what was going on.

As he neared the roof's edge, he could see the ground. There was a large crowd of cheering people, holding signs such as "The wages of sin", "It's about time", and "God hates criminals". They were quite far away — the building was at least six stories high — but Raymond felt some of them were looking directly at him, making mocking expressions and vulgar gestures. Through the din, he thought he could hear a terrified shriek, an instant after a loud banging sound, before the line moved forward again.

As he passed the roof's edge, he could see below him. There was a large metal box, the size of a standard shipping container, standing on its end, its top open. Leading into it was a sturdy-looking metal chute, open at the top. He gaped as he saw a body fall towards it, hit with a sickening thud, then slide into the container. This was a mass execution! He realized that such a fall was probably the cheapest way to kill someone. Glumly, he realized that, with all the solar panels, it was probably also the greenest method.

He reached the head of the line. Time froze for an instant. In a single motion, his manacles released and his seat pushed him forward. He watched the metal chute rush up to him. He didn't bother to scream.

About the author

Steven Boswell was born into a smog-filled dystopia through no fault of his own. He has been writing fiction since he was three years old, was a regular participant in his high school's yearly anthologies, and served as a staff writer for his college's humor periodical. Although choosing a career in the software field, his heart has never been far from the fiction writing he has enjoyed all his life.

Presently, he lives in Phoenix, AZ, and works very hard to keep airplanes from falling out of the sky.

Printed in Dunstable, United Kingdom